Charles Heathcote has always lived in Macclesfield and very rarely leaves. He is the author of the Our Doris series, northern comedy novels about a septuagenarian housewife and her schemes. Mistakes Mean Murder is the second in a series of cosy crime novels to feature Alice Valentine and Marmaduke Featherstone.

I0543623

also by the author

Mistakes Mean Murder
Charles Heathcote

VA

VARIOUS ALTITUDES

Cheshire

'Need a lift?'

He smiles as he winds the window down. It's not surprising. She must look a proper sight, drenched in her mauve anorak, and he has no idea what she's learned about him.

She doesn't plan on getting into the car with a suspected murderer, but the rain is bucketing down, and her bus won't arrive for another twenty minutes, so she accepts his offer.

They don't chat much as he drives back towards Partridge Mews. He makes a few choice remarks about the weather; it's so cold that each word is accompanied by a small puff of steam. He hunkers down and peers through the windscreen as he navigates the winding country roads.

All of this should have been enough for her to realise that it isn't the right time to accuse someone of murder, but she's always had a flair for the dramatic - she gets it from her mother. She can't quell her rising nausea and grips her knees tightly as her mind spins through all she's recently learned.

Before she can stop herself, she says, 'You killed her, didn't you?'

Silence, except for the rain battering the car.

He remains impassive, stares directly into the dark ahead of them.

She looks across at him to see his jaw twitch. With no light about them, their skin has a ghostly pallor, and she gulps because if she's proven right then she might end up becoming a phantom.

As she edges her left hand towards the door handle, he finally says, 'You have no idea what you're talking about.'

There's a grit to his tone, a tight anger wrapped around his Adam's apple.

'I don't know everything that happened, but I know you.'

'Really? You know me and think I could have done it?'

'Yes, because she was planning to leave and you're a control freak.'

'Who said she was planning to leave?'

If she tells him, perhaps he'll reveal everything he's done. However, he might go after the others, and she doesn't want any more deaths on her conscience.

'That's none of your business,' she says. 'Just hand yourself over to the police and accept the consequences.'

She doesn't anticipate the blow, the great weight of his arm slamming against her chest.

The car zigzags down the road as he whacks her repeatedly. He yells, but the words are incoherent, and she can do nothing to shield herself.

She grabs his arm, forces it back towards the steering wheel, implores him to keep an eye on the road.

He continues to hit her.

She accepts each blow against her upper body, the sound almost in time with the downpour. Focusing on her breathing, she looks around the car, just as she's seen in the films.

He doesn't notice her undo his seatbelt, even as it springs back over his body.

His assault continues, but she doesn't succumb to the pain. Not yet. She grits her teeth as dull aches bloom across her chest. She takes hold of his arm again, if only to see the road, but all she sees is the onslaught of rain.

She steels herself.

She pushes his arm away from her and wrenches the handbrake up with all her force.

The car spins.

The world is a blur. It's like being trapped in a kaleidoscope.

Tyres screech and metal crunches; then there's a slam and the sound of shattering glass.

His bellowing will haunt her nightmares; the sight of him hurtling through the windscreen will never fade from her memory and, as she loses consciousness, she knows that the dull thud and crunch as he collides with a tree will be the soundtrack to the rest of her days.

Chapter One

Alice met him at a bar because she thought that a neutral location would be best.

It also denied him the opportunity to cry. She didn't have a problem with men crying – she welcomed any man in touch with his emotions – but this particular specimen had more crocodile tears than a swamp.

If Alice wanted to argue, he cried. If she wanted to watch something other than *Top Gear*, he cried. There was even that night when they'd gone to a restaurant for her birthday and when it came to paying, he had misplaced his wallet. Granted, he'd waited until they were back at her cottage before unleashing a torrent of half-hearted sobs and drunken wailing in which he declared his apologies and called himself awful.

Then he disappeared for a few months with no contact, not even a bum dial, before texting her out of the blue with a request to meet him.

Alice had considered not responding, but she'd left a

pair of Carvela heels on his narrowboat that she could do with getting back. And so, she'd agreed to the meeting, if only to retrieve her shoes and break up with him good and proper.

With him sitting across from her, looking sheepish, Alice wondered if she'd made the right decision.

He rubbed his hands down his jeans, emitted a sigh that was somewhere between a yowl and a yawn, before saying, 'You're never going to believe this …'

'That you're late? Because that's very easy to believe considering it's one of your habits.'

'Am I?' He made an exaggerated effort of taking his phone from his pocket, tapping the screen, and staring down in feigned shock at the time. 'I don't know how that happened. No, what I was going to say is that I've forgotten my wallet.'

Alice glugged her Pinot Grigio. 'Did you bring my shoes?'

When she asked the question, Ryan looked down at his trainers, scraping the sole of the scuffed Nike Air Max's against the hardwood floor. Eventually, he said, 'They fell off the boat.'

Alice gripped her wine glass. 'How does a pair of shoes just fall off a boat?'

'I dropped them.'

'You dropped my shoes off your boat?' Alice's eyes went so wide that she resembled a lemur with a thermometer up its backside. She groaned and fell back against her seat. 'This might be the worst thing a man has ever done to me.'

'Didn't a man once hold you at gunpoint?'

'Yes, but he was a murderer,' Alice said, glancing down at her wine. 'That's the sort of behaviour you can expect.'

'It's only a pair of shoes, Alice.'

'This isn't about the shoes, Ryan,' she said. 'You ghosted me. After three months of substandard dates, average sex and that time you fed me undercooked chicken, you sailed off on your forty-foot narrowboat without an explanation. Which is fine. These things happen in modern relationships. I've ghosted so many men that I'm practically a haunted house. But then, to add insult to injury, to really pour salt in the wound, you tell me that you dropped my shoes off your blasted narrowboat.'

If anyone got to throw clothing into the canal, it ought to have been Alice. She was the wronged party. Instead, she'd washed what he'd left lying around the cottage and taken the lot to his grandmother's house. She wasn't in. Therefore, Alice had no choice but to dangle Ryan's garments from the hedgerows surrounding the property, so it looked like the hornbeams were blooming boxer shorts, but she'd returned his stuff. Besides, from far away, the boxer shorts could be mistaken for bunting; albeit bunting that was emblazoned with comic book characters.

Sitting across from Ryan, she wished that she'd just dumped his clothes into the water as well.

'It was an accident,' he said.

'Am I supposed to believe that?'

'It's the truth!' Ryan pleaded. 'I know how it looks. I disappeared and now your shoes are ruined.'

'Did you even try to get them back?'

'They're shoes.'

'*Expensive* shoes,' Alice said. 'I got them for when I had to look professional.'

'When you were a social worker.'

'Ryan, if you're about to suggest that since I'm no longer a social worker, I needn't worry about my Carvela shoes, then don't. Otherwise, you're likely to get soaked as well.' She nodded towards her Pinot Grigio, unsure if she could go through with a threat that involved the loss of wine.

'Honestly -'

'I've found that any person who starts their sentence with "honestly" is usually anything but.'

'I didn't mean to ruin your shoes.'

Alice exhaled. She closed her eyes and concentrated on the music playing throughout the bar, hoping it would calm her down. It did … a bit. Whoever oversaw the stereo had chosen some inoffensive jazz music that she couldn't place or name. She took some time before asking, 'Why did you want to see me?'

'To say sorry.'

'About my shoes?'

'And because I disappeared for three months with no contact and no explanation.'

Alice rolled her eyes. 'Right,' she drawled.

'I'm serious.'

'Why did you leave me in the first place, Ryan? We're both adults. If you didn't want to go out with me then that's fine, but some notice would have been appreciated.'

'I didn't want to hurt anyone.'

Alice paused before scowling. '*Anyone*? Who else is there?'

He couldn't meet her gaze and did that man thing of rubbing his cheeks and scratching the back of his neck. 'It's my ex.'

'It always is,' Alice said. 'Every time a man wants to break up, he blames it on his ex. I suppose you think it makes you seem more attractive, this idea that you're so heartbroken you couldn't possibly pursue a relationship.'

'I think I still have feelings for her.'

'That's what they all say.' Alice gathered her things. 'I'm supposed to be sympathetic to your plight and be all pleased that you're getting your soap opera moment of a reunion with your long-lost lover.'

'I feel like I didn't make a proper go of things with Lorelai.'

'If you're so interested in getting back with her then where is she?'

'Over there.' He pointed to a table in the far corner where a group of young women were in the throes of laughter. Alice caught sight of Lorelai immediately, looking like she'd stepped straight out of the Littlewoods catalogue. She was wearing a brown woollen dress that had been knitted to suit her measurements, as well as a pair of calf-high suede boots that made her look like the essence of autumn.

Alice grimaced and faced Ryan once more. 'Please tell me that this is just a coincidence.'

He shrugged. That was another thing about Ryan: he always looked more uncomfortable in his skin than a kitten in a bowtie. He said, 'I was going to buy her a drink when you left.'

'You forgot your wallet.'

'Maybe I'll remember where I left it by the time you leave.'

She felt the familiar tingle of anger tying a knot around the bridge of her nose. She glared at Ryan. Alice had never glared at someone so much in her life, and that included the time she'd caught Gary Taylor with her apple strudel. She swilled her Pinot Grigio. 'Are you a complete idiot, or did you only finish the introductory course?'

'You can't hate me just because I don't want a relationship.'

'You really don't understand, do you?'

Alice stood up, drink in hand, and wandered over to the table in the corner. The women immediately hushed up.

'Sorry to interrupt,' she said, 'only I've a man over there in the process of dumping me because he fancies his chances with one of you lucky ladies.'

There was a collective rolling of eyes, tutting, and pronouncing Ryan's name like it were the ugliest word in the English language.

'It sounds like you remember him,' Alice said.

'He'll be after you again, Lorelai, but you must stand firm. You'll never get used to a chemical toilet.' This came from the clear mother hen of the group, who was wrapped up in a thick cream cardigan and nursing a soda water. She raised her glass in Alice's direction and said, 'I'd usually be drinking as well, but I've a Judo tournament in the morning. I'm Becky, by the way.'

'I'm Alice,' she replied. 'I went to school with a couple of you and there's every chance that most of you don't recognise me. The fact remains that Ryan wants to - '

'You can't blame Lorelai if he's the one dumping you,' one of the women said, eyeing Alice warily.

'I don't blame her at all.' She met Lorelai's gaze and offered a smile. 'Great boots, by the way. The thing is that Ryan says he still has feelings for you, and I wondered if there was any chance of you two getting back together.'

Lorelai chuckled and shook her head. 'He invited me here tonight, but there's absolutely no chance.'

Alice sighed. 'Did he give you food poisoning as well?'

'I couldn't stand his grandmother.'

'Makes sense,' Alice said. 'Gloria is a right tyrant.'

'She is. Anyway, I'm not here for Ryan. Me and the girls have wanted to visit the bar for a while and when I saw that Elaine Closure is performing tonight, I phoned around and saw who wanted to come with me.'

Alice grinned. 'She's a friend of mine.'

'You'll have to introduce us sometime,' Lorelai said. 'Anyway, if you want Ryan then you can keep him.'

'I don't want to keep him. I just wanted to make sure that nothing was likely to happen given what I'm about to do.' She looked down at the table and saw a half-finished gin and tonic. Disregarding protests from a particularly disgruntled red-head, Alice mixed it with the Pinot Grigio in her own glass. 'I'm sorry, but I'll buy you a fresh one.'

She turned around and returned to Ryan.

He was practically bouncing in his seat; he was either excited or in urgent need of the lavatory. 'How did it go?'

'Can we take this outside for a second?'

A quick nod, and he followed her through the bar and out of the door.

Alice inhaled the smoky scent that permeated throughout the near-autumnal air. Soon enough, there would be talk of treacle toffee and toffee apples, but in that moment, she only had one thought.

She held the bowl of her glass firm, before swilling its contents and flinging the lot in Ryan's face.

He recoiled and swore, his vision impaired by Alice's

concoction. 'What did you do that for?'

'I couldn't have done it inside,' Alice said. 'Think about the upholstery.'

'Is this about the shoes?'

'For crying out loud, Ryan. This isn't about the shoes. This is because you think I've been waiting around for the last three months as some sort of wreck because you abandoned me. I do not care. I do not like you. I think you're one of the foulest individuals I've ever had the misfortune to meet, and I once dated a man who only ate chicken nuggets. If you have any sense, then go home. The only contact I ever want from you in future is through a Ouija board. Now, good night.'

Alice left Ryan wiping his face on his sleeves and returned to the bar. She ordered a gin and tonic for the red-head and a bottle of Pinot Grigio for the table. If Lorelai and her friends didn't mind, she'd join them, rant about Ryan, and find out just where she could get her hands on a pair of calf-high suede boots.

Chapter Two

Alice awoke next morning to find Jez in her living room.

'Let yourself in, why don't you?' she said, bundling the mane of hair atop her head so that it looked even more like a bird's nest than it had before she touched it.

She headed into the kitchen and filled the kettle.

Jez still hadn't said anything. He stood by the front window, staring after her, a stern expression furrowing his brow. In his tailored grey suit, he was the definition of stony silence.

Alice set the kettle to boil and stood back, folding her arms and staring back at her detective friend, playing him at his own game while also being aware that she looked nowhere near as imposing in her flannel pyjamas. In her efforts to mimic him, she cocked her head to the side.

She wasn't sure what he was up to, but his lack of conversation and impassive glare caused her chest to tighten as though her ribs were constricting, her lungs being squashed like oranges for juice.

They remained like that until the kettle boiled.

Alice made two mugs of tea and returned to the living room. She set the drinks on the coffee table and sat down in her favourite armchair, wrapping a blanket around herself. She reached for her phone, then remembered it was lying in a tangle of laundry in her bedroom. She hadn't drunk too much the night before – not enough to be hungover by any means – but she'd been merry enough that once she got in, she'd struggled out of her clothes and into her pyjamas before dropping directly into bed.

Alice had many years of practice with the silent treatment thanks to her mother. Primrose was renowned for going quiet when she felt like Alice had kept something from her, so if Jez thought that Alice was about to give in and start chatting amiably about nonsense then he could think again.

They remained in their positions for a few minutes. Alice found an old copy of *Hello* magazine beside the chair and read her horoscope. Apparently, she should've met the love of her life in June – the same month that Ryan had disappeared off the face of the earth and she'd signed up to a bunch of dating apps. She'd given up after a fortnight. There was only enough swiping a person could do before worrying about a repetitive strain injury.

Eventually, Jez took a seat on the sofa across from her. 'Aren't you going to say anything?' he demanded, eyes wide like a stern toddler mid-strop.

'I'm hoping you avoided confrontation on the thirteenth of June, because this horoscope says you were unlucky if you didn't.'

'Alice, I'm being serious.'

'I agree. It's very serious when a policeman breaks

into my home at eight o'clock in the morning, only to stand around like something out of *The Addams Family*.'

'Are you calling me Lurch?'

'If the clodhoppers fit.'

'I'm nothing like Lurch.'

'You're tall enough.'

Jez clamped his mouth shut; his lips pursed like a cat's anus. He ballooned his cheeks before exhaling and said, 'I'm here about Ryan.'

Alice slurped her tea. 'There's nothing to worry about there, Jeremy.'

'It's Jez.'

'Thanks for the concern, but Ryan's the one who ghosted me for three months. I said my piece, threw a drink over his head and spent the evening watching your husband's drag persona caterwaul her way through several of Lisa Stansfield's lesser-known hits.'

'He told me that Elaine was going to perform tracks from Naomi Campbell's album.'

'Well, she didn't.'

'Because she doesn't have the range for Lisa Stansfield.'

'No, she doesn't.'

'Ben said as Naomi Campbell was a much-maligned singer who should've had the same musical success as Grace Jones.'

'I remember the PowerPoint presentation.'

'Should I mention this to him?'

'That I criticised the power behind his falsetto? No, you shouldn't. He'd only make me go and watch him rehearse.'

'You're not wrong.'

'Either way, if you're only here to see how things went

with Ryan, that's it.'

Jez tentatively picked up his mug, staring down into its depths as though concerned that the teabag had burst. He murmured, 'It's not it though, Alice. He's been attacked. At three o'clock this morning, a milkman was on his rounds when he found Ryan unconscious at the side of a road.'

Alice dropped the magazine; its glossy pages slithered off her blanketed lap and onto the floor. Panic fluttered in her throat as though she'd swallowed a hummingbird. She rubbed at a sudden tightness in her chest because as much as she disliked the man, she hadn't wanted him to go out and get hurt.

After Ryan had left the bar, she'd thought he'd return to his boat, towel himself off and feel sorry that he'd ever been on the wrong side of her. Either that, or he'd head on back to his grandmother's house, where he could take a shower and complain about how Alice was a terrible human being and debate what he'd been thinking when he'd asked her out on a date.

Alice wound the blanket around her hands, seeking further comfort.

If Ryan died and her last words to him had been so full of vitriol, she didn't know how she'd live with herself. Guilt continued to coil through her ribcage. In an instant, she realised just why Jez was in her living room.

Concern fled her gaze, to be replaced with a glare.

He stared at her dolefully, emulating Rodin's *Thinker*. Alice wouldn't have been surprised if Jez's ancestors had turned out to be statues. She supposed that came with the territory, though. Being a policeman meant standing around like a glorified garden gnome; it was better for him to be a statue than an ornamental flowerpot.

Alice ignored her fury, pursed her lips and nodded. 'That's why you came here? Because you thought, "Alice, she's aggressive. She seems just the type to clobber a man because he preferred his ex-girlfriend." Do you honestly believe I cared enough about Ryan to risk ruining my future? My best friend's a detective constable, for crying out loud.'

'I'm your best friend?'

'You were until you started accusing me of GBH.'

'I never accused you. You didn't give me chance to. *You* jumped to conclusions.'

She averted her gaze, her shoulders raised in a half-shrug. 'It's who I am.'

'So, you're saying you didn't assault Ryan?'

Alice groaned; the sound filled with grit. She dropped the blanket from her legs and leaned forward in the hope that her words would sink in. 'I told you. I was angry, so I threw my drink over him. Then I spent the night with Lorelai and her friends, before getting a kebab on the way home. They weren't there for that. Something about keeping trim for some wedding.'

Jez ran his finger up and down the length of his mug. 'Makes sense,' he said.

'This coming from a man who hasn't touched a carbohydrate since 2005.' Alice slurped her tea.

'That's nonsense. Think of all the breakfasts we've shared at Thistlethwaite's. They're stuffed to the brim with carbs and fat.'

'That's true.' Alice sat silent for a moment, mulling over all that had been said. 'How come you immediately thought it was me?'

Jez shrugged. 'Ben was there when I got the phone call. He told me about your meeting with Ryan last night.'

'Have you questioned him yet?'

Jez started fidgeting as though there was an earwig in his underwear. 'I might have broken procedure by coming here first.'

'What would you have done if I'd admitted to battering him?'

'Did you?' He cocked his head to the side.

'No. If you think I'm lying then check the CCTV.'

He slumped back down in the sofa, his head against the back cushion. 'You don't have to treat me like a detective.'

'When you treat me like a suspect, what do you expect?'

'Alice, would you have preferred someone who doesn't know you to come around and ask?'

'No, but I expect you to accept my answer.'

'I do.'

'What if I had done it?'

'Then I'd have to arrest you.'

Alice rolled her eyes. 'I don't know what's worse, that you think I'm capable of GBH, or that you wouldn't use your position to help me get away with it.'

'That's the risk you took when you made friends with a detective.'

'Duke would help me.'

'I'm sure he would, but he's retired. He's well within his rights to take such risks.'

Marmaduke rang the doorbell and took a step back. He inhaled, pulling in his stomach so there was minimal paunch on display. He'd had the Devil's own job finding his blue tweed suit. Alice was helping him to keep the house tidy and, as such, everything was in its place – only that was never the place where Duke had left it. Then he'd put the suit on to discover that it was tight around the midriff. That was another one of the problems with knowing Alice – she regularly brought cakes around, and Duke found it difficult to refuse a slice of her lemon drizzle.

However, Mrs Cribbins had telephoned to request his assistance in a matter of the utmost discretion. Without much time to change again, Duke fastened his jacket, breathed in, and prayed to whichever deity presided over Cheshire that his buttons didn't pop.

Moments after he rang the bell, she answered the door. As with most women in Partridge Mews with a case of terminal housewifery, Mrs Cribbins dressed smartly – black trousers, whichever M&S blouse was in vogue and plain plimsolls that claimed to be orthopaedic but were more in-keeping with medieval torture devices.

She invited Duke inside and led him through to the kitchen. As much as she claimed to need Duke's help, she didn't seem to believe him worthy of her front room. Either that or she was a secret dominatrix and had some banker in there dressed in rubber and tied to her sideboard.

Probably not.

Mrs Cribbins didn't have what it took to maintain a fetish – she struggled enough to keep up with the vacuuming.

'Tea?' she asked, busying herself at the kettle.

Duke saw that a lot when he was in the force: nervous folk looking for something to do with their hands. Unfortunately for one person, it just so happened that they were fiddling with the murder weapon. That had been an easy case: wife kills husband with a cobblers' last when she discovers he's doing more than having his shoes repaired. The worst part had been the paperwork. No one had ever warned Duke about the amount of paperwork involved in murder. If they had, he might have reconsidered his life choices and become a lorry driver.

Once he'd received his cup of tea, he said, 'Now, Mrs Cribbins, just what's so awful that it couldn't be told over the phone?'

She glanced around the kitchen, as though searching for signs of possible eavesdroppers – not likely, there was too much chintz – and opened the biscuit tin.

'No thank you,' Duke said, patting his stomach. 'I think it best I start cutting back on treats.'

'I wasn't offering you a biscuit, Mr Featherstone. I didn't want to say anything, but I refuse to contribute to the obesity epidemic running rife in this country.'

His eyes practically flew from their sockets with incredulity. 'You think I'm obese?'

'It's the sedentary lifestyle. You only have yourself to blame. I think it's right for a man to have some meat on his bones, but when they get to such gargantuan proportions, I must admit to feeling dismayed about their lack of control.'

'That's right charming that is, asking a man for help and then calling him gargantuan.'

'Well, how would you describe yourself?'

'I admit to being a little overweight, but no more so than any man my age.'

'If you had a wife on hand, you'd soon be back to a healthy size,' she said. 'Look at Harold Copeland.'

'I'd rather not, actually.'

'The point is, I wasn't offering you a biscuit. I just

couldn't leave this out for anyone to see.'

'What is it?'

Mrs Cribbins handed him an envelope, cleanly opened with a letter-opener. The address had been typed onto a sticker and there was no clue to where the letter originated. Marmaduke sensed what he'd find inside. He hadn't seen a poison pen letter before – that was something usually reserved for soap operas – but that would explain why Mrs Cribbins wanted to keep it hidden.

Sure enough, the sender had torn letters from magazines and newspapers to craft their note. The collage of headlines read, "HER NAME WAS LUCY".

Marmaduke's chest constricted, and it wasn't because he was trying to confine his stomach to his shirt.

'I haven't thought about that business for nearly thirty years,' Mrs Cribbins said. 'Have you?'

His hand trembled as he brought the cup to his mouth, not caring if he spilled tea down his front. He hissed through his teeth at the scalding heat as it burned its way down his gullet.

'Was there anything else in the envelope?' he asked, struggling against the rising lump in his throat. He knew the name Lucy. If it hadn't been for her then Joanna might still be around.

Mrs Cribbins shook her head. 'Nothing. But why would someone send this to me?'

Marmaduke returned the note to its envelope. 'You're the only person who'd know anything about that.'

'Well, I'm telling you that I've no idea why anyone would send me such a note. I considered speaking to Edith Simpson but look how difficult it was for her Alf.'

'I doubt it was any easier for Edith.'

'That's as may be, Mr Featherstone, but men are permitted to disassemble after such an ordeal. Women must display an illusion of fortitude lest they be labelled weak.'

He didn't have a response. What Mrs Cribbins had said was undoubtedly true. Lucy's father, Alfred Simpson, had always been uncouth and rambunctious, a regular bloke's bloke, but he'd stopped caring about much after his daughter's death. He drank heavily, he stole from supermarkets, and he became as much of a nuisance as he could to the local constabulary without being sent to prison.

Marmaduke understood the pain well. 'Do you mind if I keep this?' he asked, holding the note aloft.

'By all means, if you think it will help your investigation.'

He nodded and slipped the envelope into his pocket. 'I'll be making tracks, then,' he said, unable to hide the solemnity in his voice.

They both stood up.

'I imagine this goes without saying, but please remain discreet. I can't have anyone believe I'm at the centre of a scandal.'

Another curt nod from Marmaduke. 'No, Mrs Cribbins, we wouldn't want anyone to believe that.'

'It's the Women's Institute, see? Most of the ladies wouldn't like to have all that business dredged back up.'

'I thought the WI was finished.'

They stopped by the front door. 'For the moment,' she said. 'However, we must look out for one another.'

'And if I have to speak to any of them during the course of my investigation?'

'I imagine you will, but I see no reason for you to

mention my name.'

'Right.'

She opened the front door to let him out.

He was halfway down the path when she called after him to add, 'And Mr Featherstone, think about it. When was the last time you saw your feet?'

'I'm not obese,' he growled.

'Bye for now.' With that, she closed the door.

The colour rose in Marmaduke's cheeks as he thundered down the road.

'Gargantuan?' he murmured. 'I'll show her ruddy gargantuan, tiptoeing around like an emaciated beansprout.'

His mobile rang and he answered. 'Hello... No, I didn't read the caller ID. It's a telephone, not the latest James Patterson... Yes, I am in a worse mood than usual. You would be too if you'd just spent five minutes with Norma Cribbins... I'll tell you later... Attacked? I'm on my way.'

Marmaduke ended the call and pocketed his phone. It wasn't even ten o'clock in the morning and he'd already been faced with a poison pen letter and an assault. He sometimes wondered if retirement was ever an option for a detective.

Chapter Three

Alice hated hospitals.

Most folk occupying their floors were ill or injured. No one would put a hospital in a travel brochure unless they were advertising its merits to hang-gliders. It was useful for people to know where the nearest hospital was when they had a hobby that occasionally involved fracturing a limb.

Not that Alice had any interest in extreme sports. She'd considered mountain-biking for a time, but that was only because Eloise Pidgeon was keen and Alice liked the idea of challenging her in some fashion, or of simply knocking her over in front of a passing 4x4.

When Alice mentioned visiting Ryan, Jez had been against the idea, worried that his colleagues might view her as a possible suspect. He'd grown more amenable to the idea when Duke had agreed to tag along, but he still seemed worried about her potential behaviour as he led them directly to Ryan's cubicle.

Alice refrained from gasping at the sight of Ryan.

His eyes were so bruised and swollen that it looked as though they'd been replaced with beetroots – weeping. pickled beetroots at that – and his cheeks bore scratches and grazes, as did his hands. He was awake and connected to a variety of machines that were rhythmically beeping; Lady Gaga could have used the ECG as an accompaniment on her next album.

His hospital gown would have made a better dishcloth. Someone had tried to clean blood from Ryan's brow but smeared it into his hair instead, where it had dried. It looked like he had the contents of a compost bin growing out of his scalp and had resorted to grim measures to style it.

'Duke,' Alice said. 'What do you say to a man who's been assaulted?'

He mulled it over for a moment. 'I don't know, what do you say to a man who's been assaulted?'

'This isn't the time or place to be making jokes,' Jez said, stern.

Alice shot a fierce look at them both. 'I wasn't making a joke. I'm not sure what you say to a man who looks like he went headfirst into a combine harvester.'

'"Hello" would be nice.'

'Shut up, Ryan,' Alice snapped.

'Or "shut up".' He attempted a shrug, but it looked more painful than it was worth. '"Shut up" is fine.'

She pinched the brow of her nose and shook her head. 'I didn't mean that. Sorry, Ryan.'

'An apology from Alice Valentine? I must look bad.'

'I don't like you right now, but that doesn't mean I wanted to see you battered.'

'Despite what you said last night?'

'What did you say last night?' This from Jez and Duke

31

in unison.

'It's good to see that Tweedledum and Tweedledee have finally woken up.' Alice averted her gaze to look at a sign on the wall about how best to deal with burns. 'I told Ryan – in my own, unique fashion – that I never wanted to see him again.'

'You said, "The only contact I ever want from you in future is through a Ouija board."'

'Yes, but I didn't expect you to go straight out and attempt to become a spirit'

'I didn't plan on getting jumped.'

'What did you plan to do then?' Alice folded her arms and allowed a scowl to simmer on her face. He might have been beaten black and blue, but there was something about his manner that had her trying to remember her mother's calming techniques.

'I planned on going home and drying off after someone threw a drink in my face.'

'It's the least I could do after you disappeared for three months, only to return and reveal that not only had you dropped my shoes off your boat, but you also wanted to get back together with your ex-girlfriend. An ex-girlfriend who informs me that she most certainly isn't interested.'

'She isn't?'

Alice noted the twinge of sadness in his tone. She couldn't be sure if his eyes were weeping due to his injuries or because of how she'd spoken to him, but her shoulders began to settle, and her ribs no longer felt like they were about to erupt from her chest in fury.

'If she'd said that she wanted to take a chance on a relationship with you then I wouldn't have thrown the drink.'

'Why not?'

'I wouldn't have wanted to embarrass you.'

Jez looked at her, agog. 'You know that you're Alice, right?'

'Where are you going with this?'

'You're renowned for embarrassing, upsetting and antagonising people. It's who you are.'

Alice turned to Duke. 'Do you think that as well?'

He was reclining on a plastic chair in the corner, an old TV Guide on his lap. 'You once stepped in front of a man with a shotgun and decided that sarcasm was the best way to go about things.'

'He was going to shoot you.'

'You could have waited for the police to arrive.'

'Once again, he was going to shoot you. And the police did arrive, and everything turned out okay because you're still here today.' She heaved a breath, gripping the strap of her handbag with enough strength to break a watermelon in half. 'Can we please stop discussing my attitude and get back to questioning Ryan?'

'I don't think you actually started questioning me.' Each word that left his lips came with a wince, most likely due to the bruising that seemed to be slowly blooming along his jaw.

Alice hated that she felt sympathetic towards him.

Jez stepped in and said, 'I feel that the question we'd all like answered is, "Where did you disappear to for three months?"'

Ryan inhaled sharply. 'I'm not sure what that has to do with me being attacked.'

'Look at it from our perspective, Mr Dewhurst. Nobody hears from you for a significant amount of time, only for you to be assaulted on the night of your return.

It could have something to do with your time away, or it could concern the reason that you fled in the first place. Therefore, I think it would be beneficial to our investigation to know your recent whereabouts.'

Alice couldn't stop herself from grinning.

Ryan allowed his eyes to wander, settling nowhere in particular. He didn't answer Jez immediately, but after some thought said, 'I went on an around-the-world cruise with my nan.'

'Would she be willing to corroborate that?'

'She can't.'

'Why?'

'She's dead.'

'What?' Alice sat down on the end of the bed and reached towards Ryan's hand. 'When did that happen?'

'In our sixth or seventh week on board. It's hard to keep track of the days when you're in the middle of the ocean. She'd been complaining of feeling poorly since we got on the ship, but I put it down to seasickness and thought she'd eventually get over it. One morning, I woke up and she was gone.'

'That's a shame, lad. It can't have been easy, stuck on that ship, folk frolicking around you while you were grieving your loss. I'd have been off at the next port, making arrangements and the like.' Duke didn't need his milk-bottle lenses to magnify his eyes; his scrutinising stare was fierce enough.

Ryan began stammering, but Jez didn't allow him to speak, asking, 'With that in mind, is there a reason you didn't leave the cruise? From your estimations, you still had another six weeks on-board. Did you contact any family members to let them know what had happened?'

Alice retracted her hand away from Ryan's. She hadn't

considered the questions that they'd put towards him; she'd simply recalled her own grief at the loss of Aunty Magdalena and tossed all animosity aside. It had been instantaneous. She could be a bolster for him as he dealt with the emotions related to the death of a loved one. Yet she realised that she'd allowed her own experiences to colour her judgement as she also wondered why he'd stayed on the ship and why he hadn't informed anyone.

Ryan looked like a dachshund with an injured paw. 'I stayed on the cruise because it was already paid for, and I couldn't afford to get back. If Nan hadn't found a special deal online, we wouldn't even have gone.'

Alice tapped her index finger beside Ryan's hand. 'Will you be able to pay for the funeral?'

'There's no point.'

'I'm sure that people will want to properly say goodbye to Gloria.'

'There's nobody.'

'There must be someone, surely?'

'No, Alice, there's no body,' Ryan said. 'Nan fell overboard. There won't be a funeral because there's nothing to bury.'

She stood up, brushed her hands on her trousers and readjusted her handbag.

Jez placed a hand on her arm and gave a warning shake of his head. 'Perhaps you could take us through the sequence of events that led to your grandmother falling overboard.'

'Our cabin had a balcony. Nan went out there to throw up and somehow ended up in the water.'

Alice guffawed. 'I've had an idea about who battered you.'

'Who?' Ryan asked, little more than a squeak.

'Gloria. When she found you going around spreading such a ludicrous story.'

'That's harsh even for you, Alice. She's dead. I'm grieving.'

'If this is grief then you're a bleeding sociopath.' She pushed Jez away when he tried to stop her from approaching Ryan. 'Everybody in this room has felt grief in some way, and from my experience, your first action isn't to break up with somebody and express your intention to try it on with an old flame.'

'We're back on that again, are we?' He scoffed and shook his head.

'Yes. Yes, we are, because that's the last thing that happened before you were assaulted.'

'And you want everyone to know it wasn't you?'

'Of course I want everyone to know it wasn't me. Who goes around wanting to be known for assaulting folk?'

'Fine, then.' Ryan turned to Jez. 'Alice didn't assault me. The person who did that was much stronger, and they were also wearing wool. It was like being attacked by a violent sheep. Also, they were much more competent than her.'

'Don't say anything,' Jez whispered in her ear.

Alice turned on her heel and headed towards the door. She stopped with her hand above the handle. 'Did you go near Italy while you were on the cruise?'

'I don't see what this has to do with the lad being attacked, Alice,' Marmaduke interjected.

'We had a couple of nights in Venice.'

'Venice? That's lovely. Did you ever think about getting me a replacement pair of shoes when gadding about one of the most fashionable cities in the world?'

Ryan shrank down in the bed. 'It's not really renowned for its footwear.'

'I know for a fact that they have Prada, Gucci and Moschino in Venice.'

'I live on a narrowboat. Do you honestly think I can afford designer shoes?'

'No,' she conceded. 'I also don't understand why you'd go on a cruise when you live on water. Wouldn't you prefer a holiday on land?'

'I just went along because the offer was for two people. Nan booked everything.'

'And then she fell overboard.'

'It seems you're getting the measure of things.'

She stared at him agog. The way he was lying there, pale and bruised in his thin hospital gown, reminded Alice of a Victorian waif – like Tiny Tim, but with an Arsenal tattoo. 'Do you honestly expect me to believe you?'

'Alice,' Jez warned.

She glared at her friend. 'I'm aware that he's been assaulted. I can sympathise with him, but that doesn't mean I have to believe his story. It's ludicrous.'

'You could at least let me look into things before accusing him.'

'That's your job. Mine is to recognise when someone is treating me as though I'm as gullible as a haddock.'

Duke chimed in again. 'What if she did fall overboard?'

'Gloria Hebblethwaite did not fall off a cruise liner. I'd be shocked if Ryan even went on holiday. It's more likely that he spent three months trying to find his way out of a paper bag.' She couldn't stop herself from glaring at him. She opened and closed her fists a few times, stretching her fingers out as far as possible in the hope that the frustration would dissipate.

'You've got a terrible bedside manner,' Ryan said. 'Are you sure you used to be a social worker?'

'There was nothing in the job description about being kind.'

'But it helps.'

'So does Pinot Grigio.' Alice snatched Jez's car keys from his pocket. 'Bye, Ryan. I'm sorry you were assaulted.'

'You don't mean that.'

'No, but if I say what I mean then Jez will think I'm a suspect.'

She left the room and headed down the corridor. Jez and Duke didn't follow her. She didn't blame them; they'd have more questions, but she knew that if she remained in the room a moment longer, she'd have a manslaughter charge on her hands.

On her way out of the hospital, Alice recognised a familiar brunette arguing with a receptionist.

'I understand that you're just doing your job, but a man has been assaulted. I wouldn't mind if he fell from a dinghy and drowned, but that's not the point.'

The receptionist's eyes were magnified behind her varifocals, and she was slouched behind the desk, reminding Alice of a bullfrog,

'That statement is one of the reasons why I believe it's safer for the patient if I don't reveal his location,' she said. 'Now, I'm going to ask you to leave before I call security. Denzel won't go easy on you because this is around the time he has his daily bacon sandwich and he's a lot harsher on those who get in the way of his daily bacon sandwich.'

Lorelai's eyes pleaded with the receptionist, who returned an impassive, glazed-over expression. Eventually, she turned around. When she caught sight of Alice, she rushed over and pulled her into a hug. 'I'm so glad to see you. I wasn't getting anywhere with that nasty pasty.'

Alice stiffened, finding herself enveloped in an embrace that felt closer to being trapped in the maw of a heavily perfumed Godzilla. 'Are you wearing crocodile?'

Lorelai adopted a stern expression, releasing Alice. 'It's vegan leather made to resemble crocodile. Do you like it? My manager says it reminds her too much of *Peter Pan*.'

'It's very you.' Alice admired Lorelai's fashion sense; she doubted she'd ever have the courage to wear such a jacket. 'Are you here to see Ryan?'

'I'd already be there if it wasn't for that gargoyle receptionist.' Lorelai sighed. 'It's not that I like him, but I felt like it was the kind thing to do.'

'I only came because I had Jez at my front door this morning asking whether I was the one who assaulted him.'

'That doesn't seem right. If you're a suspect, they shouldn't allow you to see the victim, should they? Isn't it victim intimidation or something?'

Alice pressed the heel of her palm to her forehead and breathed deeply, forcing her shoulders to relax. She hissed through her teeth. 'I didn't assault Ryan. Do you honestly believe that after I bought a kebab, the next thing I wanted to do was to batter my ex-boyfriend?'

'Last night was the first time we'd seen each other

since sixth-form, Alice.'

'Wow.'

'There's no need to take it that way. You threw a drink in Ryan's face, remember? Who's to say that you wouldn't go one step further and track him down?'

'So much for women supporting women,' she said, shaking her head.

'Look, if you say that you didn't assault Ryan and the police are happy enough to let you see him, I guess I'll believe you too.'

Alice sighed. She hated to admit it, but Lorelai was right. Of course she'd be the first suspect, even if it hurt to admit it. She'd been one of the last people to see him, and after leaving Lorelai's group, she'd been alone for the rest of the night, which gave her ample time to find Ryan and give him what for. 'Did you get home okay?'

Lorelai nodded. 'Becky gave me a lift. It's another one of the reasons why she sticks to the soda water, so she can be the designated driver. Funnily enough, I thought we saw Ryan. I wonder how long it was before the attack. Do the police have any idea what motivated someone to go after him?'

'Apart from what they thought about me, I couldn't say for sure.'

'And how is he?'

'Very bruised and swollen, but still capable of annoying me to high heavens and lying.'

'What's he lying about?'

'Apparently, Gloria has fallen off a cruise ship and died.'

Lorelai scoffed. 'He'll be happy if she has.'

'She might not have been the kindest of people, but even Ryan must like her in some way.'

'I don't mean it like that. He told me that Gloria had a huge life insurance policy with his name on it.'

'Now everything makes sense.'

'What does?'

'I don't think Gloria is dead. I thought Ryan was lying for sympathy, but now I think that he's lying in the hopes of making a quick buck.'

'He was always short on cash. I've lost count of the number of times I ended up paying for everything when we were out.'

'Funny that, he was the exact same with me.'

'Still, wouldn't Gloria need to be dead for him to claim the life insurance money?'

'I'm sure he's come up with some convoluted scheme to get around that.' Alice let the idea sit in her mind, something to return to later. 'Maybe you can ask him about it when you go to see him.'

Lorelai checked her watch. 'I spent so long trying to find a parking space and then arguing with the receptionist that I don't think I have the time. I need to get to work, and I said I'd call Becky before her judo tournament, just to wish her well.'

'There isn't much to see, anyway. He might start crying, hoping to get some sympathy from you.'

'You're probably right. Thanks for telling me about his condition, Alice.'

They smiled to one another. 'I understand why you had to come check, that's all. Send Becky good luck from me as well.'

'Will do.' With that, Lorelai gave Alice another swift hug and headed away, back down the corridor.

A quarter of an hour later, Alice was sitting on the back

seat of Jez's car when he and Duke returned. She'd been reading a Ruth Ware book on her phone, which she popped into her bag as she handed Jez his keys. 'I can understand why you thought I assaulted Ryan.'

He nodded.

Duke shrugged. 'You assaulted me when we first met.'

'That wasn't assault.'

'What would you call it, then?'

Alice considered his words. Yes, she'd thrown a number of takeaway trays at him, but as far as she was concerned, he'd deserved it. 'I was provoked. I'm not the type to assault an ex-boyfriend.'

'Just old men?' Jez said, before adding, 'Sorry Duke.'

'It's fine. I'm seventy-four years old; there's not many folk who call me young.'

'And if they do, they need their eyes testing,' Alice said with a chuckle.

Jez didn't find it funny. He gave her a puppy-dog look that had a modicum of concern behind it and said, 'This is what we're talking about, Alice.'

'What?'

'Don't you think that you can be a little abrasive at times?'

'Have you been speaking to my mother?'

Jez averted his gaze, seemingly interested in his wing mirror. 'I bumped into her at the gym. She's joined a boxing class.'

'Boxing?'

'She says she wants to try her hand at what's commonly seen as a masculine enterprise.'

'What about Nordic walking?'

'It's not on the same day. Since the WI disbanded, she has some extra time on her hands.'

'My mum is learning how to box, yet you're not accusing her of assault.'

'One, she's Primrose; she won't even pour salt on a slug. Two, she was stargazing last night with the local astronomy club.'

'It worries me how much you know about her life.'

'You only have to look at her social media. She's always on there.'

'That's good. Whenever I check social media, there's usually someone accusing me of murder.'

'Do you get my point now?'

'I am *not* a violent person!' She fell back against the seat and closed her eyes. If her Aunty Magdalena had been around, Alice would have headed to her cottage, moaned about her friends and talked it out. However, she couldn't do that because her great aunty had died nearly two years earlier, her memory confined to photograph albums and an appearance in the audience of *Bruce's Price Is Right* in 1998.

'You can't deny having a quality about you.' Jez said the words with an ease and calm that was almost persuasive.

'And what quality is that?' Alice asked, pouting like a petulant teenager.

'Aggression,' Duke said. 'Shall we go to Thistlethwaite's? My treat.'

Alice said nothing as Jez drove out of the car park. If Marmaduke Featherstone was offering to treat them to lunch, he must believe that things were serious. Either that, or he was fed up with seeing them bickering. Still, if the chance for a free meal was on the cards, then she'd take it, even if it did mean going into work on her day off.

Chapter Four

Thistlethwaite's was renowned for its reliability. Mavis hadn't changed the layout or décor of the place in at least twenty years, and Alice wouldn't have been surprised to learn that it had always been the same – one of the last vestiges of linen tablecloths, wipe-clean menus and doilies. There were rumours that when the café had first opened, they'd used oilcloths, but Mavis had quickly suppressed such accusations with threats to serve strychnine-infused scones to the Wren's Lea Mother's Union.

Since Arthur Sterling's death – and because she'd lost her job as a social worker due to Mrs Sylvia Cameron dying out of spite – Alice had taken on a few shifts at the café.

Mavis wasn't the best when it came to baking; she didn't have the patience for Battenberg and her buttercream would be better used as tile adhesive. She'd hired Alice for her culinary skills – and because the

Valentines had been supportive patrons of the place since she'd first opened decades previously.

Alice and Duke sat themselves at their usual table in the corner. Meanwhile, Jez remained in the car to answer a phone call, leaving strict instructions about his coffee order.

Having waited for them to settle in, Mavis stepped from behind the counter and headed in their direction.

Mavis Thistlethwaite looked as though she could be blown over by a hairdryer. Five-foot-nothing on a good day, she was also as thin as a lamppost, which came – she claimed – from smoking sixty cigarettes a week since the age of fifteen. Her nicotine-stained skin had the thin quality common in folk over seventy-five. Still, despite how dainty she appeared – from the uppermost curl of her perm to the soles of her Hotter plimsolls – Mavis exuded a fearsome force.

'It'll be three full Englishes, will it?' she asked.

Alice was about to confirm when Duke said, 'I'll stick to a poached egg.'

Mavis's eyes widened so much that her eyebrows nearly flew off her scalp. 'Is there something wrong with the quality of my full English? I'll have you know that you won't find better quality sausages in an eight-mile radius.'

Duke stared at his thumbs as he twiddled them. 'I thought I'd try watching my weight, is all.'

'And what's brought this on?'

'Just something someone said to me this morning. Nowt important, but I wonder if she wasn't right.' Duke reminded Alice of a child who'd been caught with a frog in his bedside cabinet; he wouldn't look either of them in the eye and his shoulders had risen so much that they were practically a stole.

'Who?' Mavis's interrogation made her seem like a cross between a concerned mother and a ferocious jaguar. She had her arms folded; her food-order pad trapped under her left armpit.

'Mrs Cribbins.'

Alice gritted her teeth. She had one or two thoughts of her own about the busybodies in town, and at that moment she was struggling to contain them.

'Norma Cribbins has no right to talk about anyone's weight,' Mavis said. 'She's been a member of Bulge Busters for so long that she should own shares in the company. Next time I see her, I'm going to remind her how many years she went without a banana and see whether she still fancies talking about someone else's weight then.'

'It doesn't mean that I shouldn't think more about what I'm eating.'

'That's all well and good, Marmaduke Featherstone, but you aren't about to do that in my establishment. Now, what are you having to drink?' She had her pen poised, ready to scribble.

Alice swallowed the ire she'd felt on Duke's behalf and said, 'I'll have a latte, Duke's on a pot of tea and Jez wants his flat white made with oat milk because he's trying to be all cosmopolitan.'

Mavis sucked her teeth.

This was the moment that Jez chose to enter the café, and silence descended as Mavis turned on him. Alice was reminded of Cady in *Mean Girls* when the entire gym was silent, although it took some thinking to imagine Mavis in an All-American high school. It wasn't just that she was a septuagenarian with a face like a walnut and a smoker's cough; she also had an aversion to anything pink.

Meanwhile, Jez look more afraid than he would've been if he'd been faced by an armed assailant. At least he was trained for those situations. Alice knew there was nothing in the police handbook about short septuagenarians with tight perms and a penchant for Kenny Rogers.

'What in the good lord's name is oat milk?' Mavis growled.

He looked to Alice, the beginnings of a frown wrinkling his forehead. 'Did you put her up to this?'

'It just seems very on-trend at the moment.' She offered a grin that was filled to the brim with menace.

'It's been around for decades,' Jez said to Mavis.

'Not here, it hasn't.' She eyed him up and down; she'd perfected her ability to bring a person down to size over the years. Or down to her size, at least.

'If it's too difficult to make, I'll just have skimmed. It's fine.'

'You'll do no such thing,' Mavis said. 'I'll have no one leaving here saying as I wasn't able to fulfil their dietary needs, even if they do turn up with faddy attitudes that are more suited to Manchester than a quiet, provincial eatery.'

Jez had been unable to remove the stunned look from his face, giving him a look of a goldfish in need of its dinner. Sure, he kept up his weightlifting regime, filling out his shirt in a fashion that made his husband blush, but when faced with Mavis Thistlethwaite, he was almost reduced to a toddler.

'Go on then, describe this *oat* milk to me. Last time I checked, oats don't have nipples.'

'It's an alternative to dairy, like all the nut milks on the market. This one is just made with oats.' Jez looked at the floor tiles as he explained it to Mavis. She had something hawkish in her gaze that had been reported to reduce many a person to cinders.

'I know how they make those and all. Sounds as though I could've strained the fluid off some porridge and saved it for you. I might have some UHT soya milk in the back from when our Theo was going through a phase, will that do?'

Jez nodded, still unable to look Mavis in the eyes.

'Sit yourself down and I'll bring it over.' Mavis sighed something about the youth of today before heading back behind the counter to get started on their order.

Jez exhaled and made his way over to the table, glaring at Alice the entire way. 'You didn't have to make such a fuss about the milk.'

'I couldn't pass up an opportunity to take the proverbial.'

'This is all because I wondered if you assaulted Ryan, isn't it?' Jez shook his head. 'I've already said sorry for that, but now I know that it can't have been you. A colleague has spoken to the owners of the kebab shop and seen the CCTV footage. We now have confirmation that you were nowhere near Magwitch Road at the time.'

'You never said that's where Ryan was assaulted.'

Jez nodded. 'I know.'

'Just in case you slipped up and mentioned anything related to the crime,' Duke said, leaning forward and planting his elbows on the table. 'I wouldn't think too much about it, Alice. He's your friend, but he's got to stick to police procedure at least some of the time.'

Jez inclined his head in Duke's direction, thanking

him for his solidarity.

Alice looked between them both in disbelief. 'I suppose this is what I get for making friends with the police force.'

'I mean, not the entirety of the police force.'

'Some of them hold on to the fact that you had our former DI sent down for murder.'

She ran her hands through her hair and sank down in her seat. 'That's just typical of people. You think that you're doing the right thing by catching a bad guy before he can strike again, but they can't see him as a murderer. To them, he's simply the godfather to their children or a man who liked an egg custard tart.'

'That's about the measure of things. Others think that he was close to retirement and so we should have let things lie.'

'He killed a fellow detective, who also happened to be his friend, and was about to kill another.'

'I'm on your side, Alice. I'm just saying as there's a few who aren't.'

She started fiddling with the edge of a doily as Mavis approached with their drinks. 'That's exactly the sort of thing that I dislike about the people in town.'

'You shouldn't let it affect you,' Mavis said. 'If anyone says anything near me, I soon set them straight. You should have heard Mrs Pigeon in the butchers. She started ranting about how she wouldn't be surprised to hear that you'd framed Clive just to cover your own tracks. I said to her that if she thought you capable of murder then she'd clearly never tried your pastry. There isn't a person on the planet who could make shortcrust so light if they were a killer. I imagine they'd have a tendency to overwork it. "No," I said to her, "Alice isn't a killer. She can be a bit aggressive at times, but that's par for the course when you were brought up by Magdalena Valentine." Oh, she could pack a punch, could Magda. It's one of the reasons why we always got on. I'd be there with my pint of bitter, she'd have her cider, and we wouldn't have to worry about any reprobates trying anything funny.'

Alice smiled. She'd grown to appreciate stories about Aunty Magdalena, even if it stung that she wasn't still around to answer questions about them. 'Thanks Mavis,' she said, taking a sip of her latte to settle the rising lump in her throat.

Mavis nodded and turned on her heel, returning to the kitchen.

'Did you only talk about what happened to Ryan?' Duke asked Jez.

'I asked if there had been any reports of a person falling overboard. Now I'm just waiting for them to get back to me.'

'If what he said about Gloria is true, do you think it could be related to his assault?'

Jez shrugged. 'Nobody saw Ryan for three months and then he's assaulted within the first few days of his return? It could just be a coincidence. This might not have been a targeted assault at all, more a case of him being in the wrong place at the wrong time, but I can't deny having my suspicions. That's entirely off-the-record, of course.'

'I'll make sure I tell no one!' Mavis called from the kitchen.

The three of them descended into laughter.

'There's someone who won't have to worry about an audiology test. She has better hearing than a dolphin,'

Duke said, while pouring himself a cup of tea.

'A dolphin?'

'Aye, a dolphin. They've got some of the best hearing on the planet. I saw it on a documentary.'

Alice blinked away her bewilderment before asking Jez, 'Has anyone reviewed the CCTV from the attack?'

He finished slurping his coffee and grimaced. 'Not yet. They're waiting on some footage. We've put out a call for witnesses on social media, but we haven't heard anything.'

'It hasn't been twelve hours since the attack,' said Duke. 'If folk were out at that time, the chances are that they aren't even out of bed.'

'I am,' said Alice.

'I meant normal people. Those who are lucky enough to still experience the joys of a hangover.'

'Just because you sleep for eighteen hours a day.'

'Be fair, Alice,' Jez said, smirking. 'There's not much for a man to do after the age of seventy-two.'

Alice grinned in his direction. 'I love it when you're sarcastic.'

Duke nodded at him. 'I agree. It's like you're finally becoming a human being.'

A few minutes later, their breakfasts were served, and the conversation shifted to the more mundane aspects of their lives. Mavis asked Alice to acquire some hash-browns before her shift the following day. The Partridge Mews Amateur Dramatic Society was in uproar because someone had stolen the makeup, so Jez had to run Ben into Manchester because they had a production of *My Fair Lady* in a month and some folk needed a hefty amount of concealer before being allowed anywhere near a stage.

Otherwise, they passed the meal in polite conversation.

Mavis joined them as they finished eating, chugging coffee from a pint mug; she took it strong with so much sugar it was a wonder she wasn't put into a diabetic coma with one sip. Alice knew she was still upset that the laws had changed over a decade earlier and that she was no longer allowed to smoke indoors; there was nothing Mavis Thistlethwaite liked more than chatting with friends over coffee with a cigarette bookmarked between the index and middle fingers of her right hand.

Chapter Five

1989

Marmaduke stood at the front gate, his right hand hovering over the latch.

He felt as though a donkey stone had taken root in his oesophagus, refusing to budge no matter how much he tried to choke it down.

Curtains twitched at the surrounding houses as folk searched for gossip in the hopes of giving their existence some meaning. Yet there he was, unable to gather the strength necessary to wander down a garden path and share the news that would ruin the lives of two friends he'd known since they'd spent their days catching newts in jam jars.

He steeled himself and opened the gate, practically catapulting towards the front door so he didn't lose any courage. One step in front of the other, shoulders back, breathe. He didn't even have chance to knock before

Edith had opened the door and was standing in front of him with an expression on her face that he couldn't decipher.

'What's he gone and done this time?' she asked.

Marmaduke was momentarily stunned. He blinked a few times behind his sunglasses before taking a handkerchief from his pocket and using it to mop the sweat from the back of his neck. 'Is he home, Mrs Simpson?'

'He's in the lounge, playing with Martin.'

He'd forgotten that Lucy had a son. 'Is there anyone who could take him for the afternoon?'

She considered his words for a moment. 'Why are you being professional, Marmaduke? What's happened?'

'I think it best if we step inside,' he said.

Edith's skin blanched, despite the heat. She beckoned him indoors and led him through to find Alf, who was sitting on the floor and playing peekaboo with his grandson – a baby who'd grow up with no recollection of his mother.

Alf's eyebrows raised in confusion. 'Just popping in for a friendly visit, Duke?'

Marmaduke breathed deeply, inhaling through his nose with all the strength of a prized bull. 'I thought it best for me to call around, but maybe I should have left it to a Family Liaison Officer.'

'It's Lucy, isn't it?' Edith said, her words high-pitched, unable to keep the fearful tremor from her voice. 'What's happened?'

'In the early hours of this morning, a body was discovered in Barraclough's Field. Having visited the scene myself, I believe the deceased to have been Lucy.'

Marmaduke would never grow accustomed to the

sound of a mother wailing over the loss of her only child.

Later, once he'd driven Alf to the morgue to confirm the corpse's identity, Marmaduke wished he'd allowed someone else to inform the Simpsons of their daughter's murder.

There were some things that a friendship could never recover from.

From The Partridge Mews Gazette

BODY AT BARRACLOUGH'S

The body found in Barraclough's Field on Wednesday morning has been identified as local woman, Lucy Simpson.

Her remains were discovered by a dog walker who alerted the police.

The investigation surrounding the circumstances of Miss Simpson's demise is ongoing, and the police ask the public not to speculate at this time.

If you have any information that may prove beneficial, please contact the station.

LUCY SIMPSON
1970-1989

Beloved daughter to Alfred and Edith and mother to Martin. She will be eternally missed. Funeral to be held at St. Michael's Church on 3rd April at 11am, followed by internment. Wake to be held at The Hare and Horse.

ARREST MADE IN CONNECTION TO SIMPSON MURDER

A man has been arrested in connection with the murder of Lucy Simpson, whose body was found in Barraclough's Field towards the end of March.

Alan Harris of Goshawk Farm was taken into police custody but denies any wrongdoing.

BLUNDER IN BARRACLOUGH INVESTIGATION

Partridge Mews Police have issued an apology to a local farmer after he was wrongfully arrested for the murder of Lucy Simpson. A spokesperson for the police said, 'Having reviewed the evidence and corroborated testimonies from certain individuals, we have released Mr Harris and apologise that his name was made public in connection to this case. We will be further investigating how the press managed to learn of his identity as we have strict confidentiality procedures in place.'

Old newspapers and photocopied police files that shouldn't have been in Duke's possession covered almost every surface of his living room. It wasn't as bad as when Alice had first met him, though. Once she'd decided that she wasn't going to slaughter him and sell his remains to Pedigree Chum, she'd helped him to tidy up. Naturally, his habit for dropping rubbish wherever he stood remained a bone of contention, but the place no longer smelt like rancid pork.

When they arrived back at the house, Duke presented Alice with the note as they were bringing boxes in from his shed. Well, she was carrying everything indoors while he supervised, having developed a convenient twinge in his back. That was a danger after seventy; suppose he slipped a disc.

Gooseflesh prickled up Alice's arms as she read about Lucy Simpson. She'd been in her late teens when she was murdered and had never reached Alice's age; her body had been left to rot among tall grass and gorse bushes. Barraclough's Field had been a source of much conversation over the decades as developers had looked to acquire the land and transform it into a housing estate, yet the farmer who owned it had always refused to sell. Otherwise, most teenagers in town had been caught getting up to mischief there. Alice remembered her own adolescence: adding cheap vodka to bottles of Coca-Cola and taking it there to drink with her friends, kissing her first major boyfriend beneath the stars as they listened to Kid Rock on his iPod. Everyone had their own tales about Barraclough's Field, and Alice was glad that her own were filled with joy as opposed to those of Lucy

Simpson's family.

Having taken her time to mull over certain aspects of the case, Alice asked, 'Is there any reason why Lucy's body was left where it was?'

Duke looked up from the file he was reading. He considered her words for a moment before saying, 'None that we ever found out.'

'And the police never uncovered her killer?'

Duke shook his head. 'There just wasn't enough evidence.'

'What about DNA?'

'It was relatively new at the time,' he said. 'Besides, whoever killed her made sure that they didn't get their hands dirty.'

Alice cocked her head to the side. 'What do you mean?'

'Digitalis poisoning. Whoever did it had clearly been reading too much Agatha Christie.' Duke closed the file and set it down on the table beside him.

'What motive could someone have for poisoning her, then?'

'I suppose you haven't got to that yet,' he said, indicating the mess surrounding them. 'Nobody knows why Lucy was killed, but I always wondered if it had something to do with the father of her baby.'

'The baby being Martin?' Alice asked, recalling the obituary.

'No. A few weeks before her death, she had an abortion.'

'And you think that if you found the father of that baby, it could lead you towards the killer?'

He nodded. 'That's why Alan Harris was arrested. His wallet was found at the scene.'

'How did you find out he wasn't the killer then?'

'He'd reported his wallet as missing at least a fortnight earlier,' he said. 'And he's gay. Not an easy thing to admit in the eighties in Partridge Mews, but if he hadn't then he could have been sent down for murder.'

'It would have taken more than a man's wallet to see him sent down, surely?'

Duke scratched his chin, tugging at the white, wiry hairs sprouting there. 'People were after blood, Alice. They didn't care who did it, as long as they had someone to blame.'

'Did you ever find Lucy's boyfriend?'

'We tried,' Duke said. 'We asked all her friends, but everyone called him her mystery man. They knew she was in some sort of relationship, but she never let on who he was.'

Alice understood that. The way that people gossiped in town left folk holding onto secrets as tightly as they could, wanting to have something that couldn't be tarnished by the snide comments of others. Thinking about the curtain-twitchers brought her thoughts back around to the note. 'Could Mrs Cribbins have known his identity? Maybe that's why she received the note.'

'Could be.' Duke shrugged. 'You know the way folk gossip in this town. You can't scratch your arm without some so-and-so from the WI telling everyone you've got leprosy.'

'So, what are we going to do?'

Duke ran a hand through his hair. It remained a wonder to Alice that he had such a substantial blonde mane atop his scalp that most men half his age would envy. It was one of the reasons why he reminded her of a big cat, along with his hair and the number of daily naps he took, although she supposed the latter could be thanks to old age.

As further proof of his possible feline heritage, he yowled and said, 'I'll go back to see her, ask if she remembers anything about Lucy's fella.'

'We could also speak to a few friends of Mrs Cribbins and find out if they've received any letters.'

'They'll probably want to keep quiet, though. Not many folks like being associated with a murder, even if it happened nearly thirty years ago.'

'I'll speak to my mum and see if she knows anything,' Alice said. 'She's part of the WI.'

There was an unmistakeable twinkle in Duke's eyes. It could have been glaucoma, but Alice hoped it was pride. 'Now you're thinking like a detective.'

'Just don't tell Jez. He gets all fussy if he thinks I'll end up interfering in a police investigation.'

'Mrs Cribbins asked me to investigate the poison pen letter because she doesn't want anyone else knowing about it. This has nothing to do with the police. We're just two people helping out an old lady.'

'She's not that much older than you, surely?'

'Anyone who still has net curtains is practically ancient, and don't you forget it.'

She returned his grin, but soon enough her thoughts flashed back to the murder of a young woman. Once more, she acknowledged all the paperwork in Duke's living room. When he'd first revealed his shed, Alice had imagined that it was a shrine to his missing niece, Joanna. Having discovered that there were articles pertaining to another unsolved case, she found herself mulling over the possible reasons. After nearly chewing off her own lips while thinking about it, she said, 'Is there a connection between Lucy's murder and Joanna's disappearance?'

Duke heaved a sigh from the depths of his lungs, his stomach practically going concave with the force. He remained quiet for a few moments and said, 'If it hadn't been for the murder of Lucy Simpson then Joanna might be here today.'

'What do you mean?'

'While the police dithered about, she decided to investigate the murder herself.'

The breath caught in Alice's throat; a sense of foreboding coiled around her trachea like an anaconda intent on suffocation. She stared at Duke, concern in her gaze. 'Do you think she was successful?'

'In finding Lucy's killer? I've no doubt about it. She's my niece. She inherited my deductive reasoning.'

'Rather that than your flatulence.' Alice hadn't planned on being so flippant, but the sombre tone permeating throughout the living room was causing the familiar ache of grief to creak in her chest again.

'I should've known that you'd lower the tone.'

'Sorry,' she said. She shook her head. 'I shouldn't have said that.'

'Don't be. Sometimes serious matters require indecent humour. I'd have expected nothing less.'

Alice offered a weak smile and rose to her feet. 'I'm going to make a cup of tea and then we'll set about clearing this place up before Jez gets here. If he sees how many police files we have in our possession, he's likely to have a coronary.'

She matched her actions to her words. After she made the drinks, she helped to return the newspaper articles and police files to their boxes. There was no air of professionalism about the way that Duke operated. He'd used anything to hand so that the important files he kept to investigate his niece's disappearance were stored in boxes meant for cheese and onion crisps, peanuts and orange squash. If Duke was ever the subject of an investigation, the confidential information he'd pilfered would appear innocuous among the rest of the mess in his shed.

Jez arrived not much later. He looked apologetic as he sidled into the living room, tapping the back of his phone disconsolately. 'We've heard back from a coastguard, and, despite some confusion, a passenger was reported to have fallen overboard.'

'And it was definitely Gloria?'

'There isn't any confirmation, but I'd say it's likely. We don't often get reports of people falling from cruise ships.'

Alice groaned and pressed the heels of her palms against her eyes. She'd pinned her hopes on the police finding Gloria Hebblethwaite sitting in front of the television, yelling at *Embarrassing Bodies* because she was sure that bicarbonate of soda was the main cause of impotence in men over the age of forty-one.

However, it seemed that she had indeed fallen from the balcony of a cruise ship and Alice was going to have to apologise. 'Ryan is going to be so smug.'

'His grandmother is dead. What's he got to be smug about?'

'That I didn't believe him,' she said. 'He'll be smug because I look like the bad guy. And if I don't apologise, I'll be seen as heartless, even though everyone knows that I can't stand to be within three feet of him.'

'I heard you got a lot closer than that,' Duke said, smirking.

'Before I realised just what a cad he is.'

'A cad?' Duke stifled a chuckle.

'Have you been watching *Miss Marple* again?' This from Jez, who'd gone from apologetic to mocking in an instant.

Alice averted her gaze, unable to contend with their needling when she was thinking about another dead resident of Partridge Mews. It felt as though all she dealt with was death. 'There was a *Marple* marathon on television last week, but that doesn't stop Ryan from being a cad,' she said.

'You could've gone with "twerp".'

'Or "nincompoop",' Duke suggested.

'I'm not averse to "numpty",' Jez said. 'But "cad" just isn't it.'

Alice stared at the ceiling and focused on her breathing. She inhaled deeply, refusing to descend to their level, before she exhaled and said, 'If I agree to apologise to Ryan, can we stop discussing my use of outdated insults?'

'I'm not sure there's any point in apologising.'

'Why not?'

'Regardless of whether you're sorry that Gloria died, everyone knows that you can't stand Ryan. I think it's best if you two stay well away from each other.'

Alice refused to give Jez the satisfaction of telling him that he was right. She might be glad to have finally called an end to things with Ryan, but that didn't mean his behaviour stung any less. She'd wanted him out of her life and had planned to spend the day forgetting about him. She was going to bake a carrot cake, practice her piping skills, and invite her mother around to watch *Gilmore Girls*. But instead, she'd awoken to find that Ryan had been assaulted, and that had just been the beginning of what was proving to be a rather difficult day.

Chapter Six

Alice decided to drive to her parents' house in silence. No sooner had Ed Sheeran started blaring from the radio than she'd switched it off and sank down in her seat. She closed her eyes and pinched the bridge of her nose. The men in her life were proving to be such nuisances that she wondered if life would be easier if she joined a convent. But she didn't have the credentials to be a nun, and she'd seen *Sister Act* enough times to know that the job might not come with the silence and absence of men that she craved. She permitted herself a few moments to bask in the solitude of her car, made sure that the doors were locked, and embarked upon her journey.

She found her father in the living room, gazing absent-mindedly at an episode of *Find It, Fix It, Flog It*. Strangely for the middle of the day, Norman was in his pyjamas. He paused the television and blinked theatrically a few times, emulating a gawping blue tang, before producing a smile for Alice. 'Don't tell your mother.'

'Don't tell her what?' She slumped down beside him.

'What's on the telly. Last time she watched an episode, I couldn't move in the back garden for shabby chic furniture.'

'That sounds about right.'

Alice sighed and leaned her head against her dad's shoulder. She'd grown accustomed to her parents' habits and their reliability. Norman would forever have an unhealthy obsession with bicycles, and Primrose was always on the search for a new hobby or activity. She'd joined a cake-making class after binge-watching the first three series of *The Great British Bake Off* in one weekend. She didn't last long; the teacher had insulted her piping skills, so she'd transferred to pottery. Then, after a kiln mishap and the immolation of a toupee, The Adult Learning Centre had refunded Primrose's money and asked her to think long and hard before applying for one of their courses again.

There was also the summer that Primrose had spent as a magician's assistant, but that all fell apart when she was tasked with tying him up – her knots were too tight, so he couldn't escape the hessian sack in time and nearly drowned. Although Primrose was a dab hand when it came to mouth-to-mouth resuscitation, she'd never worked for him again. Indeed, since so many of her pursuits had ended in a blaze, she'd agreed in future to only attempt new hobbies where heat wasn't required. She'd walked out of an upholstery workshop when they mentioned using a hot glue gun.

'Where is Mum, anyway?' Alice asked.

Norman rubbed at his eyes, pinching the bridge of his nose. 'There's a jumble sale at the church hall and someone's coming to pick up a few bags this afternoon, so your mother is using it as an excuse to clear out the back bedroom.'

'Unless she comes downstairs, sees what you're watching and decides to repurpose it all.'

'Always a possibility where your mother is concerned.' Norman yawned.

Alice noticed a greyish pallor to his skin. 'Dad, I hope you don't get offended with me asking, but why are you home? It's a workday.'

'Just a migraine and a little bit of insomnia. I've got some painkillers and sleeping pills from the doctor, so there's nothing to worry about.'

'I'm worried.'

'Well, don't be.'

'It doesn't really work that way.'

'I'm using my paternal rights to forbid you from worrying about me.'

Alice met his gaze, and they chuckled together. 'All right, then. I'll try not to worry, but I make no promises. If it gets serious, you'd better let me know. I don't want a repeat of October 2004.'

'There was nothing to worry about then, either.'

'You had pneumonia.'

'I recovered though, didn't I? Besides, I'm duty-bound to never let you worry about anything. It was in one of your mother's parenting manuals.'

'Right. Since I'm not allowed to worry, can I go and make a brew?'

'You'll have to check with your mother. She's got some new homeopathic concoction to try and heal me.' He drew his dressing gown tighter around himself and leaned his head back against a sofa cushion. 'Just pop up and ask her first. I think I need to rest my eyes.'

Alice went upstairs to the back bedroom, where Primrose was in the middle of forcing a mauve anorak into a bin bag.

'I don't think I've ever seen you wear that,' she said.

Primrose shot up, spooked, a hand flying to her chest. 'You got me there, love. I don't remember the coat at all. It's probably an unwanted gift from your grandmother. Whenever she got her hands on a Littlewoods' catalogue, she'd start ordering me clothes in the hopes of smartening me up a bit. Still, hers was a different era.'

Alice smiled. Primrose didn't like to speak ill of her mother, because she hated the idea of anyone judging her own parenting skills. She decided to change the topic and said, 'Dad told me not to tell you that he's watching *Find it, Fix It, Flog It*.'

Her mother sighed. 'Do you know the wonders that woman can do with a spot of nail polish and an old blanket box? Unbelievable.'

'I hope you're not getting any ideas.' Alice slumped down beside Primrose.

'I've been debating what to do with that Lloyd Loom chair.'

'Don't you have enough on already?'

'I thought it would make a nice weekend project,' she said. 'Something to do while your father is out with the cycling club.'

The back bedroom had become a reliquary for all of Primrose's abandoned interests. On top of one wardrobe, there was a box filled with bedazzled bodices, rope and assorted tools of the magician's trade. There were dumb-bells and boxing gloves, yoga mats and candle-making kits; there was a large plastic barrel from when she'd tried brewing her own artisanal beer. There were stools and odd dining chairs from when she'd decided to start upcycling. Indeed, the Lloyd Loom chair had been purchased from the charity shop when she'd developed a fondness for shabby chic furniture. It hadn't taken long for her to realise that she preferred such styles to furnish other people's homes.

Alice looked at the Royal Worcester figurines on the windowsill. 'Do you think that you'll ever settle on anything, Mum?'

Primrose tied up the bin bag. 'It's not about settling on something, Al. I've stuck with plenty over the years.'

'You've given up plenty as well.'

'It's not giving up. I try a lot of things because I develop an interest and want to see if it's for me. If it turns out to be a passing fancy, then I'm not disappointed because I tried something new.'

'How do you remain so positive?' Alice waded through the trash to wrap her arms around Primrose. She nuzzled her shoulder, thinking about all that had happened since she'd woken up that morning. Had she known everything that was in store, she would have stayed in bed, cocooned herself beneath the duvet and spent her time more wisely, watching make-up tutorials on her phone.

'What's happened?'

'It's just been a tough day.'

'Will a drink help?'

'It might.'

'Then it'll have to be vodka. I'm on a detox.'

'I was thinking more along the lines of tea,' she said. 'Dad wants whatever concoction you're giving him to relieve his migraine.'

Primrose laughed. 'I add a touch of honey to some ginger tea and your father acts like it's the elixir of life.'

'Maybe you just have that touch.'

Primrose exhaled and tapped Alice's right shoulder, asking to be released from her daughter's hug.

Alice followed her mother downstairs into the kitchen. She didn't have the necessary fortitude to argue with her mother about what a detox meant. Instead, she accepted the offer of Grey Goose and coke and ignored the fact that it was one o'clock on a Wednesday afternoon, because sometimes life just called for a good stiff drink.

Once Primrose had taken Norman his tea, she and Alice sat down at the kitchen counter where, over their drinks, Alice told her about the day's events.

Primrose's expression grew more alarmed as the story continued, eyes wide, pupils darting this way and that. 'My goodness, that's a lot for one day.'

Alice took a sip. 'I know.'

'And you wonder whether I can think of anyone who might have received a poison pen letter?'

'It would be really helpful if you could.'

Primrose grew contemplative. She rested her arms on the counter, stroking an index finger over the rim of her glass. Eventually, she said, 'It's not something that the ladies are likely to tell one another about.'

'Duke said that Mrs Cribbins kept hers in a biscuit barrel.'

'Exactly. However, that doesn't mean they won't gossip if given the opportunity. I'll see what I can find out.'

'Thanks, Mum.'

Primrose flashed a smile before growing sombre. 'It

must be upsetting for Mrs Cribbins to be reminded of Lucy Simpson's death, though.'

'We don't understand why the letter writer contacted her.'

'Really?' Primrose said. 'I would have thought it was obvious, but then I suppose the police weren't looking so far back at the time.'

'What is it?'

'Norma Cribbins taught Lucy at primary school. She taught me, too. She was one of the longest-serving teachers in Partridge Mews. Of course, she'd retired by the time you went.' Primrose exhaled, a small gust blowing her fringe away from her forehead.

'Was she a good teacher?'

'One of the best. She's a busybody in her old age, but there was something about her that made you feel safe in her classroom.'

Alice mulled over the new knowledge. 'That doesn't explain why someone would send her a letter.'

'Perhaps they know more than we do.'

'Do you think we should be investigating this?'

'You and Duke, you mean?'

Alice stared into the depths of her glass. She supposed that the vodka had loosened her tongue, that it was the reason why she felt the need to voice her worries. 'At first, the letter was nothing more than a note, just some scrappy piece of paper that had upset an old lady. Now I know that it references an unsolved murder, it feels big.'

'Do you want to hand it over to the police?'

'Part of me thinks that would be the right thing to do,' Alice said. 'I can't help but feel like Duke is blinkered because he sees Lucy's death as being connected to Joanna's disappearance. Maybe this note can tell us more about the case than we realise.'

'You might be right, love.'

'But Duke was a detective, and I said I'd help him find Joanna. If there's a connection, then shouldn't I be more willing to help?'

Primrose stood up. She wandered over to the sink, empty glass in hand, and said, 'I can't answer that for you. You're not a detective or a private investigator. You work part-time at a café – '

' – only as a favour to the owner.'

'I've a serious question for you now, Alice.' Primrose turned to face her. She straightened her spine and folded her arms, trying to appear as imposing as a woman with a penchant for green tea and oversized cardigans could, and said, 'What exactly do you plan on doing with your life?'

Alice couldn't mask the shock on her face. She was flabbergasted; her lips floundered as she searched for the words to respond. 'Where did that come from?'

'I'm your mother and I love you, but can you honestly say that this is the life you planned on living?'

'Not exactly, but I didn't plan on getting sacked.'

'That was over a year ago now, Alice. At first, I didn't say anything because you were grieving Aunty Magdalena, but I thought that with time, you'd consider doing something more with your life.'

'Are you forgetting that I helped to solve a murder?'

'I know that you were left a considerable amount of money, but that will run out one day, and then what do you plan to do?'

'I just don't understand where this is coming from.'

'I want to know what your plans are when you're no longer helping Duke to search for his niece.' Primrose was staring so intensely that her eyes wouldn't have looked amiss on a hawk.

Alice stared at the kitchen window behind her mother, focusing on a singular sunbeam that struck the glass. She hadn't expected such an interrogation, especially one that highlighted all her insecurities. Every day, she saw friends and acquaintances on social media announcing new jobs, pets, relationships, and pregnancies. Some had even emigrated to the other side of the world, yet she was in the same town she'd been raised in. Of course, there were the few years she'd spent in Manchester getting her degree, but all she had to show for that were the regular debt reminders from the student loans company.

She had no idea why her mother had chosen to bring up the topic; Primrose wasn't usually the type of parent to question Alice's path in life as long as she remained safe, healthy, and didn't injure anyone. 'Have you been reading parenting manuals again?'

'I'll never stop reading them, but that's beside the point.'

'Because I didn't think I was failing that badly at life.'

Primrose took a noticeable gulp. She ran her hand over her throat, her impassive gaze momentarily weakened. 'I never said that you were a failure.'

'Then where is this coming from?'

'I simply thought it might help you to make a quick decision about whether to help Duke or not.'

Alice couldn't stop herself from smiling. She sighed. 'It did. You made me feel incredibly bad about my life, which isn't something I needed today, but it helped me to figure out what I'm going to do.'

'And?'

'You'll just have to wait and see.' Alice winked at Primrose and hopped off the bar stool. After their serious conversation, she desperately needed a cup of tea.

Chapter Seven

Alice didn't believe that her string of bad luck could go on for much longer. However, she was soon proven wrong. Having agreed to purchase hash browns before her shift, she drove to Marsden's on her way to work.

The shop was as empty as always. Most people in town wondered how Sandra managed to keep the place open considering she didn't get too many customers and things sat on the shelves for so long that most purchases came with a warning about their consumption.

Sandra didn't notice Alice as she entered. She simply watched steam rise from the mug she was nursing in her hands as though it held the very essence of life.

Realising that she wasn't going to receive any acknowledgement of her arrival, Alice walked down an aisle. She held her breath so that she wouldn't inhale the invasive stench of myrrh that filled the air. Sandra said that the smell reminded her of the time she'd spent at a holistic retreat in 1984, but everyone knew she'd accidentally joined a cult and only left because the leaders wouldn't invest in central heating.

The music in Marsden's left a lot to be desired as well; an incandescent chanting in basso profondo that could have been religious, but the choristers could have been trying to sell vacuum cleaners, and Alice would have been none the wiser. All their words melded into one long, sonorous note, sounding almost like a snoring grizzly bear.

Alice debated why she bothered visiting the shop at all, considering the number of senses she was trying to dampen as she traipsed around in her search for groceries. She stopped at the end of the aisle and looked down at the floor. Everything in Marsden's was usually accompanied by a layer of dust; Sandra claimed that she didn't dust because she didn't want to disrupt the earth's natural sediment, but everyone knew that she just had an aversion to picking up a dustpan and brush.

Yet as Alice reached the freezers, she realised that someone had swept the floor. From the way it shone, it might even have been mopped – a plausible theory considering the aroma of disinfectant surrounding the area. Perhaps there'd been a spillage, although that wasn't usually enough to get Sandra cleaning. A cup of coffee was once catapulted against the wall behind the counter when she opened the till drawer, and the stain had remained for three years until she'd repainted.

Alice didn't have time to question why Sandra had chosen to clean the floor when the entire place needed an overhaul. Besides, there were a few heavy boxes scattered on top of the freezer that she wanted to get to, so it wasn't the most pressing issue. Once she heaved them out of the way, Alice lifted the lid of the freezer and stared down in disbelief.

She stood still for a few moments, not quite able to believe what she was seeing.

'For crying out loud,' Alice said. She slammed the lid shut and spun on her heel. 'No, I'm not dealing with this today. If Mavis wants hash browns, she can damn well get them herself.'

In her rush to leave the shop, she sent a tower of toilet rolls flying, startling Sandra from her reverie. That was about to be the least of the shopkeeper's worries.

Alice surged over to her car. She left the door open as she sank into the driver's seat, settling her head against the steering wheel and gripping it tightly. The sight she'd witnessed in the freezer was stamped onto her corneas. She pushed down her rising nausea and focused on her breathing.

After talking to herself for a few minutes, muttering that she'd had enough for one week and that she ought to leave it to someone else, she closed her eyes and leaned against the steering wheel. It wasn't much longer before there was a knock on the top of her car.

Alice bolted upright.

'Are you okay in there?'

Although Alice could place the voice, she couldn't remember who it belonged to. She opened her eyes to find an ursine young woman crouching down to look through the window, her curly hair almost blocking out all the sunlight. Alice thought back to where she remembered the woman from and opened the door. 'You're Lorelai's friend. Becky, isn't it?'

'It's nice to see you again, even if you're looking fed up.'

'I'm wishing I'd stayed in bed.'

'You should tackle your problems head-on, Alice. It won't do to dwell on them.'

'That sounds like something my mum would say.'

'Then she's a smart lady.' Becky smiled kindly.

Alice noticed that Becky's hands were wrapped with bandages. 'Did you get those during the judo tournament?'

She raised her hands as though seeing the dressings for the first time. 'It can be a bit rough can judo, especially when you're going up against men who think women belong in the kitchen.'

'So, you ended up teaching them a few lessons?'

'You're exactly right. I might not have won the tournament, but I did my best.'

'That's all you can do.'

'Now, are you feeling better? I don't want to rush rescuing you from the doldrums, but I've got to book a holiday for my manager's greyhound.'

Alice thought about Becky's words and about what was waiting for her in Marsden's. This wasn't the first time that she'd dealt with such things, and if she left, she might be leaving the scene of the crime. She mustered a smile and said, 'I'll be fine. Thanks for stopping and checking on me.'

'It's just what decent folk do, Alice. We look out for each other.' Becky returned to her own car and drove away, waving as she went. A warm glow rose over Alice's cheeks, and she beamed at the idea that she might be making friends.

Then she recalled what she had to do, sighed and left her car again.

A few vehicles trundled past as she stepped into the subtle warmth of the September morning, their drivers oblivious to what was going on merely feet away.

She returned to the shop to discover that Sandra hadn't moved from her spot behind the counter, so Alice had to navigate her way around a maze of scattered toilet rolls. She considered tidying up her mess but decided against it. If anything, it added to the neglected ambience of the place.

When she reached the counter, Alice said, 'Sandra, are you aware that there's a corpse in your freezer?'

She blinked a few times as though lost in a daydream. 'Is there? What species?'

'Human, of course.'

'Why did you say, "of course"? The corpse could have been that of a fish, or an Alsatian. You could have been a vegan protester.'

It was Alice's turn to stare at Sandra in disbelief. 'Why is there a dead woman in the freezer?'

Sandra shrugged, nonchalant. 'I haven't the foggiest.'

'Don't you know her?'

'I don't often communicate with the dead,' Sandra said. 'That was always my mother's thing. That's not to say I haven't had my share of visitations.'

Before the shopkeeper could head off on a tangent about her paranormal experiences – which likely amounted to a few too many shots of absinthe and a trip to the churchyard – Alice asked, 'Are you seriously telling me that you had no idea there was a dead body in your freezer?'

She supped from her mug and grimaced. 'I can't say as I did, no. It's always tough for me before midday. I've found that after forty, it's much more difficult to leave the astral plane.'

'You didn't walk the shop floor beforehand?'

More oblivious blinking from Sandra, who sat open-mouthed, giving off the appearance of a goldfish staring out of its tank. 'I never really saw the need.'

'Generally, it's a good way to see what stock needs replenishing.'

'I'm not sure my customers come here for stock.'

Alice pinched the bridge of her nose. While everything within her said not to question Sandra about the way she ran her business considering there was the more pressing matter of a corpse on the premises, she still asked, 'Why else would your customers visit?'

'I've always found it a rather calming place.'

'You could be onto something there. What if the woman was so calmed by the place that she chose to lie down in the freezer for a snooze and accidentally offed herself?'

Sandra nodded, pouting like a gorilla in agreement. 'I imagine that must be what happened.'

Alice pulled out her phone and called Jez.

Once he answered, she told him about finding the body while steering clear of any theories about its origins.

While she waited for the police to arrive, Alice returned to the freezer and took a few photographs of the scene. She'd show them to Marmaduke later and get his opinion, but the more pictures she took on her phone, the more that it dawned on her that she was wandering all over a crime scene.

The woman in the freezer looked to be in her sixties or seventies, with dark hair that had started to grey at the roots. She wore a mauve anorak and while that drew to mind the coat her mother had thrown out the previous day, Alice had no way of identifying her.

Alice stopped in her tracks and was just pocketing her

phone when Sandra turned up behind her. 'Oh, I hadn't actually believed there'd be a body in there.'

'Do you recognise her?'

Sandra leaned further into the freezer, scrutinising the corpse properly, squinting her eyes to the point at which they might as well have been closed. She stood up straight, shaking her head. 'I can't say as I know her, but then again, I've never been good with faces. I still can't tell the difference between Neil Diamond and Barry Manilow.'

'They look nothing alike.'

'So, you can understand my problem?'

Alice shook her head. 'I need some air.'

Alice waited beside her car until the police arrived.

When Jez pulled up, she grimaced at the person she saw in the passenger seat. As the two of them exited the vehicle, she asked, 'What did you have to bring him for?'

'Morning to you too, Alice,' Luke said, mustering a grin. He closed the passenger door and sauntered over.

Alice wondered if there was something written in the police code of conduct that said that their officers had to be painfully attractive. Luke was tall, dark, brooding and everything that she thought embodied the perfect specimen of a man; he also happened to be a complete and utter nitwit.

Luke had returned to Partridge Mews a year earlier, ostensibly to take on a new job but also to bury his grandfather.

There were a few issues surrounding the funeral arrangements for Arthur Sterling. It had taken the police a while to release his body, meaning that he'd been on ice for longer than an Iceland prawn ring. There was also the matter of contacting his next of kin. Arthur and his son were estranged from each other, and Luke had been deep undercover in Northumberland.

Hence, four months after one of his closest friends murdered him, Arthur was finally laid to rest. And it had been hotter than the Adult Learning Centre after one of Primrose Valentine's pottery classes. Alice recalled standing in the churchyard with Duke, waiting for the hearse to appear, wishing she hadn't worn black as a thin trickle of sweat beaded from her knee to her ankle.

'Honestly, who has a funeral in the summer?' Duke asked. 'Arthur wouldn't want to be buried in August.' He was tugging at his collar like a puppy refusing its lead.

'They couldn't leave him in the freezer much longer.'

'If he's not here soon, he'll thaw out. Luke could've saved money on a burial and left the coffin out in the street. It's hot enough that Arthur would soon be cremated.'

Alice gave Duke a wary look. 'You remember that he was your friend, right?'

'You'll find as you get older that you joke about death more. There's really not much doing between *Bargain Hunt* and *The Chase*.'

Luckily, the hearse arrived at that moment. Otherwise, Alice would have rolled her eyes, and she did that so often following Duke's comments that she worried they'd soon fall out of her head.

It had been the first time that Alice had seen Luke since the summers of her teenage years when she used to watch him mowing his grandfather's lawn, imagining the two of them together like something out of *One Tree Hill*. She wasn't sure how she'd expected their encounter to go, but she didn't imagine having to stop him brawling at a funeral – bawling, maybe.

As soon as Luke stepped out of the hearse, he was haring across the graveyard towards a tall, thin man who stood somewhat inconspicuously beside a drystone wall – the same wall that he was catapulted over when Luke landed a right hook against the man's cheek. He yelled with such rage that Alice couldn't understand a word of it, but from what she gathered, the floored man was his father.

Ian staggered to his feet, bewildered, as Luke pounced on him again.

If this was an image of masculine grief, then Alice wanted no part of it. However, as two of the younger people present, she and Jez headed over. He immediately put himself between Luke and Ian, who'd started grabbing at his son, his arms whacking against shoulders and torso, not really caring where he hit so long as he made a connection.

Alice watched for a moment. Although Jez was a policeman, he looked entirely out of place in the scenario. She braced herself and stepped between the Sterling men, yelling, 'It's a funeral, for crying out loud, so stop being idiots.' Alice pushed her hands against Luke's chest, forcing him away from his father and back towards the hearse. Once they were out of punching distance, she stopped. 'I know you don't like him, but that was shameful.'

Luke glowered at her. 'What are you doing here, Alice?'

Perhaps the heat had got to him; she knew that grief could leave you feeling the fury of seven hells and, given the temperature, she was prepared to make some allowances for his behaviour.

'I solved your grandad's murder.'

'You found a hat.'

'No one else noticed it.' Alice diverted her gaze; being scrutinised by Luke left her feeling as though she had to protest her innocence.

He raised his voice slightly, giving his tone an air of exasperation and anger, as he said, 'Because who else thinks that the detective is the murderer?'

'I kind of expected more gratitude.'

'Yes, I'm very grateful that you found out that my grandfather was killed by his friend. It really softened the blow.'

Something in his tone made her forget his grief. She balled her fists, pressing her nails against her palms as she returned his glare – ire fizzed in her veins, from her wrists to her shoulders. She inhaled, settled her shoulders, silently seething as she asked, 'Would you have preferred it to have gone unsolved?'

'Clive was like an uncle to me when I was growing up.'

'Fantastic.' Alice offered a rictus grin. 'You just made this a whole lot more Shakespearian.'

'Are you comparing the murder to *Hamlet*?'

'At least you have some smarts about you. I thought I might have to settle for *The Lion King*.'

'Why don't you make like Ophelia and beggar off, then?'

'Did you just tell me to go and drown?'

'Now look who has some smarts about them.'

'Lord, I can't wait until you disappear back to Otterburn.'

She'd chosen to leave the funeral then and apologised

to Duke when she informed him that he'd have to find his own way home. A few weeks down the line, she'd learned that Luke wouldn't be leaving town after all, having accepted a job with the Partridge Mews constabulary, taking over the role once inhabited by his grandfather's killer.

Alice still believed he'd only taken the job to spite her.

After the funeral incident, she'd made sure that their encounters were rare, short, and insignificant.

It made sense that Jez would bring Luke along to the scene of a crime, but that didn't mean she had to be happy about it. If anything, she felt downright uncomfortable. She folded her arms over her chest and tried to keep her focus on her friend, rather than allowing her eyes to wander.

She couldn't ignore Luke's grin when he said, 'Well, *Miss* Valentine, thank you for reporting this to the correct authorities. We understand the internal struggle you must have faced as you strove to solve the case yourself.'

'I just found a dead body. Surely you can show me some compassion.'

'Compassion?' he scoffed. 'I'm more inclined to take you in for questioning.'

'Why?'

'You've developed a habit of finding bodies.'

'I didn't exactly plan on it. When a person goes shopping for hash browns, she doesn't expect to find a corpse.'

'Maybe we should go inside and take a look at the body,' Jez said.

'Are you telling me how to run this investigation, Carson?'

'Give it a rest, Luke.' He sighed. 'You don't like Alice, and she doesn't like you, but there's currently a corpse inside a freezer and no one has declared this a crime scene yet. If we don't get in there soon and cordon it off, some old dear will see it and before you know it, we'll have another body on our hands.'

Luke didn't say anything to do that, and Alice smiled to see him gawping.

'Go home, Alice,' Jez said. 'I'll come and get a statement later.'

'Without him?'

'I've learned my lesson. If I put you two together again, I'm likely to be the one getting done for homicide.'

Chapter Eight

When Marmaduke stepped into Mrs Patel's living room, he was shocked to discover that there were so many different shades of red. He recoiled from the crimson drapes and scarlet walls. The carpet was plush and vermilion; even the furniture hadn't escaped from Mrs Patel's rose-tinted vision. He gazed open-mouthed as he took it all in, feeling as though he was trapped inside a glacé cherry.

Mrs Patel invited him to sit down in an armchair. She'd set out a tea tray on a Formica table and proceeded to play mother, pouring rooibos into a cup marked "Collingswoods'". When he smelt the brew, he soon set the cup and saucer down. Mrs Patel's want for everything within her realm to be red had caused her to buy a tea that Marmaduke felt was more suited to a commune than a middle-class household in Partridge Mews, but then he'd never seen the need for anything other than English breakfast tea. He supposed that if Alice had been there, she would have told him to expand his horizons. Not that she had room to talk; she spent the better part of her days insulting her mother's penchant for green tea.

Once they were both settled, Marmaduke realised that the hem around his left ankle had dropped. He reached down and folded it back up, making a mental note to locate his Uncle Tiberius's sewing kit and set to it when he got home. 'You'd never know that I've only just bought these trousers, Mrs Patel.'

'I sympathise with your struggle. It's one of the reasons that I always source my husband's clothes from Rhodes Wood in Harrogate. Of course, it might be somewhat expensive, but I grew weary of constantly having to reinforce his seams.'

Marmaduke nodded along with her. He'd lost count of the number of times he'd put on a new pair of trousers, only to walk thirty yards down the road and be tripped by the dropped hem of a hastily-stitched ankle. 'It's almost as though the designers don't care about the finishing touches anymore.'

'They certainly don't make things like they used to.' Mrs Patel nibbled the corner off a custard cream and set it down on her saucer. 'I bought this dress on a recent trip to Cheshire Oaks with my daughter-in-law – you remember Dervla – and I was utterly dismayed at the current state of affairs.'

Mrs Patel's purple dress contrasted with the room around her. If she'd also been dressed in red, she'd have blended in with the sofa, her head mistaken for a cushion. Although, Marmaduke supposed, that would be a sure-fire way to hide from the unwanted advances of an amorous husband.

'I'm not too fussy,' Marmaduke said. 'I just want a

good, strong hem.'

'It must be straight. Some of these garments look like they were stitched during an earthquake.'

'That's the problem with fast fashion, I suppose.'

'You're quite correct. I simply wish people took more pride in their work. Of course, it must be difficult earning a pittance, but does that have to mean a total disregard for saddle stitch?'

'You make a strong case, Mrs Patel. There are shoddy hemlines and then there's this fashion for torn clothing. Folk going around like they've just scaled a barbed wire fence.'

Mrs Patel smirked. 'Have you changed, Marmaduke Featherstone? You've been seen in some rather ragged costumes in your time.'

He had Alice to blame for his recent attempts at dressing smart – she'd told him that he was categorically not allowed to wear jogging bottoms outside of the house; he'd even started checking for egg yolk stains before leaving. He shrugged and scratched the back of his neck before saying, 'That's true, I'll give you that. Still, that doesn't mean I understand the trend for wearing clothes that the charity shop would throw out.'

She took another bite from her biscuit. 'Now, I don't imagine that you came to chat fashion.'

'I didn't. I'm acting on behalf of a friend of yours. They've been the recipient of a poison pen letter.'

'Excuse me for being forward, but do you mean Norma Cribbins?'

He averted his gaze, stared down at the toes of his shoes; the smudges and scuffs reminded him that he'd meant to polish them the previous Thursday but had ended up engrossed in an episode of *The Professionals*.

'That's a possibility.'

'She's my closest friend, Mr Featherstone. I commend your discretion, though I already know about the letter.'

'And what do you think about it?' This time he met her gaze, watching for any twitch, any impression that she might not be entirely honest.

'I imagine it's some cruel youth with little better to do with their time.' She punctuated her sentence by biting the remainder of her custard cream clean in half.

'Even though they're referencing a crime that happened thirty years ago?'

'Precisely. We've all moved on with our lives. Mark my words, it will be some adolescent who found out about Lucy Simpson's murder and chose to scare their older neighbours.'

Her lips were spotted with biscuit crumbs. Marmaduke offered her his handkerchief, and as she dabbed at her mouth he asked, 'Do you have any idea why they would target Mrs Cribbins?'

Mrs Patel shook her head. 'I was targeted as well. I'm not sure that what I received can rightfully be called a letter, as it's just a string of numbers.'

She stood up and retrieved an envelope from the mantelpiece.

Duke took it from her. Once again, there was no postmark, no sign of the letter's origin. He removed a scrap of notepaper, on which someone had scrawled, "13:15". He squinted and mulled it over for a moment before handing it back to Mrs Patel. 'Could be a time.'

'Or a ratio.' She returned the envelope to the mantelpiece and sat back down.

'If we suspect that it's related to the first note then we could reasonably believe it has something to do with

Lucy Simpson.'

'But what? And why contact me and Norma? While we're friends with Edith Simpson, I can't think of another connection.'

'Your Dervla was friends with Lucy, wasn't she?'

'They were school friends, but I don't know how things stood when Lucy died.'

'Was there a falling out?'

'No, nothing like that. At least, I don't think so. Things became difficult when Lucy fell pregnant.'

'Why?'

'It was their A-Level year. While her friends were studying for their exams, she was nursing a baby. Then they went off to university and she was left on her own.'

Marmaduke didn't respond immediately. He reached for his tea and knocked it back, not caring about the flavour. He wondered if Lucy's friends' departure was what caused her to start hanging around with Joanna; he'd never understood why his niece had become so intent on solving the case. She was only a teenager herself and, as far as he knew, she hadn't been acquainted with Lucy for long enough to warrant such a reaction. Yet, he also knew that everything is urgent during adolescence. Perhaps Joanna thought that he and his colleagues were going about things incorrectly. A weight of familiar guilt churned in Marmaduke's stomach; it had been his constant companion for thirty years, ever since his sister had telephoned with the news of Joanna's disappearance, and he knew that she lay the blame squarely at his door.

He struggled to drag himself from his reverie. Over the years, he knew that he'd grown comfortable with his pain, had almost developed a kinship with the shame he felt at not being able to locate one of his own.

As he slowly sank further into the depths of his memory, he grew aware of Mrs Patel's eyes on him. He blinked a few times, as everything had developed a haze during his daydream. When his eyes readjusted, he found Mrs Patel staring at him with her head cocked to the side. Concern imprinted itself into each of her words as she said, 'Whatever is the matter?'

'It's difficult thinking about all this,' he said. 'If Lucy's friends had stuck around, there's every chance she wouldn't have got involved with our Joanna.'

'We all have our "ifs" about that time. Our "what-could-have-beens". They're stacked in my mind alongside regrets and David Bowie.'

'What's he got to do with anything?'

'Nothing,' she said with a fast head shake. 'It's simply that everyone seems to love him, and I could get no further than his *China Girl*.'

'So, not related to what we're talking about in any way?'

'You seemed to be growing morose and I'm not the type to contend with morose men. It's why as soon as my husband showed the first signs of depression, I had him join the golf club.'

'I actually think it best if I go. I've got Mrs O'Malley and Mrs McBride to visit yet.'

'You'll have no luck there,' she said. 'They've been arrested. Both remain in police custody, if my sources are to correct, and they're rarely wrong.'

'What the heck have they done this time? It takes a lot to arrest someone over seventy.'

Mrs Patel smiled, ever happy to spread gossip. 'Mrs McBride wasn't too pleased with Mrs O'Malley's choice of guest speaker. Strong words were exchanged which saw jam jars used as weapons before the two of them fought like street cats in the church hall.'

Marmaduke was stunned. The rate at which folk had started assaulting one another had risen substantially since he was a detective, especially among the residents of Partridge Mews. He shook his head, rubbed his hands on his knees and decided that he'd had quite enough for one day. 'I suppose I'll head on home then and give this case a chance to percolate.'

She nodded and led him to the front door. 'Well, I hope I've been able to help your search in some way. I'm sure you'll find at least one culprit in your lifetime.'

She closed the door behind him, and he considered her words as he wandered down the garden path. It was strange how the women of Partridge Mews were able to cut him straight to his core. Mrs Patel was onto something; he'd never found Lucy Simpson's killer, he hadn't found his niece, and regardless of all the cases he'd solved over the years, he realised that folk only remembered his failures.

Chapter Nine

'Sandra says that she has no knowledge of the victim's identity. She has a vague recollection of seeing the woman leave the shop yesterday, but she can't be entirely sure as she was trying a new Tibetan meditation technique.'

Alice sighed and leaned back against the settee. Her phone sat in her lap on speaker mode. 'Thanks, Jez,' she said. 'I hope this doesn't get you into trouble with Luke.'

'I'm checking in on a member of the public who happened to find a corpse in a freezer this morning. If anyone asks, I'm also calling to find out the best time to collect a statement.'

Mavis had understood when Alice had phoned in to explain why she wouldn't be working her shift at the café. She'd also promised discretion about the body in Marsden's freezer, which meant that most of Partridge Mews would find out by supper. Alice didn't mind if her name was kept out of it.

'So, you're no closer to knowing who the woman is?' Alice said.

Jez didn't answer immediately. Alice envisaged him on the end of the line, swallowing hard enough to dislodge his Adam's apple as he fought internally over how much information he could reasonably reveal.

'Jez?' she prompted.

'The thing is, Alice…'

'Yes?'

'It's Gloria Hebblethwaite.'

Alice grabbed her phone and stared down into the speaker. 'I know Gloria Hebblethwaite, and that most certainly wasn't her.'

'Well, all the ID points to it being her.'

'Does the ID have her address?'

'No, she was only carrying her bus pass. We've looked all around the shop for a handbag or purse, but they're nowhere to be found.'

'And it's definitely Gloria?' Alice said, massaging her scalp. 'She's meant to have fallen from a cruise liner, but unless she ran into a magical sea witch, there's no way that was the same person that we know and despise.'

'It could just be coincidence that they share a name.'

'Do you really believe that?'

'We currently have nothing else to go on. Two women, both named Gloria Hebblethwaite, have died. One has fallen into the ocean, and another has been found in a freezer.'

'Before you ask, I had nothing to do with either of them.'

'Apart from wanting to buy hash browns?'

'Exactly. Maybe you should talk to Ryan.'

'Once we find out if he has any connection to this

Gloria, I'm sure we'll send someone to speak to him.'

'It must have something to do with him, surely.'

'I'm not dismissing the idea, Alice, I've just got procedures to follow.'

They said their goodbyes and Alice wrapped her blankets tighter around her. She wanted to sink into the comfort of her settee and laze the day away watching reruns of *Friends* on the television. However, she couldn't do that because she knew someone who could shed light on what was happening and, as much as she'd hoped to never see Ryan Dewhurst again, she'd have to solve the mystery to be rid of him entirely.

Despite her current feelings towards him, Alice had vowed to apologise to Ryan for assuming that he'd lied about his grandmother's death. Having since discovered that another corpse bore the same name, she was more inclined to think that she'd been right all along and that he'd spent three months getting up to some great misdeed.

She drove to the hospital, thinking about all the calming techniques she'd ever gleaned from her mother's attempts at yoga, but that simply made her chuckle at the memory of seeing Primrose spreadeagled in the living room as she struggled to achieve a downward-facing dog with a mahogany coffee table in the way.

Alice didn't plan on allowing Ryan to antagonise her again. He'd taken up too much space in her head over the recent weeks, and she'd never planned on becoming the type of woman to dwell on a failed relationship.

It transpired that there was no need to visit the hospital. Alice reached the ward to find the side-room empty and was informed by a nurse that Ryan had discharged himself against his consultant's wishes. 'He said as he needed to move his boat before he got a telling off.'

'I'm guessing he was advised not to drive a narrowboat in his condition?'

The nurse screwed up her face as though she had to realign her nose to access any knowledge. 'Is it driving or sailing?'

Alice didn't have time for semantics. She left.

There was a silver lining when she discovered that she hadn't been in the car park long enough to warrant paying. But she would've preferred to have had the conversation she'd planned with Ryan, the one where she kept her cool the entire time and didn't experiment with an ECG machine to find new and unusual methods of torture.

As Alice approached her car, she realised that she could track Ryan's location with an app on her phone. They'd decided to use the feature a few months earlier so that she wouldn't have to wander around aimlessly when searching for his boat. That was after she'd walked five miles in the wrong direction and boarded a boat to find a rather shocked older gentleman frying eggs. He was naked. Alice apologised, advised him to acquire an apron in case of spitting fat and absconded, her mind suddenly filled with images of worms in gorse bushes and potatoes so old that they grew little white hairs.

Once she was in her car, she opened the app. There were a few videos of Elaine Closure's performance and messages from Lorelai's friends checking in. Becky seemed eager for Alice to join them for an afternoon of clay pigeon shooting later in the month. She made a mental note to reply later.

Luckily, Ryan hadn't blocked her. She debated if that made her pettier than him because she'd blocked Paul Abbott on all platforms after a filthy pick-up line involving mango chutney.

She scrolled until she found him and shook her head, tutting.

Ryan was at his grandmother's house.

Alice didn't know whether that meant he was stupid or scared, but having tracked him down, she was sure she'd soon find out.

She collected Duke on the way. Not that she'd planned to. She'd been driving when she saw him kicking pebbles down the pavement like a wayward youth.

She beeped her horn and pulled up alongside him. 'What's a disgruntled man like you doing on a street like this?'

He fashioned a grin and leaned in through the open window. 'I'll let thee in on a little secret. I'm actually a high-class gigolo.'

Alice guffawed. 'A gigolo? You usually sleep twenty hours a day.'

'That's why half the widows around here appreciate my services.' He stood to his fullest height and tugged on his lapels.

'That sounds like it could be true. I suppose you charge extra because you're old enough to be considered a fetish.'

'Aye, but I'm prepared to offer you mate's rates, if you'll pardon the pun. It's £500 for tea and conversation, £5,000 for cuddling. That's it.'

Alice pushed her tongue against her teeth in an imitation of mulling over his words. She knew that the police hadn't classified the body in the freezer as being related to a crime, but she still asked, 'How much to help me solve a murder?'

His grin widened. 'Now that, I'll do for free.'

'Get in, then.'

Once he was fully situated in the passenger seat, he asked, 'So, who's carked it this time?'

'Gloria Hebblethwaite. And no, it's not the same one.'

When nobody responded to her knocking, Alice left Duke by the front door and wandered around the side of the house. She looked through the kitchen window but saw nothing more than dirty dishes in the sink and a Donny Osmond calendar on the wall. The singer was wearing leather in the hopes of recapturing his rock star days, but he looked so uncomfortable that he might have been more suited to guzzling Senokot than posing for photographs.

Even though she'd only been in the job for a few months, Alice knew from her time as a social worker that a lot of people in town left their back doors unlocked throughout the day. Alice had warned against it, due to cases where chancers had nipped into kitchens and stolen handbags, wallets, and car keys while their owners had been particularly engrossed in that day's edition of *Loose Women*.

However, it was with that knowledge that she decided to chance her luck around the back of the property.

Having made sure that no one was looking, Alice opened the gate and scurried into the back garden. Someone had taken their time to make sure that it looked appealing; the grass had been mowed and the autumn leaves raked into neat piles, ready to be disposed of later.

Whoever she'd paid to care for her garden clearly hadn't got the news that Gloria had fallen from a cruise liner.

Alice crept towards the back door, keeping low when she passed the windows. She tried the handle and breathed a sigh of relief to find it unlocked.

She slipped inside and shut the door behind her.

A strong stench of bleach filled the kitchen, as though it had only recently been cleaned. 'Ryan?' she called.

No answer.

Alice exited the kitchen into the hall. She headed towards the front door to let Duke in but saw two blurry forms through the frosted glass.

'I know she's here. Her car's right there.'

She groaned. Luke Sterling.

Alice slipped through the door to her right and pressed herself against the wall, closing her eyes. The curtains were closed, so at least he wouldn't be able to peek inside. Maybe she could return to the garden and pretend that she hadn't been able to gain access.

'Aye, well,' Duke said, stalling. 'She wanted to see that Ryan, but he wasn't at the hospital, so she came here.'

She exhaled and opened her eyes.

Alice wasn't prepared for what lay in front of her.

Gloria. The Gloria Hebblethwaite that she knew; the same woman who was supposed to have fallen from a cruise liner a month earlier.

She was sprawled in front of the mantelpiece, staring towards the woodchip ceiling. Her chest looked as though it had exploded; splinters of her fractured ribcage rose from the wound. Dry blood had crusted on her floral blouse and stained the plush carpet beneath her.

Gloria's ashen face blurred before Alice. It transformed. In an instant, Aunty Magdalena lay on the floor before her, chest ruptured, heart pulsating in the gaping maw. She turned her head and stared with eyes like pearls.

Alice stood open-mouthed, holding onto an armchair to keep her upright.

She knew that it wasn't Aunty Magdalena. She knew that her mind was playing tricks on her, that the stress of the day was getting to her. No matter how much she tried to convince herself that she wasn't watching her lost loved one writhing on the carpet – repeatedly screwing her eyes shut and opening them again – she couldn't see the reality.

Alice found that she could do nothing more than scream.

A door exploded somewhere. Arms wrapped around Alice and ferried her outside into the cold, autumnal air. It was as though the world's frequency was set to the wrong channel. She was aware of someone speaking soothing words to her, but it was lost behind a layer of white noise.

Although she had her face pressed into someone's chest, inhaling the musky scent of aftershave and a day's work, her mind wouldn't relinquish the image of Aunty Magdalena lying prone in Gloria Hebblethwaite's living room. Tears erupted as the sight played over and over again.

Chapter Ten

'It was a perfectly human reaction,' Jez said, as he carried a tea tray into the living room. He'd been tasked with taking Alice and Duke back to her cottage and collecting their statements. That had been a few hours earlier and, in that time, Jez had made copious mugs of tea, handed Alice countless tissues when a flurry of tears took hold, and listened as she opened up about how she'd found Gloria's body.

Once more, she was sitting in her armchair with a blanket wrapped around her like a cocoon, praying for it to swallow her whole and hide her from humanity. Sure, only two people had heard her wailing like Janet Leigh in the shower, but that didn't quell the shame that was currently flooding her mind.

'Can't you just let me be embarrassed, Jez?' she asked, biting a chocolate Hobnob in half, her body craving the sugar.

'These things happen, Alice,' Duke said. 'You're not

going to behave the same way every time you find a body.'

'Nope, I've had enough of corpses, thank you very much. The next person who wants me to see their remains can send a written request.' She threw back the remainder of the biscuit and crunched it with all the veracity of a jaguar eating a rabbit.

Jez and Duke shared a look.

'And you can give up communicating silently. I know it's some secret code they teach you in the force, but I'm not having any of it today.'

Jez knelt in front of her, offering a sympathetic gaze. 'This is different from the other times you've found bodies, Alice.'

'Because she'd been shot?' She knew that wasn't the reason, that she'd fallen apart because her Aunty Magdalena had suddenly been in front of her, but something told her that it wasn't common to have visions of dead relatives, and she wasn't prepared for the consequences of telling Jez about that.

'Exactly. You've found murder victims, but this is the first time you've seen anything so visceral. Even police officers struggle with some of the sights we've seen.' He took her hand in his and offered a comforting squeeze.

Alice gulped back the rock in her throat and closed her eyes against tears that burned in their ducts. She gasped and heaved a breath. She focused her mind, refusing to let it dwell on all that she'd seen since that morning, and asked herself why she'd headed to Gloria's house in the first place. 'Have you found Ryan?'

'Not yet, but we will.'

When Alice opened her eyes, she struggled to look at either one of them, allowing her vision to lose focus as she stared at the television. 'I should have just left this to your lot in the first place, but I did what I always do. I got cocky.'

'Not cocky,' Duke said. 'A little pig-headed maybe, but it's not like you were planning on finding another body.'

She opened her app and tried to locate Ryan again, but it kept saying he was offline, no matter how often she refreshed the page. There was no denying things anymore; he'd definitely played a part in the deaths somehow, and despite how she felt in that moment, Alice wanted answers.

She tossed her phone aside. 'Someone needs to contact the cruise company and see what's going on. They believe that a passenger has fallen overboard. A month later, that passenger is found shot in her own home.'

'Have you had any luck finding the gun that was used?' Duke asked, a forlorn gaze on the biscuits.

Jez rolled his eyes and handed a couple over. 'Not yet. Our firearms expert reckons that Gloria was shot at close range. It could have been a shotgun, but with no weapon at the scene, everything is currently speculation.'

'And are you viewing the crimes as connected?'

'We're not ignoring the possibility, but there's every chance that it's only a coincidence.'

Alice leaned forward, unable to contain her disbelief. 'Are you serious? A coincidence that two women sharing the same name were murdered in the same town?'

'I know it's unlikely, Alice, but we don't have anything else to go on other than their names.'

'Well, name,' Duke said. 'That'll be a headache when it comes to the paperwork.'

Jez chuckled, the weary sound of a man who's wary of what he's got himself into, like an expectant father who'd just learned that his partner was expecting quadruplets. 'Don't remind me. What's worse is that they're the same age as well.'

Alice clapped a hand to her brow, dumbfounded. 'Duke, please tell me that strikes you as odd.'

'I'd definitely put it up on the spectrum of oddities. It's right up there with Mr Methane and ratatouille.'

She looked with incredulity in Jez's direction. 'See?'

Jez tapped his fingers along the side of his mug, before setting it down on the coffee table. 'Is there ever going to be a day when you don't think you're smarter than the entire police force?'

'You've clearly forgotten that just five minutes ago, I was breaking my heart about being cocky.'

'I'm not likely to forget,' he said. 'However, I need to go and collect my husband from the gym.'

'Did he get the make-up he wanted for the am-dram society?'

'He's currently in a "creative discussion" with the director because she wants to change the colour palette, having developed a deep discomfort whenever she sees a particular shade of teal.'

Alice slurped her tea in response.

'Will you be all right getting home, Duke?' Jez asked, pulling on his coat.

Duke nodded, dislodging some of the Hobnob crumbs from his chin. 'I'll be grateful for the walk.'

Jez said his farewells and left.

Duke sidled over from his spot by the window and sat down on the sofa with a grumble that sounded like a mixture of catarrh and Roy Orbison. He swigged his brew. 'Now then, what actually happened in that house?'

She directed her words towards the wall, her cheeks flushing as she spoke 'I don't know why it happened, but I kept seeing my Aunty Magdalena in Gloria's place.'

'That's reason enough to worry, Alice. Now, I'm no psychiatrist, but do you think this could have been brought on by grief?'

Alice curled further into herself. 'It's never happened before, but I can't very well go around seeing hallucinations every time I come across a dead body.'

'There'd be no shame in going to see one of those therapist types.'

She nodded. Someone from work had given her a grief counsellor's business card after her Aunty Magdalena's death; Alice had tossed it into her handbag and forgotten about it because she didn't want to talk about her sadness. Besides, no amount of talking would make the world right again.

'I won't make any promises,' she said. 'This could have been a one-time thing.'

Duke stretched his arms above his head and emitted a yawn that sounded closer to a yowl. 'I'm just glad that you weren't so upset about Gloria.'

'She's still dead, Duke. Don't you think we should be more respectful?'

'You can, if you'd like. I'm in my seventies. I don't have to be respectful to anyone.'

'Well, it looks like she's been murdered. At least, the one that we know has been. I'm not sure what the police think about the one in the freezer.'

'You don't fancy trying to solve it yourself, then?'

'We've enough to be getting on with. If we don't figure out who's sending these poison pen letters, Mrs

Cribbins is liable to make necklaces from our bones.'

'Mrs Cribbins?'

Alice shrugged. 'Or she'll write a strongly-worded letter. Either way, that's what we're investigating.'

'And the Glorias?'

'I'm not a detective, Duke. Let's leave this one up to the professionals.'

'I *am* a professional.'

'You're retired. Enjoy it.'

Duke didn't stay long after that. He finished his brew, making more mess than a thirsty dachshund, and got ready to leave. He stood by the front door, fiddling with the zipper on his coat. 'Don't be too harsh on yourself about that screaming business. We can't be sure how our minds are going to react. At least you didn't throw up and contaminate the crime scene.'

'You sound like my mum. Always searching for the positives.'

'I could never be as bad as Primrose. She'd put a happy spin on encephalitis.'

'Encephalitis?'

'I saw it on an NHS leaflet.'

'Sometimes the way your mind works astounds me.'

'Think about what I said, Alice. Don't let it live in your head rent-free.'

He left.

A quarter of an hour later, Alice was searching for ice cream in the kitchen when there was a knock at the door. She wound her blanket around herself more thoroughly, as though it was a grey, fleece-lined toga, and answered.

Mavis stepped inside, taking a postcard from her handbag. 'Can't stop. There's an episode of *Embarrassing*

Bodies tonight that I've been waiting to see.'

'You could've called.'

'And risk someone hearing? Suppose you've had your phone tapped?'

'Who'd go to the trouble of listening in to my conversations?'

'This is Partridge Mews, Alice. I've known women to fly drones over their neighbours' houses just to see how their hydrangeas are doing. They breed them different here.'

'Right.' Alice rubbed her forehead. 'Why are you here?'

'This.' Mavis thrust the postcard at Alice, who fumbled to grab it.

She struggled to read the loops and spirals of the letter writer's prose. It looked as though it had been written by someone with a fetish for italics. Since she couldn't make head nor tail of anything, she asked Mavis to explain its contents.

'It's to do with this Gloria Hebblethwaite business.'

'I think I've had enough of that for one day.'

'That's as may be, but your Ryan said –'

'He's not *my* Ryan.'

' – that his grandmother fell from a cruise ship, yes?'

Alice affirmed that fact.

'Well, this postcard is from that cousin of mine. You remember Doris? She's away on a cruise around the world. She says that she met someone called Mrs Hebblethwaite, but it turned out that she was lying about her identity and was, in fact, the boat's owner, Mrs Veronica Ambrose.'

'Veronica?'

'That's what it says here.'

'Do you think that this woman could be one of our Glorias?'

Mavis took the postcard and returned it to her handbag. 'That's your job to figure out, Alice. Mine is to watch Dr Christian examine some hefty haemorrhoids.'

'Have fun with that, Mavis.' She opened the door and watched her elderly visitor toddle on her merry way. Alice wondered if all she had to look forward to in later life were discussions about various bodily ailments; what with Duke and his encephalitis and Mavis's haemorrhoids, it was enough to put her off growing old altogether.

She barely had chance to step into the living room before there was another knock on the door. Alice ground the heel of her right hand against her forehead and suppressed a groan before opening it.

She wished she'd left it shut. Having seen her visitor, she pinched the bridge of her nose and said, 'If you've come to scold me, Luke, can you please leave it until I've got the strength to tell you to shove off?'

'Why do you always have to assume the worst?'

'Past experience.' She slumped down against the door jamb. 'What brings you here, then?'

'I came to see how you're doing.'

'Why?'

He stepped from one foot to the other and scratched the back of his head. 'I get that I'm probably not the person you want to see right now, but I was there, Alice. I know how badly seeing Mrs Hebblethwaite affected you.'

'It didn't take long for you to change your tune.'

'What do you mean?'

'Earlier, you were all for arresting me when I found

Gloria Hebblethwaite in the freezer.' Alice shuddered at the thought of the pale-skinned corpse at Marsden's and crossed her arms over her chest.

Luke nodded curtly. 'I'm sorry. I shouldn't have done that.'

'It made sense.' She shrugged and stood up straight, putting her hand on the door handle. 'You don't like me, which is why I'm surprised to find you on my doorstep, checking in.'

'You still haven't said how you are.'

'I found two dead bodies today, both were called Gloria Hebblethwaite, and one of them is meant to have fallen from a cruise liner a month ago. I'm confused, I'm upset, and I'm fed up of having to explain how I'm feeling.'

'Right,' Luke said. 'Well, I'm only down the road if you need me.'

Alice had been set to close the door, but his words stopped her. 'You're staying at your grandad's house?'

He nodded. 'I had it on the market, but there were no takers. I thought I might as well move in, rather than keep renting.'

'Doesn't it upset you? Living in the place where he was murdered?'

'It's also where he lived, Alice. I practically grew up there. You must understand what it's like to be surrounded by the memories of a lost loved one. You're staying in your Aunty Magdalena's cottage, after all.'

'She died in Madeira, but I guess I get it.'

'Like I say, I'm just down the road if you need anything.'

Alice wanted to tell him that considering his previous behaviour, he'd be the last person she'd call in an

111

emergency, but she was too tired to entertain the idea of another row, so she simply nodded and thanked him.

Luke displayed a weak smile before turning on his heel and heading down the garden path.

As a teenager, Alice had dreamt of Luke Sterling knocking on the front door and offering his services as someone to turn to in times of crisis. Now that it had happened, she felt nothing more than sadness coiling deep within her intestines. She closed the door behind him and sank down onto the hall carpet, pulling her knees towards her chest, because she felt as though he'd only shown an interest in her when she'd proven that she wasn't as strong as she claimed. When her screams at the sight of Gloria Hebblethwaite had transformed her into little more than a distressed damsel in his eyes.

Chapter Eleven

Alice's sadness soon metamorphosed into fury.

When she eventually returned to the kitchen after her conversation with Luke, she discovered that there was no ice cream in the freezer. That had caused her fingers to twitch. She opened the fridge, hoping that there'd be a half-empty bottle of Pinot Grigio, but recalled she'd finished it the previous weekend while watching *Casualty*. That led to the realisation that she couldn't traipse down to Marsden's and acquire a replacement bottle because the store was currently a crime scene, and she didn't have the wherewithal to drive the extra mile into town to visit the supermarket. Besides, she knew how people would talk if they saw her wandering around in her pyjamas and dressing gown, only to leave with her arms full of wine and assorted snacks.

The lack of ice cream and wine added to her frustrations. She switched on the television, but the plotlines on the soaps had blended together and she couldn't remember any of the characters. The thought of Mavis's postcard kept running through her mind.

Even though she'd said that she didn't want to meddle in the investigation, her frustration towards Luke Sterling made her want to solve the case.

Alice took out her phone and searched for Veronica Ambrose. She discovered a few articles about the owner of a cruise line, talking about how she was a self-made billionaire who'd invested wisely. However, there was no mention of the name Hebblethwaite in any report or biography, no matter what Alice typed into the search engine. Although, she did find a picture of an extremely Rubenesque woman who was wearing a kaftan that looked like a tie-dyed nightmare.

Satisfied that Veronica Ambrose wasn't either of the Glorias, Alice had but one aim: to converse with the owner of the cruise line and to ask why she'd claimed to be someone else. For that, she needed contact information. However, since the internet wasn't giving that out freely, she had to involve someone who she knew was great with computers and could find out how to get in touch.

Only it was too late in the day to speak with him. Despite feeling tired, her mind simply refused to let her sleep, so Alice spent most of her time in bed staring at the ceiling, waiting for morning to come, running over the day's events.

Early the next morning, Alice was trying to decide whether to leave her bed when she heard the front door slam. Her friends and family had been telling her to get the lock fixed since she'd inherited the cottage, but it had always felt like one of the odd quirks about the place that she ought to let lie. Besides, Jez regularly entered without being invited and she thought he might be hurt if she ever mended the thing.

He usually shouted up to announce his presence, something that the latest intruder hadn't done.

Ignoring her exhaustion, Alice swallowed a bud of fear and headed downstairs. She moved slowly, avoiding floorboards that were prone to creaking and keeping to the edges of the stairs, hoping that whoever was downstairs couldn't hear her fluffy slippers shuffling across the carpet.

She entered the living room and found the person looking wary, but fashionable.

'Lorelai?'

A flash of that smile that was fit for a toothpaste advert. 'I hope you don't mind me popping around so early. I just heard what happened and thought I'd call in and see how you're doing?'

Alice squinted, feeling as though someone were pressing a knitting needle between her eyes. 'I need coffee,' she said. 'Strong coffee.' She wandered into the kitchen and set about making herself a drink before thinking to offer one to Lorelai, who declined.

'It must have been difficult to find Gloria in such a state.'

'How do you know?' Alice added a healthy dose of sugar to her coffee, something she usually only did if in shock, or hungover.

'How do I know what?'

'About Gloria. Specifically, about me finding her corpse and having such a bad reaction.' Even feeling as she did, Alice managed to muster a look of vicious inquiry.

'The Gazette keep sharing live updates on their website. It's the talk of the town. Two bodies on the same day? It's taken over from those old grannies battering each other at the church hall.'

Alice scalded her tongue as she slurped. 'And they specifically mentioned me by name?'

'No, but Becky said she'd seen you.'

'She saw me at Marsden's. How could you have possibly realised that I was the person who found Gloria?'

'Because you're Alice,' Lorelai said, matter-of-factly. 'You go looking for trouble.'

'You don't even know me.'

'We were at high school together. I never thought you'd end up uncovering dead bodies, but I remember you.'

'I didn't think you remembered me at all.'

'We were both regularly top of the class.'

'Yes, but you got on with everyone and I just wanted to get out.'

'Why?'

Alice gulped back more coffee and looked at her reflection in its depths. Alice considered Lorelai's words before replying, 'My Aunty Magdalena always warned me against the way this town operates. There are people who think they're entitled to know your business and who try to get you to behave and live in a certain fashion. It's like *The Stepford Wives*, but no one dares to say anything against it because that's just the way things are.'

'I think things are changing for the better.'

'They might be. While we have a lot of family here - '

' - and you live here now.'

She nodded. 'And I live here now. I'm grateful that my parents live in Wren's Lea. It might not be far down the road, but it's enough.'

'Besides, could you really stay in Wren's Lea after being accused of killing that woman?' Lorelai asked, her lips curling into a sarcastic smile.

Alice chuckled. 'I'll have you know, that happened in Partridge Grove, and I still think that Zumba is a perfectly healthy activity for the over-nineties.'

'You're developing a habit of surrounding yourself with dead pensioners.'

'That's the problem with pensioners. They die.' Alice necked the remainder of her coffee, releasing a gust of steam when she put her mug down. 'Still, if you know me well enough then you'll know that while I might struggle at first when it comes to finding dead bodies, I'm more than capable of quickly returning to form and being even more bloody-minded than before.'

'That's something, I suppose.' Lorelai paused for a moment. 'And do you ever think about high school?'

Alice crossed her arms over her chest. 'Occasionally, but it's not something I like to dwell on.'

'Why not?'

'Because I'm twenty-seven and too many of our classmates still behave like teenagers.'

'I know what you mean, although that's usually the popular ones, the class clowns, the ones who did well in sports.'

'Did Jamie Garrick ever become a professional footballer?'

'No. He kept saying he had a trial for Man United and ended up on trial for drunk driving.'

'He didn't?'

'He did. Went on a night out, got absolutely sozzled and drove his car the wrong way down a dual carriageway.'

'The things you miss when you leave Partridge Mews. What happened to him?'

'He moved to Aldershot.'

'A fitting punishment.' Alice smirked. 'Still, I don't know these people anymore, Lorelai. I don't really want to, either.'

'What about me?'

'We'll see. Becky's invited me to go clay pigeon shooting with the lot of you, and I don't know if I can decline such an opportunity.'

'I know my way around a shotgun, you know.'

Alice hid her shock behind a hastily-summoned grin. The memory of Gloria and her ruptured chest rose in her mind, and she swallowed hard as nausea caused her to lean forward against the kitchen counter. 'I'll remember that,' she said, wondering if it was simply a coincidence that Lorelai was boasting about her firearm skills the day after someone had shot Gloria Hebblethwaite.

She chose not to ask, though, because Lorelai said that she needed to get to work, and Alice didn't have the mental fortitude to accuse a possible new friend of being a killer.

After Lorelai left, Alice headed back upstairs. Every bone in her body protested, aching as she went about her usual business. She went into her en-suite to splash cold water on her face, but that didn't help to wake her; it just left her feeling as though she'd thrown icy needles at her cheeks. Having towelled off and brushed her teeth, she went downstairs to the kitchen and made herself another large, strong mug of coffee.

Soon after, Alice drove to Jez's house.

He shared the semi-detached on Pye Street with his husband, Ben; a man who answered the front door in fuchsia pyjamas so bright that they would've worked wonders in a military distraction operation.

Ben's grin as he opened the door quickly turned into a look of concern. 'I mean this in the kindest possible way, but you look as jittery as the Tasmanian Devil on caffeine pills.'

Alice nodded. 'I haven't slept.'

'This will be interesting.' He held the door open. 'Come in, then.'

Alice followed Ben through to the kitchen. She was so tired that her senses seemed to be magnified. The scent of Tom Ford aftershave prickled at her nostrils, causing her nose to twitch. She was soon overwhelmed by the odour of coffee; even though he'd said she looked highly-caffeinated, Ben had clearly decided that Alice needed an Americano.

Ben had a high-tech coffee machine on his kitchen counter, which managed to look mildly cosmopolitan while still seeming like something out of Star Trek. While he searched for all the required tools and ingredients to make their drinks, Alice told him about the previous evening. She focused her attention on the postcard and the subsequent search.

'Only I couldn't find anything,' she finished. 'So I came to you.'

'But you waited until my husband had gone to work?'

'He'd only moan about me interfering with the investigation.'

'Are you?'

'Blame Mavis Thistlethwaite.' Alice sat down at the kitchen island, leaned her elbows on the counter and pressed her forehead into her fists. 'And Luke Sterling.'

'Still pining, are we?' Ben queried as he ground coffee beans, the noise eliminating any chance to retort. After a few minutes of pressing buttons and steaming milk, he presented her coffee.

'Do you always have to be such a showman?'

'As a drag queen with a degree in theatre who spent his late teens and early twenties working at coffee shops, yes. Yes, I do.'

'Well, I plan on taking advantage of different skills today.'

'That sounds ominous.' He eyed her as he sipped his drink.

Alice's hands wrapped around her mug as she attempted a doting gaze that came across more doleful. 'Since you work in computers, I thought you could find Veronica Ambrose.'

'And then?'

'See if you can arrange a video call,' she said with a shrug.

'So, I shouldn't hand this information to the relevant authorities? Not even my husband?'

'Exactly.'

'I've seen a lot of people lose touch with reality before. Usually, it's when they look in the mirror and think they're serving Kate Moss but they're closer to Hatchet Face.'

'I'm firmly in touch with reality.'

'Last night, Jez said that you were distraught and would happily let the police do their jobs. What changed?'

'Luke Sterling.'

'You had another row and now you're planning to illegally investigate the murders?' Ben couldn't contain his grin.

Alice scowled. 'There wasn't a row. He came around pretending to be concerned and I wasn't having any of it.'

'How can you be sure he was pretending?'

'Because this is Luke I'm talking about. For the last few months, he's gone out of his way to prove how much he dislikes me.'

'He's in charge of a murder investigation now, Alice. There's protocol to consider. Perhaps that's why he was checking on you.'

'I don't want him checking on me. He can act like he cares about my wellbeing after seeing how I reacted to finding Gloria's body, but I'm not some princess that needs rescuing.'

'Who's the wicked witch?'

'Didn't you hear?' Alice said. 'Gloria Hebblethwaite is dead. Although, I don't think a handsome prince had anything to do with it.'

'Mildly catty, but I'll allow it. It's a bit of a conundrum though, isn't it? Two women with the same name declared dead on the same day.'

'I used to watch *Only Connect* with Aunty Magdalena. I'm pretty sure I can figure it out.'

'I just need to arrange a video call with this Veronica,' Ben said.

'Exactly. I'm glad that you're coming around to my way of thinking.'

'I'm not, but Jez isn't likely to ever involve me in a murder investigation and I don't have much on today.'

121

'Hence the bright pink pyjamas.'

'It's a fuchsia lounging suit, Alice. Don't be such a pleb.'

She stuck around for long enough to hear the latest about Ben's difficulties with the local theatre company. He'd found all the make-up required to turn a six-foot rugby player into a convincing Maria Von Trapp, but the dates clashed with an important match and the committee was considering diverting to *Whistle Down the Wind* instead.

'I had to remind them that I'm not their employee,' he said. 'I'm only helping them out because someone stole from their makeup department, and if they continue to speak so awfully to me, I'll take a leaf out of Gloria's book and have Jez take me on a cruise. I could perform as Elaine Closure, and he could have a break from the old biddies of Partridge Mews.'

'Speaking of which, I said I'd take Duke to visit the O'Malleys and the McBrides.'

'Rather you than me. I can't think of anything worse.'

Chapter Twelve

Marmaduke waited for Alice to stop her car before climbing down from the wall. He wasn't one for daring feats of adventure anymore, but he'd had some time to kill and so he'd assessed the height of the wall, squatted and lunged a few times to limber up his joints, then hefted himself up. Memories of his mother warning him against haemorrhoids echoed through his mind, but he ignored them. He swung his legs back and forth against the bricks, leaned his head back and enjoyed the breeze on his face.

Then Alice had driven her car around the corner and blasted her horn, tearing him from his reverie. He swore, almost toppled backwards but kept his balance – and his cool – and hopped down, ignoring the twinge in his left knee as he did so.

Perhaps he was allowing himself to think too much about what Mrs Cribbins had said to him a few days earlier. He knew that was how women of her age talked, but her words had struck a nerve, and he thought that if they'd affected him so much then she might have been right and that maybe it wouldn't hurt for him to lose a few pounds. Not that he was about to admit that to anyone.

Marmaduke eased himself into the passenger seat. He looked across at Alice and pressed his tongue against the back of his teeth – it was never a good sign when she tied her hair up in a ponytail. She looked paler than could be healthy, as though all the blood had fled her body, and her eyes looked sunken in their sockets.

'You don't look well,' he said.

Alice attempted a glare but winced and pinched the bridge of her nose. 'Good morning to you, too, Duke.'

'Couldn't sleep?'

She nodded. 'Mavis brought something round and I stayed up half the night researching it. Don't worry, though. I've handed it over to Ben.'

'Ben?'

'Jez's husband.'

'I know who Ben is. I just don't understand why you'd show something to him before me.'

Alice blinked a few times, her mouth opening and closing like an astonished flounder. 'No, I didn't give the postcard to Ben.'

'What postcard?'

A few minutes later, he'd managed to extract the entire story from her. She even went so far as to remove the postcard from her pocket and to hand it to him. 'And you said you didn't want any more involvement in the investigation?' he said, feeling the faint twitches of a smile at the corners of his mouth.

She groaned a groan that he'd come to know well. 'I

didn't, but then Luke had to turn up at my front door and annoy me again.'

'Are you planning on solving the case out of spite?' Marmaduke asked. 'Because he does have more resources than we do.'

'He has more resources, but once we speak to Veronica Ambrose, we'll be ahead of him.'

'Only if she can shed some light on the Gloria Hebblethwaite situation.'

'When did you get so pragmatic?'

'Around the same time that you lost touch with reality.'

'You're the second person to accuse me of that today.' Alice checked her mirrors and pulled back onto the road. They drove for a few minutes in silence before she said, 'Do you think that the poison pen letters have anything to do with the dead Glorias?'

Marmaduke considered her words for a moment. 'I don't. Only because our Gloria didn't live in Partridge Mews when Lucy was murdered.'

'There goes my theory of Gloria being the culprit, then.' Alice sighed and turned down a side street.

Marmaduke didn't like to shut Alice's ideas down immediately considering all that she'd been through of late. There was also the fact that she'd solved Arthur Sterling's murder, and she hadn't allowed friendships to blind her when it came to the culprit's identity. He sometimes wondered if he was doing the right thing in letting Alice get involved in his investigations – unlike her, he'd had the proper training and supposedly knew how to converse with folk. If Alice hadn't had three arguments before breakfast, then her day was off to a bad start.

Either way, Alice could drive, and Marmaduke's license had been revoked years earlier. It had been a great miscarriage of justice that involved several pints of Boddingtons, two dozen mallards and a local drug dealer, but Marmaduke hadn't appealed the decision. There were times when he regretted not being able to drive anymore, but he had his bus pass and enough acquaintances that he could cadge a lift in at least three counties.

He also couldn't compete with Alice's parallel parking.

A quarter of an hour later, as she reversed into a space, Marmaduke clenched his jaw and ground his fingernails into the passenger seat, clawing like a lion after a gazelle. When she stopped the car, he exaggerated an exhale, expelling enough air to dismay an asthmatic.

Alice glared. 'You'd better not be one of those men who thinks women can't drive, Marmaduke Featherstone. Otherwise, I'm likely to drop you off on Bodmin Moor and let you walk home.'

'I never thought you couldn't drive, and I never *said* you couldn't drive. As a matter of fact, I was about to compliment you on your parking.'

'Go on then.'

'What?'

'Compliment me.' She looked at him expectantly, a mischievous glint in her near-bloodshot eyes.

'That were some proper good parallel parking there, Alice.'

'Thank you, Duke,' she said, smirking. 'Now, let's go and see if the O'Malleys have received any notes recently.'

They received little resistance from Derek O'Malley.

He was in a rush – something about Carlisle, a traffic jam on Junction 29 and a prior engagement – so he handed over an envelope as though it were as inoffensive as junk mail. Not that the contents seemed threatening.

Marmaduke removed an A5 sheet of notepaper from a plain brown envelope.

Alice read its contents over his shoulder. 'Fancy a scrap?'

'No idea what it means,' Derek said. 'I guess that's where you two come in. It's a bit like cryptic crosswords, I could never get my head around them either.'

With that, he bid Marmaduke and Alice farewell.

There were no identifying marks on the note, and the words on the page had all been torn from magazines.

'Let's hope we have more luck with the McBrides,' he said.

Fifteen minutes later, they reached their destination. Once they were both out of the vehicle, Alice locked it. Marmaduke didn't feel that was entirely necessary, considering the estate on which they found themselves was filled with Audis, 4x4s and Porsches. There was little chance of anyone wanting to steal Alice's car with so many luxurious alternatives. Indeed, after he glanced around at the cottages - each of which came with open windows, twitching net curtains, and the silhouettes of residents eager for gossip – he wouldn't have been surprised if someone had called the police and labelled it a highly suspicious Ford Fiesta.

Alice had also noticed the number of eavesdroppers because she said, 'I'd like to take this moment to reiterate that while I despised our Gloria, I didn't kill her.'

'I never thought you did.'

Alice nodded. 'I know, but there's plenty that will call

me a killer just to have something to chat about over a game of whist.'

He looked at her, perplexed. 'Folk still play that?'

'According to Mavis, they do. She's forever going on about some old dear named Pat and how her cataracts have spoiled the whole thing for her.'

'And I thought that went out of fashion with salad spinners,' he said as they continued down the pavement towards the McBrides'.

'What?'

'Whist.'

'Oh. Anyway, Mavis thinks that Pat's faking her illness so that more people will let her win.'

'Sounds like a neat trick. I'll try it the next time I play dominoes against Moira Janowski.'

'She's a bit rough, isn't she?'

'You're not wrong, but she's a good person to know.'

'Could she shed any light on the poison pen letters?'

Marmaduke shrugged. 'Maybe. She isn't usually the type to muddy her own hands, though.'

'And we wouldn't want to risk anyone else hearing about the letters.'

'Once we've got some clues about the sender, maybe we'll start asking around.'

The McBrides lived on the outskirts of Partridge Mews in a four-bedroomed detached house, a middle-class monolith that faced "The Pool" – a beauty spot where locals walked dogs that were too posh to poo. The front garden looked like it had been cultivated by Monty Don, as though *Country Life* might arrive at any moment and offer them a feature. A black BMW was parked on gravel in front of a garage that seemed to be more for show than for any practical purpose.

Marmaduke came from old money. The McBrides did not. They were part of a tribe of rich people who believed themselves to be better than others simply because of their wealth – who felt the need to flaunt it and who treated expensive cars like ornaments for exhibiting the weight of their bank balance.

Alice strode up the path and Marmaduke followed. She pressed the doorbell, one of those new contraptions where the homeowner could see their guests via a camera.

'Is that Marmaduke Featherstone?' A voice emanated from the doorbell's speaker.

'And Alice Valentine,' she said. 'Is that Mr McBride?'

'What do you want?'

'Is Mrs McBride home?'

'Look, we have a solicitor involved. We don't need help from two people who ought to know better. Especially you, Miss Valentine. Shouldn't you be at work?'

Alice plastered a smile on her face that wouldn't have looked out of place in a horror film and said, 'We're not here because your wife has been arrested for battery. We're here because we believe that she's received a poison pen letter. Now, we can continue to chat through your doorbell and let all your neighbours hear how your wife is so uncouth that she's at the centre of two current police investigations, or you can let us in.'

Marmaduke grinned at Alice as she stepped back to stand beside him.

Moments later, the front door opened.

Graham McBride was wearing beige chinos, a navy Gant polo shirt and a pair of crocs. He looked every inch the gentleman-golfer, minus his niblick.

An overwhelming gust of aftershave filled the air, catching at the back of Marmaduke's throat. He coughed a few times, but it did nothing to lessen his reaction. He hoped they'd find any evidence quickly, with no need to search.

Graham's brow was scrunched so tight that his forehead was invading his eyes.

'Now, I've only let you in because you started making outlandish claims and I didn't want you to make fools of yourselves in front of my neighbours.'

Marmaduke gauged the situation, looking at Alice's fists to see if she was about to thump Graham. However, it had already gone further than that because she'd adopted a fearsome gaze like a stoat after a chicken.

'Perhaps your wife is in the business of keeping secrets from you, Mr McBride,' Alice said. 'After all, you've proven to have quite a temper. Maybe Valerie feels as though she can't share her worries with you, fearing how you'll react.'

'That's nonsense.'

'Is it? Suppose I tell Mrs Cribbins my concerns. She's the reason that we're here, after all. She'd like to know why we were obstructed from carrying out our investigation.'

Alice looked to Marmaduke and grinned before turning back. 'Unless, of course, you don't have any answers because Mrs McBride is the writer of the poison pen letters.'

'Why would Valerie want to send such rubbish to a bunch of old nutters?'

'I don't know,' Alice said with a shrug. 'Maybe they annoyed her at the last jumble sale. She's still in custody after her fight with Pandra O'Malley. Suppose she chose to attack the committee because she believes they haven't had her back.'

Marmaduke had to give credit to Alice; she could be fearsome when crossed, like a ewe protecting her lambs from a badger.

Graham stared at Alice, aghast. 'Valerie didn't write any letters, poison pen or otherwise, and nor has she received any.' His gaze shifted as he reached the end of his sentence, looking towards a sconce above them.

'Since she's not here to ask directly, could we look around and see if there's anything she might have hidden from you?'

'No. What a stupid question. You aren't a detective anymore, Marmaduke Featherstone. If you'd like to pretend otherwise, that's entirely up to you, but you've no authority. I'm sorry that my wife's friends are being harassed, but we've got enough to be going on with without worrying that someone might send us a rude note.'

Although Marmaduke had been in the business of interrogating people for years, it was always interesting to watch them change colour as their emotions got the better of them. Graham McBride – always mild-mannered unless he was on the golf course – grew so outraged that his skin turned a glorious shade of puce.

'You're quite right, Mr McBride,' Alice said. 'I'm sorry for getting carried away. I didn't realize how outrageous we were being. We'll be on our way immediately, but do you mind if I use the facilities first? Only I'm having some troubles of a feminine nature that I'd like to see to before going anywhere near my car's upholstery.'

Graham rapidly paled, the puce turned to alabaster as though Graham was auditioning to be an understudy in

Casper the Friendly Ghost. He stammered a few times before muttering his agreement and directing Alice towards the lavatory.

She disappeared to perform the necessaries before leaving the two of them in an awkward silence as they awaited her return.

Eventually, Graham hissed at him, 'What are you doing, Marmaduke?'

'What do you mean?'

'You've lived your life. You can go around playing the detective and acting the fool, but why drag Alice into this? She has her whole life ahead of her, but rather than try and return to the job she's trained to do, you have her for a sidekick.'

Marmaduke balled his fists. 'Alice is no sidekick. Besides, she has a job.'

'Throwing gravy around for Mavis Thistlethwaite? That's a bit below her pay grade.'

'What business is it of yours where Alice chooses to work?'

'It isn't any of my business. I just hate to see someone with such promise throwing their career away for the sake of an old man who should know better.'

Marmaduke discouraged the rising ache in his throat and headed towards the front door. 'I'm going out for some fresh air because there's none left in here. It's all been obliterated by the stench of aftershave. A word of warning to you though, McBride. I've always thought that those who spray such copious amounts of perfume invariably have something to hide.' He slammed the door behind him.

As soon as Marmaduke reached the end of the garden path, he heard hissing. He glanced around for the source and found the McBrides' next door neighbour peering over a boxwood. 'What're you doing, Elvis? You sound like a hosepipe with a blockage.'

Elvis reminded most people of a mole; it was the way that he shuffled around, hunched over, eyes usually hyper-focused on the toes of his M&S brogues in case they got scratched by an errant pebble. His voice was little above a whisper when he said, 'Is this to do with Mrs McBride's arrest?'

Marmaduke used a phrase that had saved him from such questions for decades. 'I'm afraid that I can't discuss such matters with the public at this time.'

'Only, I have some information that might be important to the case.' He raised his head, revealing watery eyes hidden behind square-framed spectacles. Elvis really was a pillar of ill-health and misfortune; when he was in hospital having his tonsils removed, his third wife ran away to Abergavenny with a yoga instructor. She emptied the house save for one tub of vanilla ice cream. Elvis had always maintained that Sonia couldn't have hated him too much to leave him one tub of vanilla ice cream; however, folk often pointed out that it would have been kinder if she'd left him a freezer to keep it in, and if he hadn't been lactose intolerant.

Rather than telling Elvis Shatwell that everyone and their hamster believed they had important information when it came to a crime, Marmaduke said, 'Go on then. What do you have to tell me?'

'It's about Bianca Thistlethwaite.'

'Now there's a name I haven't heard in a while. Are you sure you mean Bianca?'

Elvis nodded. 'It were her, all right. I recognised the bomber jacket.'

'Why the heck would Bianca Thistlethwaite come here?' Marmaduke asked. 'She hasn't visited Partridge Mews in thirty years.'

'That's for you to find out. All I know is that others have seen her around town as well. Penelope Haycroft says as Bianca owns one of those bungalows on Wells Crescent.'

'I don't suppose you got the house number?'

'This is Bianca Thistlethwaite we're talking about. Just look for the motorcycle. There can't be too many octogenarians going around like the Hairy Bikers.'

Marmaduke thanked Elvis for the information and wandered back to the car. He and Bianca had been close friends in their heyday, regularly holding up the bar at The Blind Cat and ranting about the interfering busybodies at the Partridge Mews Women's Institute. As he leaned against the car door, he recalled something Bianca had said to him many moons before.

They'd been in the pub at the time. Bianca had necked her snakebite and ordered another round before Marmaduke had sipped his bitter. Once they'd reached their regular table, Bianca had revealed that she'd had some bad news from the doctor – something to do with heart disease and it being life-limiting. That had been followed by an evening of alcohol and food so full of fat and carbohydrates that it was a wonder that her heart hadn't given out there and then. By last orders, the pair of them had been trapped in a drunken haze of time that moved both too slowly and too quickly, and Bianca had said to him, 'I'm leaving again, Duke. I haven't got as much time as I'd hoped, and I need to see more of the world. Now, I don't plan on being gone forever. One day, some so-and-so calling himself a cardiologist is going to tell me that I'm dying properly and that's when I'll come back to settle some scores. I've let folk get away with too much for too long to keep our Doris happy, but when it's my time to go, this town will know all about it because Bianca Thistlethwaite is going out with a bang.'

She'd always been able to handle her drink better than he had. She'd had the landlord book a taxi to take him home. By morning, she'd left town.

Marmaduke hadn't considered that she could be a suspect. Surely Mavis would have told him if her cousin had returned. Or would she keep things quiet so as not to tar herself with the same brush? He didn't have much time to dwell on matters because Alice was stomping towards him.

He wouldn't tell her about Bianca just yet. Alice already lampooned him enough about one of his friends being a murderer. If she found out that another one was possibly the writer of several poison pen letters, she might start questioning the criminality of all his other acquaintances.

Alice's decision to search the bathroom had been based on the actions of a former client. As a social worker, she'd visited an older woman who'd had a particular fancy for vanilla fudge. No matter how hard her husband had tried, she'd always managed to get her hands on the stuff and had refused to give it up, stating, 'There's nothing good on the television anymore. We haven't had sex in so long that should the opportunity arise, I'm likely to spring a leak. I'll probably be dead within the next six months, so you can bleeding well let me have my vanilla fudge.'

But her husband had continued trying to stop her

consumption of sweet treats. He'd searched the house and removed every trace he could find, yet he still kept finding his wife in her wheelchair, making her way through a bag of fudge with all the voracity of an Alsatian in a butcher's. She never did tell her husband where she hid the sweets, and after several fruitless weeks, he'd given up.

Alice had been unable to let it lie, and so she'd asked the woman where she hid her contraband. 'In plain sight,' she'd replied. 'If that man ever replaced a toilet roll, he'd find my stash. You can hide anything you like in a bathroom cabinet because they seem to be invisible to the eyes of men.'

Years later, Alice was hoping that those words proved to be true.

She entered the bathroom and found herself momentarily stunned. Everything in the McBrides' bathroom was white. Sunlight beamed through the window onto polished tiles that were so bright that Alice had to avert her gaze to avoid being blinded. The McBrides clearly had a solid cleaning regime in place, because Alice saw herself reflected in every surface. It was like being in a funhouse, minus the scent of urine and regret.

Alice staggered back slightly when she saw what hung above the toilet – a portrait of Mrs McBride in a filigreed white frame. The only modicum of colour in the bathroom was the dark red of Mrs McBride's hair. From the looks of things, she spent a lot of money on its upkeep.

That splash of colour against the stark décor called only thing to Alice's mind: blood.

Alice didn't have much time, so questioning how the

McBrides chose to furnish their lavatory would have to wait until later. She might even visit her mother and discuss the ordeal over a bottle of Pinot Grigio.

She scanned the bathroom and considered checking the cistern as she'd seen in so many television dramas, but then she thought better of it. On the one hand, cisterns seemed to be the place to hide drugs or burner phones, and Mrs McBride was above such things. On the other hand, it seemed like such a common place to hide something.

Considering her former client, Alice headed to the cupboard beneath the sink; footsteps echoing as she walked.

Not wanting to leave any fingerprints or smudges on the handle, Alice wrapped a towel around her hand before opening the door. She grimaced as she was immediately assaulted with a gust of astringent odours from the cleaning supplies within. She held her breath and began pushing aside bottles. Eco-friendly disinfectant sat on the shelf next to bleach and something with no name but a corrosive warning; Alice didn't want to think about why the McBrides had *that* in their bathroom cabinet.

It didn't take long to find what she was looking for.

It wasn't a note, but having seen the portrait above the toilet, she knew that it was related to the investigation.

Alice quickly took a few photographs on her phone before shutting the cabinet doors and hoping that she'd left everything as she'd found it. Trying to add a level of believability to her story, she flushed the toilet and washed her hands before leaving the bathroom and making her way back to Marmaduke.

She stopped at the top of the stairs when she heard Mr McBride mention her name. When she heard what he had to say, her grip on the hardwood banister tightened, her nails clawing into the varnish. She waited the conversation out, breathing and focusing on the wallpaper across from her – she'd seen something similar when decorating her cottage, but she'd ultimately decided against it as she thought it was too plain and would be prone to showing dirty marks.

Once Marmaduke had left the house, she descended the stairs. She took each step slowly, hoping that her very presence in his home might make Mr McBride uncomfortable.

As soon as she saw him, Alice glared. 'What business is it of yours if I choose to play detective and throw gravy around for Mavis Thistlethwaite?'

Mr McBride looked stricken, clearly more comfortable lambasting men. 'When I see a young person throwing their life away, I think it's my duty to comment.'

'Why?'

'To steer you in the right direction?'

'Who gets to decide what the right direction is, Mr McBride? See, I already own my home.'

'We all know that your Aunty Magdalena gave that cottage to you.'

'And there are plenty of richer people than me who've had more given to them than I ever will. So, what's your problem?'

'You had a promising career, Alice. Why give that up to go traipsing about town at the behest of a pensioner?' He had his hands on his hips, attempting to look imposing but looking more as though he had trapped wind.

'It seems to me that your problem is that I'm not living my life the way you think a life should be lived,' Alice said. 'If it were up to you then I would work until I married, have a child and then spend my life being utterly miserable until such a time as I could retire and do nothing more than spend every living moment on a golf course until I inevitably died, hopefully around about the eleventh hole so as I could have a nice view of the ladies cloak room.

'Well, that might be a good life for you, Mr McBride, but I'm aiming for something different.'

'At least you have some aim, then.'

'I do, and it doesn't involve spending time with interfering busybodies who think they can dictate how I ought to live my life.'

'Interfering? That's a bit rich, coming from someone who's only visiting so she can ferret around my house and ask intrusive questions.'

Alice didn't retort immediately. She allowed her shoulders to settle and drew a breath. 'I can't deny that, but if it's how I choose to live my life then it's none of your business.'

She made her way to the front door.

'Leaving now, are we?' he said, grinning churlishly.

'Nothing would give me more pleasure than to punch you in the face right now, but I already have a reputation for clobbering OAPs and so I'll restrain myself,' Alice said. 'I have one more thing to say, however. I'm the only person on this planet who's allowed to give Marmaduke Featherstone any grief. Should I hear so much as a whisper that you've insulted, belittled or berated him, I'll tell this entire town what you get up to on your golfing away days.'

Mr McBride gulped. 'I don't know what you're talking about.'

Alice smirked. 'She might have only been a member for a few months, but my mum remembers everything she saw in that bunker.'

She tapped him on the shoulder and left the house, leaving him to mull over her words. Sure, they'd been drunk on rhubarb wine when Primrose had told her about their golfing away day to Lytham St. Anne's, but that didn't mean that the threat was any less real.

Alice smiled at Duke as she unlocked the car. 'Too full of hot air?'

'That's about the measure of things. Did you find anything?'

She shared the pictures when they got into the car. Duke's brow furrowed; it looked as though a furry worm was crawling across his forehead.

Mr McBride hadn't been lying when he'd said that no poison pen letters had been delivered to his wife. Instead, whoever was targeting the WI committee had sent her a box of ash blonde hair dye. The sender had also left a post-it-note stuck to the box on which they'd scrawled the message, "COVER UP THOSE GREYS".

When she asked Duke if he had an inkling as to who the culprit might be, he said, 'It could simply be that the writer is mad at the Greys.'

'There's a lot of people who fit the bill.'

Most people in Partridge Mews knew the Greys. Doug and Violet had been at the forefront of social gossip for decades. A year earlier, their marriage had disintegrated after it had been revealed Doug had been having an affair for decades. Violet had fled town and sought sanctuary with her sister. No one had seen hide nor hair of Doug ever since.

'They've upset a lot of folk over the years, that's for sure,' said Duke.

'But if the person behind these notes knows what happened to Lucy Simpson, we need to find them.'

'I don't like to agree with Graham McBride, but it could be that some kids have found out about the case and decided to scare a few old ladies.'

Alice sank down in the driver's seat, rubbing at her temples. In all her excitement, she'd forgotten that Mrs Cribbins had employed them to find the writer behind the poison pen letters. Despite everything that she and Marmaduke had collected, it felt like they were no closer to solving the mystery.

After she returned home, she spent the remainder of the day lounging on her sofa, devouring enough chocolate hobnobs to offend a diabetic, washed down with copious amounts of tea. She paid little attention to what was on the television; she just switched on ITV3 and allowed nostalgia to fester as she watched all the shows that she used to enjoy with her Aunty Magdalena. *Hamish Macbeth* gave way to *Wycliffe* and transformed into *A Touch of Frost,* a favourite of her mother's. Primrose Valentine had a longstanding adoration for David Jason that Alice regularly worried would end in a restraining order.

In the evening, she ordered herself a takeaway, because the idea of walking a couple of feet to the kitchen made her entire body ache. She supposed the stress of the past few days and exhaustion from not having slept had finally taken its toll on her.

Indeed, after luxuriating in a hot bath for over an

hour, Alice went to bed and enjoyed a rather vivid dream that involved Robert Carlyle, a raspberry sponge cake, and some delicately placed whipped cream.

Chapter Thirteen

Even without the poison pen letters, the Partridge Mews Women's Institute had been in disarray for at least a year. After the exposure of her husband's affair, Violet Grey had fled town and handed the job of interim chairwoman to another local busybody, Mrs Doris Copeland. Either of them could have received missives; indeed, they could have been the letter writer themselves.

Violet had supposedly gone to visit her sister, but after making a few calls around town, Marmaduke had discovered that no one had any way of contacting her and, if they did, they certainly didn't plan on handing her details over to him. Having heard about the postcard that Mavis had received, he knew there was no chance of interviewing Mrs Copeland for at least a fortnight.

Therefore, he decided to visit her daughter. Although she'd been married for the better part of twenty years, to Marmaduke, she'd always be Angela Copeland. He hadn't considered visiting her before because while she was the daughter of a prominent member of the WI, she'd never shown any inclination of joining their ranks.

Unable to settle at home, Marmaduke found himself wandering the streets in the hopes of calming his mind down. The walk helped him to get his thoughts in order, and before he knew it, he'd stopped outside the gate on Steerforth Street. Soon enough, he'd gone up the garden path and was ringing the doorbell.

When she opened the door, Angela smiled. 'Afternoon, Mr Featherstone. I wondered when you'd be paying a visit.'

She led him down the hallway into a large kitchen that still felt homely; the cupboards and drawers were painted white and had knobs made from pine. Highly polished granite countertops reflected the numerous appliances situated about the place; given the opportunity, Angela could have turned her hand to any culinary delight.

Marmaduke almost wished he'd brought Alice along, just so she could marvel at the place. One of her only peeves about her cottage was that she had a kitchen the size of a two pence piece.

Angela seated him at the breakfast bar with a view out onto a well-cultivated garden. She'd clearly learned a thing or two from her father, Harold, who was renowned for being a keen gardener. Some folk said that it was no wonder he chose to spend so much time outside, given the wife he had.

They chatted amicably while she made them both a drink before bringing them to the bar and sitting down across from him. 'I think I know why you're here, so why don't we get started?'

Marmaduke was momentarily stunned as he said, 'I've been asked to investigate a "delicate" matter by Mrs

Cribbins.'

Angela eyed him over the brim of her mug, then set it down on a coaster and said, 'The poison pen letters?'

Marmaduke clucked his tongue. 'I should've guessed that you'd know about them.'

'They're the worst kept secret in Partridge Mews, apart from Sheila Hartingstall's wig. You know how much folk in this town love to gossip. If you cough at lunchtime, they'll have everyone thinking you've got bronchitis by supper.'

'So, all the ladies have told each other?'

'Off the record, naturally.'

'Did your mother receive one?'

Angela shook her head. 'She's given up with the WI now. I thought she'd keep at it until her heart conked out at a jam competition, but the other ladies were determined to oust her.'

'Was that because of the community service?'

'Partly, I think. Not that many people care for Janice Dooley, so they didn't much mind Mum knocking seven bells out of her. The other ladies disliked that Mum was made chairwoman without an election, so when that happened, they gave her the boot.'

Marmaduke glugged his tea deeply, giving himself time to avoid asking the question that was pinching his brain. 'Could she have had anything to do with the letters?'

'From what I've heard, these are barely notes. Any letter my mum writes goes on for about seven years. She couldn't constrain herself to poison pens.'

'You don't mind me asking?'

Angela chuckled. 'We're talking about Mrs Doris Copeland here. If she wasn't on a round-the-world cruise, she'd be your main suspect.'

Marmaduke smiled wryly. Although he hadn't seen much of Doris in recent years, he regularly read her letters to the Partridge Mews Gazette; one that lingered in his mind was when she'd lambasted a new café in town that had the audacity to call itself a trattoria when they were little more than a greasy spoon full of wipe-dry menus, where even the foie gras was served with chips.

No, Angela was right. Her mother was too grandiloquent for poison pen letters.

The next line of questioning had Marmaduke staring at his trousers, straightening fabric at the knee and making sure that his hems hadn't dropped. If he let the silence build for too long, it was liable to grow more uncomfortable, so, after a gulp of tea, he asked, 'Do you know what the letters are referencing?'

'I don't, but from the way you're examining your knees, I can't imagine it's good.'

'It's Lucy.'

Angela exhaled. 'That's something they didn't mention about the letters.' She gulped and reached for her tea with a trembling hand. 'Even after all these years, it hurts to hear her name. You'll know what that's like.'

'At least we know what happened to Lucy. When it comes to Joanna, she just disappeared. No trail, no nothing.'

'I've always used that as a reason to hope that she's out there living her best life.'

Marmaduke averted his gaze again and gave a curt nod. 'I try that sometimes, but then I think, well why couldn't she live her best life here?'

'It was tough on all of us, Mr Featherstone. First, we lost Lucy, and then Joanna. Ash found it so difficult to cope that he left town, and the rest of us drifted apart. Every time we met, it was another reminder of who was missing.'

He knew exactly what she meant. After Lucy's death, Marmaduke had believed that he'd eventually rebuild his friendship with her parents, but he'd become the man who'd taken their daughter away from them. They were civil enough on the streets, but he could no longer pop round on a Saturday afternoon to sup on Special Brew and watch reruns of *Rawhide*.

When Joanna went missing, he'd wondered if they welcomed his loss, if they saw it as some sort of karmic retribution. He'd avoided them after that, drawn the curtains of his cottage and kept them that way for nearly thirty years.

If Alice hadn't steamrolled into his life, he might have left them shut.

Although he hadn't heard of Ash before, he could understand them choosing to leave Partridge Mews. He'd considered it himself many times because the town was full of memories, and therefore full of grief, but he'd never been able to take the plunge in case Joanna returned and he wasn't there to greet her.

A few tears burned as they escaped from their ducts. He dabbed his eyes on his handkerchief and cleared his throat. 'I never gave much thought about how it all affected their friends.'

'I suppose it was easier because we weren't here.'

'Could be. I were too busy ruining my own friendships to think about anyone else's.'

'I think that university played a role. Lucy was left behind with the baby. That was a shock for all of us, not least Mrs Simpson. When she found out, I thought she was going to vaporise half of Rochdale.'

'Why Rochdale?'

'She's never been a big fan of Lisa Stansfield.'

'How did Edith come around to the idea?'

'That was thanks to my mum, actually. She saw how conflicted Lucy's pregnancy had left Mrs Simpson, so she went around and said to her, she said, "Most women wouldn't have the bravery to do what you've done. So often, we hear of teenage mothers tossed out onto the streets as though they're being left for the rag and bone men. To stand by your daughter and be there through what will be a terrifying time for her takes great courage and I hope more women in this town take note of what it means to be a mother in the 20th century."'

'That doesn't sound like Doris at all.'

Angela nodded as she hastily swallowed from her mug. 'It might have challenged her sensibilities, but she'll do anything to help a friend save face.'

'So, Lucy gave birth to Martin and you all went off to university. Who else was in your group?'

'You had me and Lucy, Dervla Rowley – but she's a Patel now – and Batty McBride.'

'Batty?'

'Well, we couldn't go around calling her Bathsheba, could we?'

'And to think Graham McBride has the gall to question my life choices when he has a daughter named *Bathsheba*.'

'It was nothing to do with him.'

'No?'

'No. Mrs McBride went into labour watching *Far from the Madding Crowd*. She wouldn't go to the hospital until she'd seen Terence Stamp playing with his sword in front of Julie Christie.'

'That's no reason to call a poor lass Bathsheba.'

'Mrs McBride always said too many children were named Julie after that film, and she wasn't about to give her daughter a name that everyone else had.'

'She did well then, because no other beggar would flaming want it.'

Angela offered a glare that could have melted titanium strength. 'Your name is *Marmaduke*,' she said. 'You have no right to talk about ridiculous names.'

His neck retreated into his collar as she spoke. He coughed and sat up straight, somewhat gingerly. 'Aye, that were a stones and glass houses situation, but you can't have drifted apart too much if you're still so defensive of her.'

'There was never any falling out. If we stayed away from one another then we didn't have to think about Lucy. It sounds terrible to say, but I think we all wanted to forget that it happened.'

'And no matter what you do, something will always come along to remind you.'

'She was killed on my birthday, Mr Featherstone. Did you know that?'

'I know that she was on a night out.'

'The summer before uni, we all agreed to get back together for my birthday weekend. Lucy arranged everything while we were away, scoped out the best places for us to go and kept in contact to make sure that we'd all come back.'

'Do you remember much about the night?'

'You know my mother,' Angela said, meeting Marmaduke's gaze. "If I ever turned up blackout drunk, she'd have exiled me to a convent for the rest of my years. No, I remember everything. We were glad to be back together and avoided talking about university when we realised it was upsetting Lucy. Then she had to leave early. That's something I've thought about for years. She said that she was off to meet her "mystery man" and wouldn't let us go with her. I wish we had.'

'Who could have expected that she was off to meet her murderer?'

'I could have asked my Aunty Bianca to follow her.' Angela chuckled at a memory, but her face soon regained its sombre expression. 'Mum was worried about me going out in town for the first time, so Aunty Bianca came with us. She always knew how to party. Even when the bouncers said she was too old, she snuck in through the bathroom window.'

Marmaduke couldn't withhold a grin. 'It's been a long time since I saw Bianca. When she wasn't arm-wrestling landlords, she was drinking them under the table. Last I heard, she'd gone adventuring on that motorbike of hers.'

'She never could settle down. I invited her to Theo's Christening. She sent a St. Christopher, but she didn't come.'

'I never had Bianca down as a churchgoer,' Marmaduke said. 'I doubt she'd have left a club to follow a young girl who was supposedly on a promise.'

Angela shrugged. 'You're not wrong. It's simply one of those things you do after a tragedy. You can't help wondering how you could have done things differently. We always stuck with the pack, see? We never met Lucy's mystery man and so of course we had our suspicions, especially when Ash upped and disappeared a few months later. That would have been at around the same time that Joanna went missing. Did you ever think that there might be a connection?'

Marmaduke tapped his index finger on his knee and tried some of the breathing techniques that Primrose harped on about whenever he got irate about the snooker. His mind focused on the box of hair dye that Alice had found in the McBrides' bathroom. There was one fact that he couldn't deny. 'I don't know an Ash.'

'Nobody knew Ash,' she said with a sigh. 'His parents sent him off to boarding school and they spent every break on holiday somewhere because Violet didn't want him associating with the plebs of Partridge Mews.'

'Hang on a minute there, Angela. Are you telling me that this Ash was the Greys' son?'

She nodded.

There it was, the post-it note on the box: *cover up those greys*. Perhaps it was more straightforward than he'd originally thought. 'And you think he was Lucy's secret boyfriend?'

'It just seemed likely. He'd finished uni, and he and Lucy both worked for his dad's firm.'

'Doug Grey gave Lucy a job?'

'Lucy was his assistant. He made a big song and dance about being a modern man who wouldn't see his friend's daughter disgraced by small-minded attitudes that were entirely out of date.'

Decades had passed since Lucy's murder, and Marmaduke had never tasted that morsel of information. 'Did you ever think he could have killed her?'

'Who?'

'Ash.'

'We all did.'

'What changed your mind?'

151

Angela glanced away with a shudder. She stared into empty air for a moment, refusing to meet Marmaduke's gaze; then she steeled herself, her shoulders back and her spine rigid. 'You're not investigating Lucy's murder, are you, Mr Featherstone? You were just asked to find out who's been writing letters to the committee.'

'Now, there's an unexpected change in tone.'

'I want to know the truth as much as anyone. I'd love for you to finally have answers about Joanna, but the facts remain that the police never found a killer and two more teenagers disappeared, one of whom no one even remembers.'

'Rather than help to solve it, you want to leave the case open and focus instead on who wrote a bunch of nasty notes?' A growl escaped as he ended his question.

'I seem to recall that you were taken off the case back then. What would happen if I contacted the police to say you were interfering again?'

His glare was magnified by his milk-bottle lenses, giving him the appearance of a particularly angry hawk. 'Strange how folk always go straight to threats when they're hiding something.'

'Find out who's writing the poison pens and leave Lucy alone.'

Angela reached across the table and took his mug. She turned around, crockery in hand, and headed towards the kitchen sink.

Marmaduke stared at her back, allowing the silence to build between them for a few minutes. He picked at a hangnail and admired the zinnias in the back garden. Eventually, he said, 'What if the writer is also Lucy's killer?'

At first, she didn't say anything; she simply continued

washing their mugs. His question proved to be too much, however, and she turned around, drying her soapy hands on a dishcloth. 'Why would they incriminate themselves?'

'Guilt, maybe. I've an idea you know what that feels like.'

This time, Angela's glower was filled with so much fury that Marmaduke was reminded of being called to the headmaster's office for dropping a newt down the back of Jerry Algernon's polo shirt.

There was an acidity to Angela's voice as she spoke; she'd clearly been taught the art of dismissing a guest by her mother. 'I've just recalled a prior engagement. I'm ever so sorry, Mr Featherstone, but I'll have to ask you to leave.'

'Angela, there's no need to be like this.'

'I'm sure we can reschedule something. Maybe when an arctic blast freezes Sydney harbour.'

Marmaduke was hustled out of the kitchen and down the hall.

Angela ignored his protestations and attempts to butter her up. She didn't slam the door behind him, no doubt because they both knew how the town would gossip about that. The only farewell he received was the soft click as she locked him out.

He hadn't even had chance to pull his coat on properly, so his fists were balled against the elbows of his sleeves, giving him the look of a crab with deflated pincers. Once he'd adjusted himself, Marmaduke set off down the garden path, wondering why the mention of Ash Grey might have inspired such a reaction, and just who he'd been in the first place.

Being thrown out of a person's home came with the

territory, as far as Marmaduke was concerned. Folk didn't like being questioned. They always reverted to adolescence, where interrogation led to punishment. Even the innocent got agitated when everyone had their own version of the truth.

Marmaduke had no issue with being escorted out of Angela's house. What snagged was the further mention of Bianca Thistlethwaite.

Bianca had rebelled against authority figures since her childhood. She'd demonstrated her right hook on her first day of school, giving the teacher a black eye and fleeing the playground. She'd been found tending to Mrs Perry's geese. The event proved indicative of how Bianca would live her life. In Partridge Mews, she'd been in more fist fights than Giant Haystacks; elsewhere, she proved to be charitable and hardworking.

Many wondered if it was what the town represented to Bianca that caused her to behave with such animosity towards its residents.

Her mother had been arrested for assault in the late fifties; it hadn't necessarily been the subsequent trial and imprisonment that had proved too much for Bianca, but the gossip around town and the whispering and sidelong glances wherever she went. Bianca had left her younger sister in the care of relatives and fled town.

Marmaduke knew from experience that Bianca wasn't the type to get along with the housewives in town – those who spent their lives fraying net curtains as they peered out of their front windows in their efforts to be perpetually nosy – but, she had been around on the night of Lucy Simpson's death and, since she hadn't been seen since, he wondered just what she knew about the murder that made her family so protective.

Chapter Fourteen

Alice was languishing at home, contending with the housework.

She wasn't a domestic goddess by any means, but she needed something to take her mind off things. Ordinarily, she'd bake some cakes or have a bash at choux pastry. However, she'd recently read a book in which a person cooked their feelings into their food, and this had put Alice off baking in case she accidentally served someone a Battenberg that tasted of fear and was iced with homicide. Specifically, the recollections of homicide, because the more she tried to forget, the more the image of Gloria's gunshot wound burst into her mind.

From time to time, she checked Ryan's location through the app, but he seemed to have gone AWOL because there was no sign of him. He certainly knew how to disappear.

Alice was humming along to Radio 2 as she scrubbed

her skirting board when a shadow fell over her. She scowled at the source and switched off the radio saying, 'Just because the front door doesn't lock correctly, it doesn't mean you have permission to let yourself in whenever you feel like it.'

'I knocked,' Jez protested, looking as earnest as a toddler in want of a doughnut.

'Are you sure?'

'I'm putting the kettle on.' He headed into the kitchen and Alice staggered to her feet; glad he was facing the opposite direction so that he couldn't see the way she rose unsteadily like an infant giraffe.

'I suppose the music was a little loud,' she said.

'I didn't know you're a Luther Vandross fan.'

'That's who that was?'

Jez did little to hide his look of incredulity. 'Sometimes, your lack of musical knowledge astounds me.'

'We didn't all spend our childhoods spinning around houses twirling a baton to hits of the 1970s.'

'I regret ever introducing you to my parents.' Jez blushed, a subtle pink mottling his cheeks as he opened the cupboards over the kitchen counter in search of his mug. Following her Aunty Magdalena's example, Alice had assigned him one she'd found in the January sales – porcelain, with penguins painted on the sides. She thought it apt; he found it mildly offensive to policemen but liked that he had his own mug when he visited.

Once he'd made the coffees, the two of them went and sat down. He took the armchair by the window, and Alice settled down on the sofa.

'We've been establishing the final movements of the Gloria Hebblethwaite you uncovered at Marsden's. It turns out that she spent the evening at her local church hall helping to prepare for a jumble sale.'

'And where's local to her?'

'Wren's Lea.'

Alice mulled that over. 'That's nearly nine miles away. For someone of her age to be travelling that distance at night, she must've had some important business to attend to.'

Jez pressed his feet firmly into the carpet as he sat forward, intent. 'We're currently trying to find out what. She left the church hall at eight o'clock. We're currently waiting for CCTV and traffic cam footage.'

'Any chance she was followed from the church hall by a grumpy adversary?'

'It's possible. Then we have to ask the question, "Why would someone follow her such a distance just to push her in a freezer?"'

'Why travel ten miles just to visit Marsden's? It doesn't make sense. The shop closes at five. If Sandra had remembered to lock the door, then Gloria wouldn't have been there in the first place. Who did she meet? Why did they push her into the freezer?'

Jez averted his gaze, focusing on the wall as he nibbled on his thumbnail. After a few moments of imitating a hamster with a pumpkin seed, he said, 'There's every chance that she simply fell into the freezer and the boxes collapsed, trapping her inside.'

'Really?'

A shrug. 'We've got to consider all possibilities.'

'It's suspicious that she was found on the same day as another woman with the same name.'

'I don't disagree with you. We found something else in her pocket that might be of interest. It's with forensics, and I can't say more than that.'

'So, our local constabulary believes that Gloria suffered an unfortunate accident?'

'Currently, yes.'

'Despite the fact that the floor at Marsden's had recently been swept. Sandra has avoided cleaning so much that there were Opal Fruits wrappers pressed into the lino.'

'Gloria could have slipped on the wet tiles and fallen in.'

Alice looked at him incredulously as she slurped her coffee. She swallowed hard, rubbing her chest as the heat bloomed and feeling like a glassblower had set up their furnace in her sternum. 'Do you honestly believe that?'

'I'm simply saying that it could have happened. Our focus is primarily on the second Gloria. We need to speak to Ryan and find out the truth about his grandmother falling from the cruise liner.'

'I told you he was lying straight away and now look where we are.' She didn't tell Jez that his husband was helping her to track down the boat's owner. Quite frankly, she could do without another warning about interfering with a police investigation. Besides, Ben hadn't found anything yet.

'There's also the matter of the missing shotgun that was used to kill our Gloria.'

'I don't suppose the killer left an easily identified gun cartridge behind.'

'How do you know about gun cartridges?' Jez asked, his left eyebrow raised in such a fashion that it looked set to leap from his forehead.

'I did some research after what happened with Clive Constable,' she said nonchalantly. 'Also, my mum spent a summer clay pigeon shooting.'

'An entire summer?'

Alice gulped her coffee. 'You know how she gets with her hobbies. Every time I went home, she was in the lounge polishing her barrel.'

'Why did she give it up?'

'She says it was tinnitus, but my dad says she accidentally shot down a drone that was capturing footage for a particularly tense episode of *Escape to the Country.*'

'I'm not really sure you should be saying that to a detective.'

'You're giving me details about an ongoing police investigation, Jeremy. I'm not sure you'll be telling anyone about my mother's struggles with a firearm.'

'It's Jez.'

'That's what I thought,' she said with a smug grin. She considered their conversation, but something continued to poke at her mind. 'Are you sure about the floors, though? Sandra never tidies.'

'Apparently, her daughter was in the shop during the day complaining about the state of things, but she only had time to clean the floors.'

'It feels like too many coincidences.'

'What else do you want me to say? Police resources are tight, and we have to choose a focus. Right now, that's the woman who was shot. Ryan told us she was dead, was assaulted on the same evening, and is currently missing.'

'You're no closer to finding him, then?'

'Narrowboats might travel slowly, but we've no idea which direction he went in.' Jez shook his head. 'It isn't looking good. He has a reputation for going missing, now.'

'Is he a suspect?'

'Alice, at one point, even you were a suspect.'

'That's charming, that is.'

'But understandable.'

She sighed. 'It is. It's not very nice, but it makes sense.'

'You took being a possible murder suspect a lot better than you took being accused of assaulting Ryan.'

'I'm just getting used to being accused of things I didn't do.' Alice pulled her legs up onto the sofa and stared down at the remainder of her coffee. She'd hoped that when she next saw Jez, he might have some answers, but he'd only added to the number of questions. It was like watching an episode of *Only Connect*, thinking that she'd figured everything out just to discover that she was on the wrong wavelength from the beginning.

Jez pulled her from her reverie. 'We're testing for gunpowder residue on Gloria's clothes. The frozen one.'

'Tactful as always, Jez. Considering our Gloria has a great blithering gunshot wound to her chest, I didn't think it would be her. It would be a waste of police resources considering it's so bleeding obvious.'

Jez rolled his eyes. 'Sometimes it's easier if you just let me talk. That way, you won't come across as so stupid.'

'I hope you don't talk to all your witnesses like that.'

'Other witnesses don't give me so much lip.'

Alice grinned. 'Go on then, Detective Carson, what else did you want to say?'

'We're testing the clothes of the body in the freezer, because we've established a connection to the Gloria Hebblethwaite that was shot.'

'I'm guessing it isn't just her name?'

Jez nodded. 'It's to do with a name, though. Her next

of kin is listed as Sandy Dewhurst.'

'Who are they?'

'No idea. The number listed is for a landline that's no longer in use, but once we find out we'll have the difficult job of sharing the news of Gloria's death and asking questions.'

'Hopefully you'll employ some of the tact that you've just so masterfully exhibited.'

'There's something else, as well.' Jez ran his index finger around the rim of his mug. 'Have you seen the paper this morning?'

'The *Gazette*? Doesn't that just showcase the grievances of every housewife in a ten-mile radius and give the occasional recipe for plum chutney?'

'Ordinarily, yes, but today it's reported some information that we were hoping to keep from the public for a while longer.'

'And what's that?'

'It's to do with the victims; specifically, gunshot Gloria.'

Alice allowed a moment to pass. 'Gunshot Gloria?'

'Yes. I thought it was an easier way to differentiate.'

'That's even more tactless than "the frozen one". Do all members of the police force do this?'

'It's what we've been calling them down the station.'

Alice shook her head. 'And I'm the one people slam on social media.'

Jez waited a moment to see if Alice had anything more to add before saying, 'Either way, we've established that she isn't Gloria Hebblethwaite at all. Her real name is Gwen Mainwaring. She was released from prison a year or so ago.'

'What was she in for?'

'Fraud.'

'Do you think Ryan knows?'

'We'll have to find him to ask him. I don't suppose he's contacted you?'

She shook her head. 'He's switched off his location as well.'

'We'll be doing things the old-fashioned way, then.' Jez sighed. 'That'll be good news to break. Can you imagine finding out that the woman you believed to be your grandmother isn't who you thought she was?'

'It's like *Little Red Riding Hood*.'

'Only both grandmothers are dead in this case.' Jez slurped the remainder of his drink.

Alice clamped her mouth shut; eyes wide as she recognised the truth of his words. She let them percolate in her mind as she sipped her drink. 'We don't know if Ryan knew about the identity theft, but why was Gwen pretending to be Gloria?'

'We're going to talk to the company where Gwen Mainwaring worked. Now that we've established Gloria's next of kin, we just have to find them.'

'How long will it take to find Sandy Dewhurst?'

Jez shrugged. 'It's a piece of string scenario. If Ryan were around, we'd ask him.'

'It's strange when you think about it,' Alice said. 'Ryan never mentioned any other family. Sure, we weren't going out for long, but aren't parents and siblings usually a first date topic?'

'I can't remember. I've been with Ben for over a decade. Most memories of our first date involve sweaty palms, braces, and Tom Hanks.'

'Since Ryan never said anything, do you suppose Sandy is a woman's name? Could it be his mother?'

'I've been in this career for long enough to not suppose anything.'

'You sure can be a detective about things, sometimes.'

'I know,' he said. 'Great, isn't it?'

'That's not the word I would have used.'

'I agree that it would be helpful to establish what the connection is between Gloria, Gwen and the Dewhursts.'

'And don't forget, there's still the Gloria who supposedly fell off the cruise ship.'

'I wouldn't be surprised if that was faked, too.'

Alice beamed. 'I love it when you come around to my way of thinking.'

He left soon after that, telling her that Luke wanted him back at the station for a briefing and he needed to pick up some Nair along the way. Alice didn't ask any questions.

Once she was sure that Jez had gone, she pulled out her phone and typed "Sandy Dewhurst" into the search engine. As always, there were thousands of results, including social media profiles, employment histories and an article about an Anglican priest who accidentally drank absinthe and rehomed a dozen bantam hens.

She knew that the murder was none of her business – that she should just let the police get on with things until they found some answers – but that didn't stop her from opening the Free Births, Marriages and Deaths Register on her phone. She'd discovered the website a few months earlier when trying to create a family tree, only to realise that the Valentine family had more than enough branches to strangle itself without her finding more.

If Sandy was Ryan's mother, then Alice guessed that she'd been born in the sixties or seventies. She entered that information and scrolled through the results.

Her eyes widened when she reached an entry where the mother's maiden name was listed as Hebblethwaite.

Gooseflesh sparked down Alice's arms. Unless Ryan used his mother's name then Sandy wasn't related to him that way. She scanned the entry again.

"SANDRA DEWHURST".

Of course: Sandy was a nickname.

Alice knew that she shouldn't operate on a hunch. However, there had been a lot of coincidences recently, and considering that a body had been found in a freezer that was owned by someone of the same name, Alice searched the marriage register.

Once more, she scrolled through the results, and when she found what she was looking for, her breath caught in her chest. She pressed a hand to her throat as her oesophagus played pinball with her ribcage. Her hunch had been right.

Alice couldn't be sure if the shopkeeper was a killer, but she did know something else.

Sandra Marsden was the daughter of the frozen Gloria Hebblethwaite.

Chapter Fifteen

Alice's mum walked through the front door as her daughter was preparing to leave.

In fact, Primrose all but fell in, staggering beneath the weight of the rucksack on her back like a tortoise with a hoarding problem. She heaved deep breaths as she unstrapped the bag and let it drop to the floor, where it thudded and clattered. After leaving her Nordic walking poles in a nook on her way into the living room, Primrose inched across the carpet and dropped onto the armchair. Her face looked like luncheon meat, albeit sweaty luncheon meat that had been forgotten at a picnic in the middle of a heatwave.

She closed her eyes, her chest rising and falling rapidly.

'I was just heading out,' Alice said. She took Primrose a glass of water, hoping that she'd down it in one and be on her way.

Primrose's hand trembled as she took the glass and

brought it to her lips, spilling water across her face as she glugged it down. Then she smeared her arm across her mouth and leaned back against the chair again.

'I'm sorry if I scared you, love,' she said, gasping as she did so. 'This is simply one of the benefits of Nordic walking with a Le Creuset casserole dish strapped to your back.'

Alice returned the glass to the kitchen, asking as she went, 'Why did you go Nordic walking with a casserole dish strapped to your back?'

'Mrs Drummond has gout.'

'Okay?'

'Well, her Stan is perfectly fine at making himself a sandwich, but he finds more substantial meals a bit of a struggle. Since I had some time on my hands, I took them a tuna pasta bake.'

'One, you never have time on your hands. Two, why does that mean you had the dish on your back today?'

'They asked if I could call in. While I didn't consider the weight of the casserole dish before carrying it around for the better part of three hours, since I will have burned many more calories than usual, I plan to treat me and your father to a takeaway and a bottle of Pinot Grigio this evening. Would you like to come?'

Alice thought about her plan to visit Sandra Marsden. Seeing as she and Duke regularly got accused of being hot-tempered, it might help to have someone like Primrose around to keep the peace. Indeed, if her mother hadn't been around when she'd first met Duke then Alice might have been doing time for assaulting a septuagenarian.

She smiled at Primrose in the fashion that's common among children who require something from a parent.

'That sounds great, but first I need you to help me with something.'

It was as though a switch had been flicked in Primrose's brain. Suddenly, she sat bolt upright and started rubbing her hands down her waterproof trousers. 'What is it, love?'

'How would you like to help me to question a suspect?'

Primrose's shoulders slumped slightly. 'Is it legal?'

'We'll say we're just chatting to a friend who recently endured a trauma.'

'Should I bring my rucksack? With the added weight of that casserole dish, it will make an excellent weapon.'

Sandra Marsden lived in a stone cottage on the outskirts of town, surrounded by pastures where sheep grazed and dawdled in the early autumn sun. Alice welcomed the sound of sheep bleating in the countryside – it added to the rural ambience and made her feel closer to nature – but she could barely hear them over the sound of wind chimes.

Although Sandra only had a small front garden, she'd planted trees, and erected bird houses and metal poles upon which she'd hung the tubular bells. There was only a slight breeze, but it was enough to have set the instruments banging against one another; the sound was tinny and sonorous and set Alice's teeth on edge.

The air was filled with an odour that could have cannabis or cat urine. Alice couldn't be sure; she simply knew that it wasn't a scent that was commonly associated with muck-spreading.

Alice and Primrose made their way down the small stone path through the garden to the front door.

It took a few minutes for someone to answer. They heard lumbering about inside, the spraying of an aerosol and the opening of windows before they were eventually greeted.

Sandra didn't answer the door; instead, they were greeted by her daughter. Indigo was wearing a cream top and brown trousers, both linen and oversized. She reminded Alice of a latte. She'd never liked the way that linen creased, felt as though it made people look unkempt, but it suited Indigo as it added to the bohemian flair that she exuded from the blonde hair in a messy bun to the Birkenstocks on her feet.

'You'll get no sense out of her.'

Indigo led them down the hall and into a room that gave a whole new meaning to the word "lounge". The space was populated by giant beanbags in assorted colours, and a lawn table and chairs stood by the window. Sandra was sprawled in the middle of the beanbags, her eyes barely open and bulging like overripe peaches breaking through their skins. She had an almost greenish pallor to her that was reminiscent of pistachios. She wiggled her fingers through the fog of marijuana smoke as it spiralled slowly towards the recently opened windows. Sandra moved her hand languorously as *Naima* by John Coltrane echoed out from the record player beside her.

Alice had once taken a puff of weed during a house party in her university years and, after coughing so much that she was surprised not to dislodge her spleen, she'd decided it wasn't for her. She'd always thought that getting high was an adolescent occupation; seeing Sandra practically performing the backstroke towards nirvana, she realised how incorrect her supposition had been.

A grin slowly stretched across Sandra's face, revealing strings of saliva between her teeth. 'H'Alice,' she said, her words slurred with a grogginess that was commonly associated with the heavily sedated.

Primrose placed a hand on Alice's shoulder. 'Maybe this isn't the best time, love.'

'If I don't speak to her now then Jez will come around here, and things will get a lot worse.'

'But that's his job.'

'You wanted to come, too.'

'That was before we found out that Sandra isn't really in the mood for guests today.'

'She's been smoking non-stop for days,' Indigo said. 'We haven't been able to open the shop while the police investigate, so naturally my mother has decided to hole herself up in her "studio" and to smoke herself into oblivion.'

'It must have been difficult for her.'

Indigo leaned against the door frame, pinching the edge of her nose. 'She's such an embarrassment. Why am I always the one that ends up mothering her?'

'I'm sure your mum tries her best, Indigo.'

Alice gripped Primrose's hand in hers and met her gaze. She shook her head. 'Not now,' she whispered. She knew that Primrose couldn't bear to hear another parent criticised; she'd always insisted that if children only knew how difficult it was and gained some perspective then they'd understand.

'No, it's fine,' Indigo said. 'Everyone who meets my mum sees her as this kind, airy-fairy woman who goes about without a care in the world. The problem is that it's true. She cares about herself so much that she forgets that I exist.'

'I'm here, Indi,' Sandra said, although it was hard to take her seriously considering it sounded like she had a mouthful of plums.

'You're high, Mum.'

'Buh I'm here.'

Indigo heaved a breath. 'Why did you want to see her?'

'They're my guests, Indi. Go away.'

'You're in no state to be left alone,' she said. 'Especially when it sounds like they're going to be asking questions that should be left to the police.' She folded her arms and tilted her head back slightly, clearly attempting to look intimidating but only achieving a look of holding back snot.

Alice faced Sandra and asked, 'Why did you lie to me?'

She attempted to rise from the beanbag but, after a few moments of floundering, gave up and reclined back. 'Perhaps just an unspoken truth.'

'You said that you didn't recognise the body in the freezer.'

'I did.'

'Is that a yes, you said you didn't recognise the body in the freezer, or you did recognise the body??'

'I did not know the body.'

'Which is a lie.'

'Isn't. I'm no good with faces.'

'A convenient excuse.'

'Excuse? You're trying to confuse me.'

Primrose stepped in and said, 'Alice isn't trying to confuse anybody, Sandra. We're just a little bit concerned because you say you don't know the woman in the freezer, but we have it on rather good authority that she was, in actual fact, your mother.'

Alice had hoped to be the one to deliver the news. Her shoulders slumped and she exhaled.

She looked at both Marsdens to gauge their reactions. Indigo had given up trying to look imperious and had instead wrapped her arms around herself. She wavered, seemingly unsure as to whether to go to her mother or to remain hovering in the doorway.

Meanwhile, Sandra jerked her head, her brow furrowing as Primrose's words sunk in. 'I don't know my mum.'

'Then why are you listed as her next of kin?'

'Next of kin?' Sandra pushed herself up. Once she reached a seated position, she used the table as a lever and rose to her feet. She staggered into a lawn chair and pressed her hands against her face. 'Indi. Water.'

Indigo rushed from the room, returning within what felt like seconds to plonk a glass of water onto the table alongside a strip of paracetamol. She stood in front of the table like a sentry guarding her mother.

Sandra knocked two pills back and drained as much of the water as possible. 'I haven't heard from my mum in forty years.'

'You really didn't recognise her?'

Shaking her head proved too much trouble for Sandra. She held onto the back of her neck. 'Why would I?'

'You didn't have an inkling it was her? Not even when you saw her name in the paper?'

'Look, my mum has told you that she didn't recognise the body,' Indigo said. 'Besides, she doesn't get the newspapers. They always make her upset.'

Sandra managed a nod. It looked like her head was about to drop from her neck like a bowling ball being balanced on a plastic fork, but it was a nod. 'Why me?'

'Well, she used the name Sandy Dewhurst,' Alice said. 'I thought it was Ryan's mum at first because he's gone missing, and it was another connection. Then I found out that you're Sandy.'

'Ryan?' asked Sandra.

'My ex.'

An aura of rage emanated from Indigo. She leaned forward, one arm folded across her stomach, the other being used as an implement to punctuate her sentences. 'I see what's happening here. You've had a bad break up with some lad that might have a loose connection to my mum. A woman we've seen neither hide nor hair of in nearly half a century is found dead and you've decided to pin it on him. That's fine, we've all been there, but most of us don't go around accusing other people's parents of being a killer's bleeding accomplice.'

'That isn't what I'm doing.'

'Well, you did think Sandra could have been the killer, love.'

'You're not helping.'

'My mum wasn't even at the shop that night.'

'The police told us.'

'Right. The police. Because this is a matter for them. I'm sorry that you've split up with this Ryan lad, and I'm sorry that you found a dead body at our shop, but that doesn't give you the right to come around here and start making wild claims.'

'You're pretty protective of Sandra considering minutes ago you were complaining about how selfish she is.'

'That's what daughters do, Alice. We might get annoyed by our mums, but we're not going to watch

172

them get hauled over the coals.'

Primrose grinned and Alice glared at her. When she caught sight of her daughter's gaze, she shrugged. 'I'm sorry, Al, but it really is nice to see such a healthy parent/child relationship.'

'So, we're just supposed to believe it's a coincidence that it was her mother's body in the freezer?'

'It might not be a coincidence, but that doesn't mean that Sandra knew Gloria's identity.'

Alice was about to respond when they became aware of another sound. They were silent as sirens overwhelmed Sandra's music and the incessant rattle of wind chimes. Soon enough, several police cars pulled up outside the house.

'Did you invite them?' Indigo scowled at Alice.

'I didn't know anything about this.'

The four of them headed outside as the police officers came towards them, led by Luke Sterling and Jez.

'What are you doing here, Alice?' Jez asked, his voice full of concern.

'I didn't expect you to figure it out so soon.'

'It's our job, Alice.' Luke said. He stopped still, and the officers followed suit.

Alice was reminded of a standoff, she just hoped that it didn't go the same way as *Gunfight at the O.K. Corral*. She considered her words, not wanting to dob Jez in with his superiors, and said, 'I was trying to find out if Gloria had any more family members who could give us Ryan's location. When I looked into things, I found out that Sandra is Gloria's daughter. Well, she's the daughter of the Gloria in the freezer. I've no idea how she's related to the other one.'

'That might just give us some motive.'

173

'What do you mean?'

'We found Sandra's fingerprints on Gloria Hebblethwaite's coat.'

'That's enough, Carson.' A purple tinge flourished on Luke's cheeks as he growled. 'Let's just get this over with.'

Sandra stood frozen on the garden path, shuddering. 'But it wasn't me. I didn't know she was my mum.'

'Don't say anything without a solicitor present, mum,' Indigo said. 'I'll ring dad and have him send Mr Murgatroyd down to the station.'

They watched as Sandra was read her rights and taken away.

Once they police cars had receded into the distance, it turned out that Indigo had more to say. 'She didn't do it. Mum's prints are on the body because she was moving something to protect me.' Red blotches bloomed on her cheeks, and she struggled to catch her breath.

Primrose took Indigo in her arms and led her back towards the cottage. 'Everything is going to be all right, love.'

'It's not. No matter what happens, my mum interfered with a crime scene, and it's all just got worse because it turns out that we had a connection to the corpse.' She heaved a breath, but it did nothing to allay the tears streaming down her face.

'Why were her fingerprints on the body?'

'Now isn't really the time, Alice,' Primrose warned.

'Sandra has just been charged with murder. I don't think that there is a right time.'

Indigo nodded her head. 'I've been using the shop as a front for selling drugs for years. It's the worst kept secret in town. Mum moved the body because there was a load of weed beneath her. We didn't know that she was my grandmother. She was just a regular buyer who said she volunteered at the local hospice on Thursdays and would take pot brownies in for the patients. I'd leave the goods in the freezer, "accidentally" leave the front door unlocked and then she'd visit during the night and collect them.'

Alice looked to her mother and exhaled. 'That's a lot.'

'I need to ring my dad.'

'Did Gloria never give her name?' Primrose asked.

'No.' Indigo sniffed and wiped away her tears on her sleeves. 'She signed all her texts, "Mrs H". What reason could she have for not telling us the truth?'

'Forty years is a long time,' Alice said. 'Maybe she thought too much time had passed to be thought of fondly.'

'Well, she's dead and my mum's been arrested, so I'm not exactly thinking the kindest things about her right now.'

'Neither of the Gloria Hebblethwaites has turned out to be the nicest of women. I wonder if it's something to do with the name.'

Indigo pushed her hair away from her face as she blinked back tears. 'It's happened again.'

'What has?'

She breathed deeply and said, 'My guess is that there aren't two Gloria Hebblethwaites. Back in the seventies, Gloria's brother married a woman named Gwen. Somehow, Gwen pretended to be Gloria and mounted up tons of debts in her name, as well as emptying her bank accounts.'

Alice didn't know what to do with that information. She staggered back, theories flying through her mind like seagulls after chips. 'Jez said that Gwen had recently been released from prison for fraud.'

'She still likes to dabble, then.'

'That's awful,' Primrose said. She laid a hand on Indigo's shoulder and offered a conciliatory smile. 'You could write to *Take a Break*. I'm sure they'll have some advice.'

Indigo turned her attention to Alice. 'Is she always like this?'

'She's only trying to help.' Alice paused. 'Did you know that Gwen still lived in Partridge Mews?'

'The last we heard from the Hebblethwaite side of the family was that my great-grandmother had recently died, and Gloria was trying to sell the place.'

'Where was this?'

When Indigo gave them the address, Alice gawped. 'That's where Gwen was staying.'

Indigo chuckled. 'She was definitely up to her old tricks.'

'What do you mean, love?' Primrose asked.

'It just seems so obvious to me. Gwen gets released from prison, finds out that Gloria has a big inheritance and so she pretends to be her in the hopes of scoring a boon.'

'Is Gwen the reason why your mother lost touch with her family?'

Indigo hugged her arms around herself. 'After Gwen's antics, Gloria was left with nothing. She fled town, got married and had kids, but Mum said that the trauma of what had happened to her proved too much and she did a midnight flit. Grandad couldn't cope and sent Mum to live with his sister.'

'What about Sandra's brother?' Alice asked.

'We don't have much to do with my uncle. We're friends on social media, but that's about it. There's no ill will, we just keep our distance. Do you think my cousin was involved?'

'So, Ryan is your cousin?'

Another nod from Indigo. 'But last I heard, he was living it up in New Zealand with his wife and daughter.'

For some reason, nausea overwhelmed Alice's senses. She gulped. Her forehead felt like it was being slowly crushed.

Primrose called her name, but it seemed to be coming from a distance. Alice reached into her pocket and removed her phone. Her hands shook as she scrolled to her photographs, navigating back through them until she reached a photo she'd taken with Ryan when they'd gone to Marple on his narrowboat.

She showed the phone to Indigo, struggling to keep her voice steady as she said, 'This is Ryan. Is he your cousin?'

Alice stared directly into Indigo's eyes, feeling tears rise like pinpricks of fire beneath her corneas.

'Ryan might be my cousin, but I've no idea who this lad is.'

Alice had known the answer before she'd even shared the image. Her throat constricted as though a hastily swallowed humbug was lodged there. She longed for the simplicity of a week earlier, when the worst thing that Ryan had done had been to drop her shoes off his boat, as opposed to the complicated present where it turned out that he'd lied about his identity and got himself inveigled in murder.

Chapter Sixteen

'Does everyone in this blasted family come with multiple identities? I've just spent nearly half a year wasting my time on a man I thought was called Ryan, and it transpires that he might be an overgrown squirrel named Frederico.'

'I'm just as shocked as you are,' Lorelai said. 'If you're going to steal an identity, why Ryan's? It's not like he's got anything going for him. He doesn't even have a proper toilet.'

'That's a real sticking point for you, isn't it?'

'I think that Lorelai is onto something though, Alice. Why steal Ryan's identity? It must have something to do with the fake Gloria Hebblethwaite, otherwise why spend so much time with her?' This came from Becky, who'd tagged along to Thistlethwaite's claiming that she was there to support Lorelai. Alice thought that she was only there because she wanted a vanilla slice.

Once she'd taken her mother home, she'd felt the

need to rant at someone who knew first-hand the perils of dating Ryan Dewhurst, or at least the person who was claiming to be him. Lorelai was amenable to taking some time away from work, citing a family emergency to her manager.

'Do we think that our Ryan knew that Gwen was pretending to be Gloria?' Alice asked. She had a pulsing ache between her eyes from trying to untangle the threads of stolen identities, familial dramas and murders; she'd have had more luck with an expert Sudoku.

'How are we supposed to know?'

'We could call him,' Lorelai said.

'You can give it a go, but he won't answer the phone to me.'

Mavis came over with their drinks, her eyes focused on Becky. 'Don't I know you from somewhere?' she asked, handing over a hot chocolate that was piled high with whipped cream and marshmallows.

Becky's shoulders seemed to shiver involuntarily. 'I just have one of those faces.'

'No, I definitely recognise you. Were you one of those who came to try my mega-breakfasts a few years back?'

'I don't even know what that is.' She crammed her mouth full of cream, smearing it over her lips.

'You must do,' Mavis said. 'It were one of them food challenges. If you ate the entire breakfast, you got it for free. I had to stop serving it because too many people were saying that it was too much of a challenge. They wrote to the *Gazette*. I said to them, "Most folk these days would be able to swallow a dozen pork sausages without batting an eyelid, but them around here have gone too soft, moaning about *cholesterol*. It wouldn't be much of a challenge if there wasn't a chance of someone having a heart attack in the middle of it, would it? It's not my fault that they missed the message about our country's obesity epidemic.'"

'I hope you're not saying that I remind you of the obesity epidemic.' Becky scowled, wiping her mouth on a serviette.

'Calm down, Brunhilda, I'm talking about the newspaper. I saw you in the newspaper.'

Becky averted her gaze and mumbled, 'No you didn't.'

Mavis grabbed a copy of the *Partridge Mews Gazette* from another table, rifling through the pages before showing them the article about Gwen Mainwaring stealing Gloria's identity. A photograph showed a group of women sitting around a table, smiling to one another; the paper had directed a red arrow towards Gwen, but beside her, albeit younger and slightly slimmer, was Becky.

'You knew that Ryan's grandmother wasn't who she said she was?' Alice asked.

Becky pushed aside her hot chocolate. She breathed deep and said, 'I used to work at the same company as Gwen Mainwaring, but we didn't work together.'

'You're looking pretty friendly here.' Mavis sat down in the remaining seat at the table.

'That's a promotional photo from the company website. We came from different departments. Gwen was in HR and I was an admin assistant, but the CEO wanted something to advertise that we had a diverse working environment.'

Alice examined the photograph further, noting the truth of Becky's words as she did so. Whoever had overseen the photo had endeavoured to make the company look as diverse as possible. 'That doesn't answer whether you knew that Ryan wasn't who he claimed to be.'

'Becky never met Gloria.' Lorelai had a glare like a disturbed heron. 'I'm sure that if she had, she would have told me that Ryan's grandmother was actually a renowned fraudster named Gwen.'

Noting how protective Lorelai had become, Alice retreated back into her seat. Something within her warned her not to lose this potential friendship before it had even begun. 'Sorry, Becky,' she said, eking out the words as they seemed determined not to pass her lips.

'I'd have asked the question as well, but Lorelai is right. If I'd known that Gloria was Gwen, I'd never have let her near.'

'Who?'

'Lorelai. I would have made sure that she never went back to that house.'

'Surely you'd give her the information and let her make the decision herself.'

Becky shook her head, seeming pained. 'You don't understand.'

Alice looked to Mavis for support, but she simply shrugged and rose to her feet. 'Don't look at me. I've got a meat and potato pie to check on.'

As she headed back into the kitchen, the other two women smiled at each other and drank from their mugs. Lorelai closed her eyes. 'That is a great cup of coffee. I can't believe we've never visited before; we'll have to bring the girls one day.'

Alice wondered if she'd done enough to be considered one of the girls, or if these meetings would end when the assorted mysteries had been solved. She also couldn't get past Becky's comment. She watched them both, somewhat bewildered, as they chatted.

Eventually, Lorelai seemed to notice Alice's silence and asked, 'What's the matter?'

'Does Becky really have so much control over you?'

'It's not control. I'm looking out for a friend.' Becky looked like a bouncer as she said those words, or a rhinoceros in cashmere.

'It's what girls do.' Lorelai shrugged. 'We stop each other from making bad choices.'

Alice considered their words, tearing at the edge of a napkin. 'I suppose my closest friend at the moment is Jez.'

'See, stick with us, Alice. We won't see you wrong.'

'Who's Jez?' Becky asked, a high-pitched twinge to her voice.

'You remember Jeremy Carson from school?' Lorelai said. 'Blonde. Played badminton. Glued pictures of Halle Berry to his planner so we'd think he was straight.'

'You met his husband at the bar. Elaine Closure.'

Becky nodded, knocking back her hot chocolate as though it were a yard of ale on a stag night. 'What's this Jez up to nowadays?'

'He's a policeman,' Alice said, gauging Becky's reaction. 'Detective Sargent, to be specific.'

If Becky was affected by the news, it didn't show. She nodded once and smeared more hot chocolate onto a serviette, bruising her lips like windfall apples. 'Tough job. I wouldn't want to do it.'

'Where do you work now?'

'I do admin for an accountant in town. It's menial work, but it pays the bills. Is Jeremy investigating the murders?'

'It's Jez, and yes, although he doesn't tell me anything

about police business.'

'I'm pretty sure that's how it's supposed to be,' Lorelai said.

'I get annoyed when it feels like the police haven't found any new clues or evidence. It would help if they could find Ryan.'

'Have you any idea where he could be?'

'No. He's switched off the location on his phone.'

'There's nowhere special he used to take you?'

'Marple, maybe,' Lorelai said, twirling a strand of hair between her fingers.

'He took you there as well?'

'Men are creatures of habit, Alice. Ryan will have had a successful date once and recreated it with every subsequent partner.'

Alice wasn't sure how to respond. She saw the sense in what Becky had said, but that didn't stop her from sinking further into her seat.

The most romantic thing that Ryan had ever done for Alice was to invite her onto his narrowboat and sail down the canal to Marple. It had been a warm spring afternoon, hot enough that every movement felt languid, as though the day had slowed down so that the pair of them could appreciate every moment. It had seemed like every person on the towpath had a smile and a wave for them. Enthusiastic children had raced along beside dogs of all breeds; it had been the sort of day promised by Hallmark movies.

A gentle breeze had caressed Alice's cheeks as they'd travelled towards their destination. Ryan had held her in his arms as he'd steered the narrowboat, nuzzling into her neck and leaving her feeling like her lungs were doing somersaults behind her ribcage.

Once they'd reached Marple, he'd moored the boat and ran to a nearby chippy. It had been one of the few times that he'd paid for something, arriving back a few minutes later with fish, chips, and mushy peas for them both. They'd sat on the roof, sharing furtive glances and the occasional grin while glorying in the day.

Ryan had opened a bottle of Prosecco, and one thing had led to another.

It had been one of those dates that Alice liked to remember. Regardless of how she felt about him, Ryan had made her feel special.

Except that his name wasn't Ryan, and it turned out that she wasn't the only person he'd taken to Marple on his boat. She imagined it was how he tried to woo every girl, and she'd been silly enough to believe that he wouldn't have done it for anybody else.

'I thought it was somewhere special for the pair of us.'

'So did Lorelai. So did every other person that's ever had the misfortune to go out with him.'

'And it turns out that we don't even know his real identity.' Lorelai leaned back in her chair and stared at the ceiling. 'Or why he felt the need to hide it.'

Alice grimaced. 'He's certainly no superhero. We know that much.'

Lorelai met Alice's gaze. 'Do you think he's the murderer?'

'I'm not sure he's smart enough,' Becky said.

'He's smart enough to have tricked us into believing he was someone he isn't. What else has been an act?'

The three of them remained quiet for a few minutes, mulling over Alice's words but coming to no real conclusion. Soon enough, Lorelai and Becky claimed that they needed to return to their respective jobs, said their goodbyes and made their exits. Not that there was anything else to add.

Alice had hoped that chatting to Lorelai would assuage the rising anger at being lied to yet again by Ryan. It didn't. Learning about Marple had left a sour taste in her mouth, something akin to jealousy, not something she could ever reveal to anyone because her naivety was nobody's fault but her own.

She was debating asking Mavis if she needed help with anything in the café when she received a message from Ben, who'd arranged a video call with Mrs Veronica Ambrose. New hope swelled in her chest. Maybe this would provide the answers she needed, even though every answer seemed to lead into another labyrinth of questions.

Chapter Seventeen

The following afternoon, Marmaduke bought a bicycle. He was walking through town when he spotted it leaning against a charity shop window, its yellow price tag dangling from the handlebars. A bespectacled volunteer had been demolishing a lemon bun when he entered, eating with a gusto that Marmaduke admired. She was thrilled that he wanted to purchase the bike; apparently it was a right beggar to get back into the shop at closing time.

Marmaduke handed over his money and wheeled his acquisition away. It had been decades since he'd last ridden a bike, and he wasn't about to embarrass himself in the middle of the high street.

No matter how much he tried to forget them, Marmaduke found that Mrs Cribbins's words had affected him. Of course, he knew that the waistlines of most men expanded when they reached his age; he just didn't think that it applied to him. Earlier in the day, he'd only eaten two chocolate digestives with his brew for elevenses and felt like he was starving himself.

He knew that he wasn't and that biscuits didn't count as health foods, but he was amazed at his willpower considering he could polish off a pack of digestives in a quarter of an hour if he wasn't paying attention and there was a particularly interesting bowl on *Bargain Hunt*.

Marmaduke hadn't always led such a sedentary lifestyle. He'd played for local cricket teams as a lad and still revelled in the memory of Archie Middlemiss getting a concussion because he was too focused on Miss March's French Fancies.

Marmaduke hadn't played in years.

He could no longer run without his knees twitching or his hips aching so much that they didn't feel like they were connected to his body. Someone had once recommended a cricket team for the over-sixties; there was no running involved, and the ball was soft to avoid anyone getting injured. Marmaduke said that took the fun out of it and joined the waiting list for walking football.

The fact of the matter was that Marmaduke had stopped caring after Joanna's disappearance. Nearly thirty years had passed since then, and he'd spent most of that time re-reading all the articles and notes surrounding the case and getting nowhere.

Until Alice came along, he'd dedicated his days to wallowing under the pretence of finding his niece. He'd ignored having to buy the next size up whenever he went shopping for clothes, swapping out belted trousers for the elasticated waists of jogging bottoms while dreaming of meat and potato pies. He'd thought that no one had noticed the weight gain – had believed it was just the way that bodies transformed with age – until Mrs Cribbins had called him gargantuan, and it itched at his mind alongside his need to find out who was writing the poison pen letters.

If Elvis Shatwell was telling the truth, then they had something to do with Bianca Thistlethwaite.

She'd left town around the same time that Lucy was murdered, and Joanna went missing. He assumed that the horrors had made her want to resume her travels across the country, but now that he knew she'd visited the McBrides' home, he wasn't as certain.

Which is why he'd decided to visit Mavis.

Since he hadn't told Alice about possibly finding the culprit, Marmaduke decided to cycle to Wren's Lea. An eight-mile ride through the countryside would be child's play for a seasoned cyclist; for Marmaduke, it was something of a struggle.

The roads leading out of Partridge Mews were mostly flat – practically built for the less-than-energetic OAP. However, after heading out of town, he learned the meaning of "uphill struggle" as he attempted to climb towards the country lanes that would take him to Wren's Lea. He huffed and puffed like a wolf after some pork, while sweat glued his shirt to his lower back. He edged towards the grass verge as vehicles careened by and was almost tossed into a hedgerow when a Vauxhall Corsa full of adolescent layabouts zoomed by. They leered out of the windows and swore at him.

'Darn hooligans,' he cursed.

Admitting defeat, Marmaduke clambered off the bicycle and sat down on a drystone wall. He scraped his left shoe against his right to dislodge some wet leaves, before staring across at a squashed squirrel on the opposite side of the road.

He nibbled his thumbnail, mulling over his options; if he went home, he could telephone Mavis to see if she knew that her cousin was back in town, or ferret around in search of his bus pass – Alice would have tidied it away somewhere. It was nice to have a tidy home, but he always seemed more capable of finding whatever he was looking for when the house was in disarray. He supposed he could hitchhike; he'd simply have to hope that he wasn't picked up by a trucker who wanted paying in kind and had a fetish for old men.

The solution to Marmaduke's dilemma arrived a few minutes later. He was growing aware of his buttocks becoming damp and cold from sitting on the wall for too long, when a Land Rover rattled by. Its exterior was pitted and scratched, and it sounded like it had some mechanical form of emphysema. Blotches of rust broke through the paintwork. The driver stopped and beckoned Marmaduke over.

'Trying to recreate the good old days of bobbies on bicycles, Uncle Duke?' Luke Sterling heckled, grinning wide enough to make an orthodontist proud.

'Beggar off with your "good old days" nonsense. I might've taken early retirement, but it wasn't that long ago.'

'Do you need a lift?'

'I was hoping to go to Wren's Lea.'

'Right then.' Luke switched on his hazard lights and drew in as tightly as he could to the verge. 'Best sort your bike out first.'

Once the bike was situated, Luke helped Marmaduke into the passenger seat.

'Where shall I drop you off?'

'Thistlethwaite's café will do nicely.'

'Alice too busy to take you? Or is she remaining true to her promise and steering clear of playing detective?'

Marmaduke bristled. 'Look, lad. I don't want to fall out with you, but why do you keep on insulting her?'

Luke's shoulders sagged slightly. He sighed. 'It's something I can't control. Ever since Grandad's funeral, when I see her, I get this overwhelming urge to goad her.'

'Goad?'

He nodded. 'Goad.'

'That's not we called it back in my day. How many girls have taken you up on your offer of a pleasant goading?'

Marmaduke smirked as Luke's cheeks flushed. 'I've got no idea what you're talking about.'

'Course you do. This is Katie Henderson all over again.'

'And look how well that went. I never did find the courage to re-watch *Bruce Almighty*.'

'I warned you about ordering a large strawberry milkshake beforehand.'

Luke no longer appeared to be the stoic detective in the middle of a murder investigation. As he groaned and sank down in his seat, he reminded Marmaduke of the lad with frosted tips, sagging jeans that revealed his underwear whatever the weather, and the overpowering odour of Right Guard. 'You used to use so much deodorant that folk nearly choked. Do you remember that little phase you went through?'

By that point, they were idling down the country lanes. Luke gulped a few times. 'We've all done embarrassing things as teenagers.'

'Aye, but we haven't all gone around spraying

ourselves with Clinique perfume so that our mates thought we were spending our time in the arms of some amenable lass.'

Luke groaned. 'Can we talk about something else, please?'

'Why? I'm having fun reminiscing.'

'So, can we talk about your youth as well?' Luke asked. 'What did you get caught doing behind the cricket pavilion?'

It was Marmaduke's turn to blush. He averted his gaze, staring out of the passenger window, but he could feel the warmth rising up his neck. 'I get your point. What do you want to talk about, then?'

'Have you found out who's harassing the WI committee?'

'Mrs Cribbins told me that it was of the utmost importance to keep it a secret, and it turns out that the whole town already knows.' Marmaduke shook his head. 'I shouldn't be surprised.'

'I've lost count of the number of times you've ranted about them. Didn't Violet Grey once try to get you to sign up to her garden safari?'

'People sneaking about my house, all under the guise of complimenting my hydrangeas. I gave her short shrift and all.' Marmaduke furrowed his brow so much that his forehead practically blanketed his eyeballs.

'Well, the whole town is talking about these messages. They don't want the police involved because of the scandal, but they've no problem saying that we aren't fit for our jobs since we haven't found the culprit.'

'Sounds about right.'

'So, have you?'

'Have I what?'

'Figured out who's behind all this.'

Marmaduke mulled over what he'd learned at the McBrides' house. 'I'm following a lead, but I can't be sure.'

'At Thistlethwaite's? You don't think it's Mavis, do you?'

'I wouldn't put it past her, but no. I just want to consult her about a few things.'

'You could have just told me you were visiting a friend. Going for a chat. Isn't that what the elderly always do?'

'Charming, that is. I've no idea why you and Alice don't get on. You both take great joy in mocking anyone over seventy.'

'You started it.' Luke struggled to contain his grin. After a period of companionable silence, he said, 'Once you find the person responsible for these notes, what will happen?'

Marmaduke scratched the back of his head, wincing as he tugged a knot of his hair. At his age, he was surprised that he'd managed to maintain such a long mane. 'I'll speak to them and find out why they've brought up Lucy's murder again.'

'You're hoping they have answers, aren't you?'

'I think she must.'

'So, it's a she, now? Who do you think it is, Uncle Duke?' He paused for a breath. 'Actually, don't tell me. I've enough going on with this double murder.'

'Yet you're giving your godfather a lift in a clapped-out, old Land Rover.'

'Don't let Floella hear you say that.' He ran his hand along the steering wheel. 'This is her pride and joy.'

'Floella's back in town?'

'She's going to be looking after the farm, since your sidekick ran Uncle Bertie and Aunty Flo out of town.'

'He was hiding the identity of his brother's killer.' Marmaduke smirked. 'Don't think I didn't notice how fast you turned the conversation back around to Alice.'

'Let's not start this again. I was just explaining why Floella is up at the farm.'

'I might have to pop in sometime.'

'When you've solved your crime?'

'If it can even be called that. Is it a crime to deliver the wrong shade of hair dye?'

'In Partridge Mews? It's more than likely.'

'You're not wrong there. If I'm right about the culprit, then I'm sure she'll have her reasons.'

'And hopefully some answers about Lucy and Joanna?'

'I suppose it's very transparent what I'm doing.'

'I don't blame you. If this proves to be a lead, the local constabulary might start looking into things again.'

Marmaduke rolled his eyes. 'As if they'll ever find the inclination or resources for that.'

Within ten minutes, they were outside Thistlethwaite's. Luke offered to drop the bicycle off later before heading on his way.

Mavis was sitting at the counter, mulling over the crossword in the *Daily Mirror*. She looked over her spectacles at him. 'You're too late for food, Duke,' she said. 'I'm just about to shut up shop.'

'That's why I'm here.'

'You've got another weight loss tip? Arrive at a café after they've stopped serving?' Mavis chuckled and shook her head. She tapped her pen against her newspaper as though she was knocking ash from a cigarette.

Marmaduke latched the door. 'I think I know who's writing the poison pen letters, Mavis.'

She set her pen down and met him with a steely gaze. 'You best come through then.'

He followed her into the kitchen, telling her about his investigation but saving the most pertinent piece of information for the end. 'Elvis Shatwell said he'd seen your Bianca delivering something to the McBrides.'

Mavis set about making drinks. 'She was never really my Bianca. Me and Doris always got on. Bianca was too flighty. Look at how she upped and left when Aunty Lizzie was in prison. No, we've never had much to do with each other.'

'So, you've no idea where I can find her.'

Mavis smiled at him. 'I didn't say that.'

'Where is she, then?'

'Here.'

'Here? In the café?'

'In Wren's Lea, you daft 'apeth. She's been back a month or so. I'll look up the address.' She made herself a black coffee, packed full of sugar, and brought a mug of tea over to Marmaduke. 'I've had our Angela on the phone. She says you've been questioning her.'

'She threw me out.'

Mavis rifled through a drawer until she found a scrap of notepaper. 'She's only looking out for her mother.'

'There's no way that your Doris could be sending these letters though, is there?'

She copied an address down and handed the paper over to Marmaduke. 'There isn't. Her husband might be a fool, but even he wouldn't let her start harassing people back home when she's meant to be enjoying a cruise.'

'Then what's she protecting Doris from?' Marmaduke slurped his drink, grimacing at the lack of sugar.

'See what dieting does for you, Duke? It makes you dislike a perfect beverage.' She pushed the sugar bowl towards him. He relented. 'Anyway, I've no idea why our Angela thinks she needs to protect her mother. Perhaps she thinks that our Doris has been through enough in the last year. She lost her hair last bonfire night because of a firework gone rogue.'

'I was asking after Lucy's murder.'

'Well, bringing all that up again is as good a reason as any to throw you out.'

Marmaduke ballooned his cheeks, sighed and said, 'I think your Bianca is the one behind these poison pens.'

'I wouldn't blame her.' Mavis shrugged and sipped her coffee. 'I think the ladies of the WI could do with having the wind put up them.'

He nodded. A lot of people in town believed that the Partridge Mews Women's Institute had done more harm than good in recent years, and he himself thought they deserved all the criticism they received. However, the more he wondered if they knew more about Lucy's murder than they were letting on, the more questions he found spiralling around his mind.

'Have you spoken to Alice today?'

'She rang me earlier about visiting Sandra Marsden, but I had other things to do.'

Mavis gave him the hawk-like look that she'd spent decades mastering. 'That's not like you. She was breaking her heart in here earlier.'

'About me?'

'She found out something about that man of hers

that's left her upset. Forget that, though. I think folk take her more seriously when she has you with her. You're actually a detective. She's going to get in trouble if you're not with her.'

'I don't think she's that bad.'

'You're good for one another. I'm fond of Alice, but she can be a little like her Aunty Magdalena, always running into things without considering the consequences.'

Marmaduke recalled how she'd run in front of a loaded shotgun to confront a murderer, how she hadn't waited around for him recently before going off and questioning possible suspects. 'She's not a detective.'

'She isn't, and I worry what will happen if she doesn't get her head around that fact sooner rather than later.'

Marmaduke knew that Mavis was right. He'd lost Joanna because she'd ignored the police investigation and attempted to solve Lucy's murder herself; he wasn't sure how he'd cope if it happened again. Yet if he warned Alice, there was every chance that she wouldn't listen to him anyway.

He didn't have anything more to say to Mavis; he accepted the address when it was offered and considered his options.

Chapter Eighteen

'So, Gloria is Gwen, Ryan isn't Ryan, and the actual Gloria Hebblethwaite is the body in the freezer at Marsden's?'

'That's about the measure of things, Duke.' Alice stared down into the grim depths of her coffee. She'd made it too strong and too sweet in the hopes of getting rid of the ache between her eyes, but it had done nothing.

Part of her said that she should leave the investigation up to the local constabulary, but another part told her that she was already in so deep that she might as well keep going.

After leaving Thistlethwaite's, she returned home and made an apple crumble because she required the comfort of nostalgia. Apple crumbles reminded her of Aunty Magdalena. She recalled being eight years old, standing on a stool so she could reach the kitchen counter. Aunty Magdalena's palms had wrapped around her hands and guided her as she sifted ingredients into the bowl until they created the perfect breadcrumbs. She'd stewed the apples on the stove with sugar and cinnamon so that the cottage would smell like autumn – her favourite season for its promises of nights snuggled on the sofa beneath blankets, listening to classic records and re-reading her favourite books.

She ate a slice of crumble with custard – the latter was store bought because she'd never mastered making it herself – while watching an episode of *Only Fools and Horses*. It did little to diminish the ache in her throat. In the past, she would have chatted about any issues with men with Aunty Magdalena, but she couldn't. The reminder of all the things she loved only emphasised what she'd lost.

The next day, she walked around to Duke's. Dark clouds filled the distant sky, and a biting wind ambushed her as she went, piercing her cheeks with ice-cold needles so that she had no choice but to burrow into the woolly collar of her brown leather jacket.

Half an hour later, they were sitting at the table in his living room, where she finished telling him about the events of the previous day.

Duke reclined in his chair and sighed. 'Well, at least we've proved that Ryan was definitely a twerp.'

'If his name is even Ryan.'

'Whether it is or isn't, it doesn't make him any less of a twerp.'

'You're not wrong.' She slurped some more of her coffee, unable to stop her face from contorting with disgust. 'Have you got any further with identifying the writer of the poison pen letters?'

'Do you think Ben will give me a lift into Wren's Lea when we're finished here?'

'I could drive you, or am I not invited?'

'Not this time,' he said, a gruff authoritative tone to his voice. 'I've found a lead, but it's a bit delicate. If it turns out all right, I might bring you along next time.'

'Maybe it's for the best,' she said. 'The way things are, Luke Sterling is probably looking for any reason to throw me behind bars.'

'So, you're drinking bad coffee to prepare yourself?'

'I'm just trying to wake myself up before we speak to Mrs Ambrose.'

They didn't have to wait long for Ben to arrive. Even though he claimed to be exhausted, he'd managed to pull together an outfit that Alice could never have dreamed of: a purple silk shirt with a multi-coloured geometric pattern, a frilled black suede jacket and jeans in a complimentary shade with silver, glittery cowboy boots. Apparently, he'd been listening to a lot of Shania Twain.

He set his laptop up on the table and the three of them crowded around it to await the video call. 'Well, it's about time we spoke to the owner of this cruise liner. What do you say, Duke?'

'Can you give me a lift into Wren's Lea afterwards?'

'He won't let me,' Alice said. 'He's got some secret business to attend to. I just want to collect my car.'

Ben stared towards the ceiling. 'I suppose this is my penance for getting involved with would-be sleuths.'

'If anyone is a would-be sleuth, it's Alice. I'm a former detective.'

'And a current pain in the backside.'

'Don't be mean, Alice. Duke is one of the few friends you have left.'

Before she had chance to respond, Ben's laptop notified him of an incoming call. He answered and they were all shocked to find a woman of giant proportions facing them. Mrs Veronica Ambrose filled the screen. She'd covered her face in so much foundation that she looked like her skin was melting. Clearly, she'd never been filmed in HD before, because if she had, she'd have known to step a few feet away from the camera.

Although Alice had seen a photograph during her research, she was still astonished to see such a figure up close.

'Am I speaking with Ben Weatherill?' she asked. She was so close to the camera that her breath fogged up the lens.

'You need to sit back, Mrs Ambrose.' This came from someone out of shot.

She looked across the room, her beady, bottle-green eyes practically firing daggers at someone in the background. Mrs Veronica Ambrose scratched her chair across the floor, edging backwards until she wasn't close enough for them to see up her nose. 'Please forgive my assistant. I asked them to keep quiet, but they apparently don't know when to keep their mouth shut.'

'That's no problem, Mrs Ambrose,' Ben said, taking the lead. 'I'm Ben Weatherill. I contacted you regarding the story that one of your passengers had fallen overboard.'

'I know perfectly well why we're here.' She sighed, closed her eyes, straightened her shoulders, and sat back in her chair. 'I'm sorry. I'm currently undergoing some treatment, and it isn't having the best effect on me.'

'We all have our off days.'

'Well, thank you for your understanding. In your original message, you said that you received a note that claimed that a Gloria Hebblethwaite had fallen from one of my cruise liners? Then someone else reported that I was that passenger?'

'That's right. I'm Alice, by the way. I saw a postcard from Mrs Doris Copeland saying that you and Gloria Hebblethwaite were one and the same.'

Mrs Ambrose beamed; her smile was radiant and showed a thick line of pink lipstick on her front teeth. 'You never said you knew Doris. We haven't known each other long, but she's become a good pal of mine. Well, if she's told you about Mrs Hebblethwaite, I ought to tell you everything.

'When a young man reported that his grandmother had fallen overboard, we immediately started our search and rescue operations. We pinpointed her location, and do you know what we found?'

Alice looked to Duke and Ben, but one shook his head and the other shrugged. She sighed. 'No idea,' she said.

'A mannequin. It was a well-dressed mannequin, wearing clothes that would suit an older woman with some fine costume jewellery that I wouldn't have minded myself, but it was a mannequin nonetheless.'

Alice gripped the arms of her chair, scraping her nails against the woodgrain. 'Did it happen to be wearing any shoes?'

'It did, as it happens. I have a photo somewhere to share with you.' She glanced over the top of her computer again. 'Ellis, come and give me a hand. Sitting over there like piffy-on-a-rock-bun.'

A uniformed person blocked the view of Mrs Ambrose for a few moments, clicking away on the computer until a picture appeared on-screen. It showed a rather bedraggled, sodden mannequin on a ship's deck.

Alice immediately saw the mannequin's footwear. Anger uncoiled across her face; her nose screwed up with rage. 'They're my shoes!'

'As sad as it is to have lost a *smart* pair of shoes,' Ben said. 'Can we talk about the fact that Ryan chose to fake his grandmother's death?'

Duke leaned forward and waved. He may as well have been shouting, given how loud he spoke. 'Did anyone on the cruise witness Gloria Hebblethwaite?'

Mrs Ambrose readjusted the purple turban atop her head and fluttered her eyelashes towards the camera. 'She was seen boarding in Liverpool. After that, her grandson claimed that she was too ill to leave their cabin. He refused offers of care from the ship's medical team, before eventually attempting this trick with the mannequin.'

'What happened once you found him out?'

'We sent word to shore that we'd rescued the passenger, and all was well. Frankly, I thought that the young man had made an utter fool of himself, and that was punishment enough. When we arrived at our next port, we kindly asked him to leave the ship and helped him to make arrangements for his safe return to England.'

'Then why did you pretend to be Gloria?' Alice asked.

Mrs Ambrose blinked as though only just remembering that there were people present in the room other than Duke. 'The passengers had to be notified that we were heading back to find someone who'd gone over. I'm so rarely seen outside of my suite that I could gad about being Mrs Hebblethwaite and turn all the events into nothing more than a rumour.'

'And Ryan?'

'That's the second time I've heard such a name, and I must say that I have absolutely no idea who you're talking about.'

Anticipation tingled at the base of Alice's skull. She tapped her fingertips down the sides of the chair to hide some of her excitement. 'This is where you could prove even more useful, Mrs Ambrose.'

'How's that?'

Duke took over, taking on the role of lead detective. 'It transpires that the young man you knew as Mrs Hebblethwaite's grandson gave us a fake identity. He's a person of interest in an ongoing murder investigation, and any information you can share would be greatly appreciated.'

'You're a proper dick, aren't you?' Mrs Ambrose grinned. 'I was always a big fan of Maigret in my youth, and I must say that there's a touch of Rupert Davies about you.'

Duke blushed. He tugged at his shirt collar and stopped slouching. 'Well, we're always thankful for compliments around here, but if you could tell us what you know, I'd be most grateful.'

Mrs Ambrose nodded so frenetically that her turban almost fell off, a wisp of brown hair straggling down her forehead like a frizzy noodle. 'All the documentation provided to us, including the cabin booking, was in the name of Mr Thomas Mainwaring of Wren's Lea, England.'

'Thomas?' Alice shot up in her chair. 'He looks nothing like a Thomas.'

'He looks a downright rascal from what I remember,' Mrs Ambrose said. 'As far as we're concerned, he's Mr Thomas Mainwaring.' She clicked her mouse and scans of documents appeared on the screen alongside her.

Alice leaned in closer and saw his registered address. She'd been raised in Wren's Lea and knew the road well, and as she read all that was on the screen, plans began to formulate in her mind. Then something else hit her. 'Mainwaring!'

'That's right. She was definitely here for boarding, but we didn't see her after that. I knew that young man was up to no good the second I found him with a makeup kit. He had absolutely no idea what he was doing when it came to blusher.'

'I think that's all we need from you today, Mrs Ambrose,' Duke said. 'Thank you for taking the time to talk to us.'

Mrs Ambrose tittered once more. 'I'm just happy that we could shed some light on the situation. I can forward scans of our paperwork to the relevant authorities if that's any help.'

They gave her Jez's contact details and – after she said that she planned to one day visit Partridge Mews so that Duke could show her the sights – they disconnected the call.

Ben closed his laptop. 'That might just be the fastest we've ever got answers. We know what happened to Alice's shoes. We know that while Gwen boarded the ship, it seems that she didn't stay on there. And we know that Ryan is Thomas.'

'Thomas *Mainwaring*,' Alice said. 'He has the same surname as Gwen.'

'So, we can safely assume that they're related.'

'It's been over forty years since Gwen conned Gloria Hebblethwaite,' Ben said. 'That's enough time to remarry.'

Duke nodded. 'I'm not sure that anyone could remain married to the person who'd conned their sibling. It seems likely that Mr Hebblethwaite divorced Gwen, leaving her to do what she knew how to do best.'

Alice braced her elbow against the table and lay the side of her head against her palm. 'What if Thomas is actually Gwen's grandson and that crime runs in the family?'

'It's a possibility,' Duke said.

'Every time we get answers, we end up with about fifty more questions. It's like algebra all over again.'

'It's been at least a decade since you ever went near algebra,' Ben said with a smile.

'It still hurts my head to think about it.'

'Do you want a lift to Wren's Lea as well, then?'

Alice shook her head. 'I've got a few places to go today, but I hope you get your answers, Duke.'

'If you go to Sheppard Street then be careful, Alice.' There was something in his gaze, which was magnified behind his milk-bottle lenses, that left Alice feeling uneasy.

'What's the matter?'

'I just don't want you running into anything too hastily. Someone out there has already killed two people.'

'It's all I've been able to think about recently.' She rose from her seat and headed towards the front door. 'I don't want to argue with you, but I need answers.'

'I think that Duke can understand that more than most.'

Alice appreciated Duke's concern, but she couldn't allow it to stop her. She didn't look back at them as she left the cottage, her mind whirring with the news about Ryan's real identity and what it might mean.

Chapter Nineteen

Sheppard Street in Wren's Lea was characterised by a row of redbrick terraced houses. After struggling to find a parking space between the vehicles and assorted potholes on the road, Alice got out of her car and inhaled a scent that caused her to grimace; the stink of smoked haddock enveloped the area, with undertones of urine and the occasional hint of marijuana.

She wandered towards number nine, keeping an eye on the pavement so that she didn't trip on an upturned slab, step in dog muck, or become entangled in the yellowing weeds that seemed to populate every crack between the paving stones. Sheppard Street gave an entirely new meaning to disrepair.

As Alice neared the house, she groaned.

Leaning against the front door, looking as smug as a Dobermann who'd caught a weasel, was Luke Sterling. He stood up straight and smirked. 'You seem surprised to see me, Miss Valentine.'

'I didn't think that Mrs Ambrose would have sent the paperwork over so quickly.' She stopped in front of number nine.

'I don't know any Mrs Ambrose,' he said. 'Your local police force isn't entirely incompetent. This is the home of the woman found shot at the Hebblethwaite property, Gwen Mainwaring.'

A rock formed in Alice's throat. She laid a hand on the house, needing the sensation of rough brick against her palm as a reminder that it was real.

'What's the matter?' Luke's expression exuded concern.

'I just found out that Ryan is actually called Thomas Mainwaring.'

'Then it seems that the only thing the pair of them didn't lie about is that he is her grandson.'

Alice attempted a nod, but it came with a shudder. She'd been holding onto the hope that everything she knew about Ryan had been a lie, because if it was then she could pretend she hadn't ever dated him, shared his bed, or enjoyed his company. A chill rose from the base of her spine and threaded around each vertebra until it had a firm hold of her shoulders. She'd thought that Ryan was a little insensitive, a little stupid and mildly mindless. She couldn't reconcile that with Thomas Mainwaring, this man who'd pretended to be somebody else, who'd attempted to fake the death of his grandmother only for her to end up murdered anyway. She considered something she'd avoided thinking about. She hadn't wanted to share the idea with Luke Sterling, but he was the only other person present, so she said, 'Could Thomas have killed his grandmother?'

'We'll explore every possible avenue when it comes to

finding the perpetrator of these crimes. Regardless of your misguided notion that as a former partner of a missing person you should be told everything about my investigation, I'm not about to discuss an ongoing case with you.'

'Will you let me see inside the house, at least?' She stood up straight, brushing the dust from her hands.

Luke sighed and shook his head. 'No, Alice. If you were to enter the house, it would count as trespassing. It's also an active crime scene.'

'What do you mean?'

'Did you honestly believe I was standing here in anticipation of your visit?'

'Kind of,' she said.

'Well, I wasn't. We received reports of a disturbance last night, and our officers arrived to find that the place had been ransacked. I'm waiting for back-up, and I suggest that you leave before they get here.'

'Have you any clue who did it?'

Luke pinched the bridge of his nose. 'That's all the information I'm going to give you. Please, take some further advice from me and stay out of this. Otherwise, we'll have no choice but to arrest you.'

'You've had plenty of chances already and haven't done so.' Alice folded her arms and pressed her tongue against the back of her teeth. She wasn't feeling too confrontational, but she also wasn't prepared to let Luke Sterling get the better of her.

'Look, if Marmaduke Featherstone wasn't close friends with the PCC for Cheshire, there's every chance that you'd already be in a cell.'

She dropped her arms to her sides. 'What?'

'But that only affords you a certain amount of

protection, Alice. Do yourself a favour and stay out of this.'

Alice exhaled and raised her hands in defeat. 'All right,' she said. 'All right, I'll go, but can I tell you why this is important to me?'

Luke shrugged. 'I should think that finding a murderer is important to most people, and they usually don't have any problem with leaving that to the *proper* authorities.'

'How would you feel if you found out that someone you'd been dating wasn't who they said they were? How would you feel if it turned out that they were lying about their identity and there's every possibility that they're a killer?'

'I don't think anyone would feel good in such a situation, but that doesn't mean they get to interfere in a police investigation. I'm sorry if you're frustrated and feel that it isn't moving along quickly enough for you, but that's all I can offer you right now.'

Alice despised the sincerity in Luke's words. She couldn't stand to look at his doleful gaze, or the way his mouth no longer sneered with disdain for her; if anything, his lips had a downturned, worrisome air.

She didn't say another word; she simply turned on her heel and headed back towards her car. At least it hadn't been an entirely wasted trip because if someone had gone to the trouble of ransacking Gwen Mainwaring's home, it meant there was something worth finding.

Indeed, she'd intended to follow that train of thought, but when she returned to her car, she found several missed calls from Lorelai's friend Becky. It wasn't long before the phone started ringing again. Alice answered with a tentative, 'Hello?'

'Have you seen Lorelai? I can't find her anywhere and she isn't responding to my calls.'

'I sent her a message earlier, but I haven't had anything back.'

'This isn't like her.'

'Do we really need to worry? It's only been a day since we saw each other.'

'Look, I know all about your need for *adventure*. I don't understand why you put yourself in harm's way, but that doesn't mean you get to drag Lorelai into it.' There was a harsh, judgemental tone to Becky's words that didn't go unnoticed by Alice.

'There's every chance she's just having a busy day at work.'

'Even if that's the case, she gets a break, and Lorelai never puts her phone down. She should've answered me by now.'

Alice pressed the heel of her left hand against her scrunched-up forehead. 'Is there any reason you think she could be in trouble?'

'You were there when she mentioned Marple. What if she's gone to find him? This is all your fault. She sees that her new friend has previously been involved in a murder investigation and has decided that she wants in on the action. If anything happens to her then I'll lay the blame firmly at your door, Alice Valentine.'

'I'm not doing anything right now.'

'There's a surprise.' Alice could practically see Becky rolling her eyes through the phone.

'Okay, that's rude,' she said. 'I know where she's talking about. I'll drive there now and see what I can find.'

'I should think that's the least you could do.'

'This is really odd behaviour from a friend, regardless of how close you are. I understand worry, especially when there's a murderer about, but I'm sure Lorelai can defend herself.'

'What if Ryan has something to do with her disappearance?'

Alice gritted her teeth. 'She hasn't disappeared. I won't ask if you've called her workplace because I can tell from your behaviour that you've pestered them a lot today.'

'I just care about my friends.'

'You're the type of girl who used to suffocate hamsters, aren't you?'

'Did Lorelai tell you about Mr Tickles?' Becky asked. 'That was supposed to be a secret.'

Hearing a horrified Becky had Alice smiling. 'She didn't say anything about Mr Tickles, but it's good to know when I've got the measure of someone. Bye, Becky.'

She disconnected the call and looked into her rear-view mirror. Luke was still standing outside number nine. She bolstered herself and left the car once again because she had a favour to ask of the local constabulary.

It took a few tries to locate the boat. Once Alice had guessed that he would have taken his boat to Marple, she had to find the thing, which meant ambling down the towpath for miles in both directions before she eventually found it hidden in the shade of an oak tree.

Valkyrie was a forty-foot narrowboat painted in a shade of teal that had always left Alice thinking of mallards. Net curtains hung over every window. Coal smoke gusted from the chimney; the scent had an appealing, homely quality that Alice thought was synonymous with autumn.

Alice inhaled with a smile before stepping onboard. She rapped her knuckles on the roof.

It didn't take long for him to open the doors. She followed him into the saloon. There was a fetid stench to the place as though he hadn't aired it out in a while, like a teenage boy's bedroom – all stale sweat and anxiety.

'Before we get started, what should I call you? Is it Ryan, or is it Thomas?' Alice moved a few copies of *Men's Fitness* off a wicker chair and sat down.

He switched on the kettle. 'You know, then?'

'You're getting quite the reputation for ghosting people, Tommy Boy,' she said. 'It's a bit more serious when it's the police force.'

'Tea or coffee?' he asked tremulously, his face as pale as blancmange.

Alice pushed away any feelings of sympathy. 'Tea.'

Thomas nodded and set about making the drinks. His hands trembled as he stirred milk into the mugs. 'I didn't mean for any of this to happen.'

'Any of what? Stealing another man's identity, faking the death of an old woman or murder?'

He handed over her drink. 'Have you been playing the detective again?'

'I found both bodies. I planned to leave it up to the police, but then you let me back in.'

'Me?'

'When I found out that you were pretending to be someone else.'

'What do you think I'm guilty of, Alice?' He had a pleading look that reminded her of a labradoodle after a saveloy.

She sipped the tea to buy herself some time before saying, 'Why don't you tell me why you and your grandmother pretended to be Gloria Hebblethwaite and her grandson?'

He gulped. 'What do you know about Gwen Mainwaring?'

'Other than being related to you? Nothing.'

'Then I'd best start at the beginning.'

'Before you do, can you explain how you're related to Gloria Hebblethwaite? Your family tree is starting to look like a Spirograph.'

'Gloria isn't related to me. She's my grandmother's former sister-in-law. I'm Gwen's grandson from her second marriage.'

'So, you're not related to Sandra Marsden or Indigo?'

He shook his head. 'Gloria told me that she couldn't cope with being in Partridge Mews after everything Gwen did to her. Apparently, folk still believed that she must've had something to do with the money Gwen stole in her name. Mud sticks and all that. So, Gloria left town. She married Reggie Dewhurst, and they had two children, Raymond and Sandra. A few years later, she tried to persuade her husband to move to Australia so that she could get away properly. He refused, so she left her family behind.'

Alice sat back in her seat. 'It sounds like you know a lot about the real Gloria. What's been going on, Thomas?'

He ballooned his cheeks and released a hefty exhale. 'When I was ten, Gwen disappeared from my life. It turned out that she'd been playing the long con and had managed to steal the entirety of my grandad's savings. He lost everything – money, car, house, all gone in a matter of months because of her. She had a heart attack from all the stress and wasn't found in time.

'Dad searched for her, but it was like she'd never existed.

'A few years ago, I saw a newspaper article and I recognised her immediately. She'd been at it again, got a job at some company and conned them out of £30,000 in gift vouchers. This time, she got some jail time. They only gave her six months, but at least there were some consequences for what she'd done. What she did to my grandad wasn't even seen as a crime because they were married, and his signature was on everything as well.

'While she was in prison, I used the time to see if I could find out more about her. The article gave her address, so I went to Wren's Lea. Have you seen the house? It's a dump. I have no idea what she's done with all the money she nicked over the years, but she hadn't invested it into her home.

'It turns out that I wasn't the only person who'd seen the article, because when I reached Sheppard Street, Gloria Hebblethwaite was there, staring at my nan's front door.

'My mum always says that the universe moves in mysterious ways, and I wondered why it had decided to push me and Gloria together. We shared our stories.

'Gloria's brother divorced Gwen after the Hebblethwaites discovered the fraud. However, they spent years having to pay back the money she'd borrowed.

'Last year, Gloria's mother died. Gloria came back to help sort out the estate, only things started taking longer than they should have done. Then she saw the article and decided to stick around a bit longer. There were too many bad memories attached to Partridge Mews, so she rented a place at a retirement home in Wren's Lea.

'Gloria and I came up with a plan to get our own back on Gwen.

'First, I sent a visitation request to the prison, and she accepted. It was awkward at first. I struggled to hide how angry I was, and she didn't bother asking for forgiveness. She just said that being a grifter was all she knew. For the plan to work, I had to let that slide.

'Fast forward a couple of months. She got out on good behaviour, if you can believe it, and I waited to pick her up at the gates. Well, we arrived to find that her house had been trashed. Gloria's handiwork. So, I told Gwen that we could spend the night at my place.'

'Only it wasn't your place?' Alice hadn't intended to interrupt Thomas when he was so invested in the flow of his story, but she couldn't contain her thoughts.

'Exactly. Gloria had me take Gwen to her parents' house and present it as mine.'

'Didn't Gwen say anything when you arrived? She would have recognised it.'

'I saw her go a bit wide-eyed, but she kept quiet. I made up some story about it being a steal because the former occupants had died.'

'You were lucky then.' She took another slurp of her tea and grimaced. That was another thing on the long list of things that Thomas couldn't do: make a decent cuppa.

'Stupid, more like. Now that I look back on it, of course, Gwen knew that something was going on straight away. She'd spent her entire life in the game, but me and Gloria had only been playing at it for five minutes.

'She played along. I acted like the dutiful grandson for a few weeks, helped her get integrated into the

215

community, and eventually we decided that she might as well stay.'

'What about your narrowboat?'

'That factored into the plan as well. I'm a continuous cruiser, which meant I'd have to leave Gwen in the house on her own. We hoped that it might make her a little uneasy, especially when we started having post delivered to the house in the name of Gloria Hebblethwaite.'

'And did it?'

Thomas shook his head. 'If anything, it had her itching to return to form and have another go at conning people. Once, I got back to the house and she was on the phone giving her name as Gloria. I didn't do anything at first because I didn't want to ruin anything. We'd been planning on scaring her, on getting her to admit that she'd wronged us and maybe to pay some compensation, but seeing how things were going, we decided to change tack and go with the whole "if you can't beat them, join them" way of things.'

'That's when you became Ryan?'

'I made her think that it was all her idea, said as she couldn't tell everyone that she was Gloria Hebblethwaite and have people thinking I was Thomas when a quick internet search would reveal her actual grandson is called Ryan Dewhurst.

'She liked that it would add a sense of truth to everything, and I suppose somewhere deep down she might have thought we were connecting with each other, that she could pass down some tricks of the trade to her grandson. Maybe it was her way of apologising for all she'd put the family through. I try not to think too much about her motivations.'

'Then how did the cruise come about?'

'Gloria got tired of waiting, so she came up with the life insurance plan. We'd take out the policy, naming Gwen as primary beneficiary, and wait a while. I suggested it to Gwen as though it was my idea, and she was keen for us to go ahead. We'd both head to Liverpool and get on the boat, but she wouldn't be there when it set off.'

'That's why you stole the mannequin and my shoes.'

'Sorry about that. You'd left them on my boat, and they worked perfectly for the plan.'

'I just don't understand why you threw a mannequin overboard. It's difficult for ships to locate a body, so it would have worked out better if there hadn't been anything for them to find.'

'That was my mistake. Gwen said not to use the mannequin.'

'Nothing makes sense to me. If the life insurance policy was in the name Hebblethwaite, wouldn't you just be scamming Gloria again?'

'Gloria said to do it that way. Once the money went into Gwen's bank account, she'd go to the police.'

'What happened after the crew located the mannequin and threw you out at the next port?'

'We didn't know that was how things would go. Gloria said to collect the life insurance money once I was back in town, only when I returned to the house, Gwen wouldn't let me in. Somehow, she'd found everything out. She commended me on my efforts but said that I should've realised not to mess with someone who'd been in the game for as long as she had.

'I called Gloria and told her that we'd been found out, and then I got in touch with you.'

'So that you could properly break up with me?

217

Because disappearing for three months without a word felt a lot more criminal at the time.'

'No,' he said. 'I thought that you and Mr Featherstone might be able to help, but then you started going on about your shoes and I saw Lorelai, so I said that I fancied my chances getting back together with her, rather than saying what was actually going on.'

'Regardless of everything you had going on, you were a terrible boyfriend. There was all the crying when you didn't get your own way. You consistently *misplaced* your wallet. You regularly forgot to empty the chemical toilet on the boat. Those are just a few of the issues.'

'Like I said, I hoped that you'd help me.'

'But you didn't ask for help. You were late, had no money of your own and told me you were interested in another woman.'

'I admit that wasn't the best way of going about things, but you threw a drink in my face.'

'You deserved it!' Alice steadied her hand and set her mug down on a bookcase beside her and leaned forward, making sure that she met his gaze. 'Look, *Thomas*, I'm glad that I finally know who you really are. I'm sorry to hear about everything that happened to your grandad, but I don't understand why you killed them.'

'I didn't kill anyone!'

'Gwen Mainwaring confronted you about trying to con her and then turned up dead.'

'Technically, I did con her.'

'What do you mean?'

'Who do you think paid for the cruise?'

'Great, so you went one step further than your grandmother? You stole her money to pay for a cruise and then killed her.'

'I just told you, I didn't do it.' Thomas stood up and paced towards the kitchenette. 'I planned to go back to the house, if only to collect the things I'd left behind, but I didn't make it.'

'Because of the assault?'

'Exactly. I wondered if it could have been Gwen, or someone related to her.'

'Then why did you leave the hospital? Surely, you'd have been safe there.'

'Whoever rang 999 knew me as Ryan. I didn't want anyone checking their records and seeing that I wasn't him, so I made my excuses and signed myself out.'

'You realise that looks a little suspicious when both women turned up dead?'

'I didn't know they were dead, did I?' Thomas leaned against the counter. 'I went back to the house to collect my things and that's when I found Gwen. Things didn't look good for me, so I scarpered.'

'A likely story.'

'It's hard to believe, but I'm telling the truth.'

'What did you do with the gun?'

Thomas shrank further away from her. 'Whoever killed Gwen and Gloria is trying to set me up.'

'I think you've done a pretty good job of that yourself, Thomas.' Alice stood up and headed towards the door. 'Your grandmother's actions led to your grandad's death, and that set you on the path to revenge. She found out about it and you killed her. Maybe you killed Gloria because she could have implicated you in the murder. It's like something out of Shakespeare.'

'I'm telling you again, I didn't kill them.'

'And I'm telling you again that I don't believe you. You're terrible in bed and a terrible liar. You can choose which one to explain to the police.' Alice stepped out to find Jez waiting beside the rudder. 'He's all yours,' she said as she hopped onto the towpath, leaving Thomas to answer for all he'd done.

Chapter Twenty

Marmaduke had never been the fondest of public transport – due to an unfortunate event involving labyrinthitis, vomit and a young mother singing … *Baby One More Time* to a wailing infant – therefore, he was grateful when Ben agreed to take him to Wren's Lea.

They pulled up in front of a row of bungalows. 'Do you want me to stick around, Duke?'

'If you can wait out here, this shouldn't take too long.' Marmaduke climbed out of the car. He took in the whitewashed brick bungalows with their solar panels and manicured front gardens. He couldn't look at them without feeling a pang of fear in his chest. These homes were often the penultimate resting place for the elderly before being summoned by death.

He reached Bianca's bungalow and knocked. He had his fingers crossed that he'd be proven wrong and that she wouldn't be back in town. Yet, there was a screeched 'Hang on a sec!' before the door was opened and he saw

Bianca Thistlethwaite for the first time in decades.

She didn't look well.

Her skin had a greyish quality that put Marmaduke in mind of uncooked haggis; with an odour emanating from her body like cheese left in direct sunlight. She was wearing a shapeless pilled jumper that had pulled threads dangling from it.

She managed to fashion a bawdy grin while shaking a heavy glass bottle in his face. 'Duke, long time no see. Care for a Smirnoff?'

Marmaduke followed her into the living room. 'What are you playing at, Bianca?'

'Question for a question? Some things never change.' She chuckled and slugged back her drink. After smearing her mouth on the back of her hand, she asked, 'How the devil did you find me?'

'I'm a former detective and you're a creature of habit.' Once he'd removed a pile of musty laundry from an armchair, Marmaduke sat down. He met Bianca's gaze. 'You're finally dying, then?'

She shuffled through a pile of rubbish on the floor – newspapers and junk mail threatening to trip her up – and Marmaduke found himself reminded of his own home before Alice had come along and helped him to tidy up. He wondered if Bianca needed someone to lend a hand.

Bianca sagged into a dining chair, her chest rising and falling rapidly, hoarse wheezes accompanying every breath. It was like being in the same room as a broken accordion.

'I haven't told anyone I'm here, so you can't tell anyone. How did you know I was back?'

A shrug. 'There have been these nasty little notes

going about town, and Mrs Cribbins asked me to investigate things. Now, these notes are all related to the murder of Lucy Simpson. You can understand why I ended up speaking to your Angela, who just so happened to remember that you were there on the night of Lucy's murder. Then Elvis Shatwell said that he saw you in town.'

'So, you didn't solve the mystery at all?'

'You can't exactly say you were trying to hide. After I met Elvis, I remembered something. I was having a drink down The Blind Cat with you years ago, and you'd just had some bad news from the doctors. I hoped that when I knocked on your door, there'd be no answer, but here we are. So, is it you, Bianca? Have you been terrorising the WI again?'

She kneaded her chest with her gnarled hands, her yellowing fingernails long enough to tear through the bobbled fabric of her ratty jumper. 'Course it's me, Duke. I'm surprised it took you so long to figure it out.'

'How could I suspect someone I haven't seen in nearly thirty years?'

'I've never been able to cope with this town, with all of its venom wrapped up in politeness. That's why they've never found Lucy's killer.'

Marmaduke nodded. 'Back then, the police kept being given false leads because the public had their own vendettas against folk.'

'By "public", you mean the WI?'

'I was having a go at this polite lark myself.'

She allowed him a smile. 'I had my own go at hounding the police. First, you arrested Alan, and we all knew it couldn't have been him. Then I heard about the WI working hard to make sure that the police arrested

Walker McEwan, and that just didn't smell right to me.'

'I don't know that name.'

'That's what I mean. No one ever associated Walker with Lucy. There was no evidence, but mud sticks in this town. The WI used his name because he was a bit of a tearaway, and I'm guessing they wanted him to be kept away from their daughters.'

'Where is he now?'

'Oh, he ended up in prison,' she said. 'Not for murder. Something to do with cars.'

'Do you think the WI gave the police his name to pull the attention away from someone else?'

'You know how they like to think they run this town.'

'Are you thinking about Ash Grey?'

There was a glimmer of surprise in Bianca's eyes, but she quickly caught it, running her tongue across her cracked, dry lips. 'Our Angela clearly had a lot to say.'

'Not much after that. She kicked me out.'

'She must have had her reasons. What did you expect, after dragging up that business about Lucy?'

'That was your doing, not mine.'

'I'll give you that,' she said. 'But I have my reasons. The doctors can't say how long I have left, and I need one final go at finding Lucy's killer.'

'Do you think it was Ash Grey?'

'After all these years, I'm not sure.'

'Did you know that our Joanna obsessed over Lucy's death before she went missing?'

Bianca sighed and set her bottle of vodka on the table with a clunk. She rubbed her hands together, clearly mulling something over. 'I know a lot more than I can tell you right now.'

'Why?'

'Because I have an appointment,' she said. 'Come back tomorrow afternoon.'

She went through the difficult process of rising from her seat, using the table as leverage.

'Who are you trying to protect?' Marmaduke asked.

'There's only one person on this planet I have left to protect, and that's our Doris. I've made sure that she's never had anything to do with all this.'

'But you were happy to involve her daughter?'

'I'll tell you everything I can tomorrow, Duke.' She staggered back towards him. 'This is all for me. I've been blaming myself for thirty years. I should have followed Lucy out of that club and taught her that girls stick together. Instead, I was underneath a table with a DJ who didn't know how to handle his decks.'

Marmaduke rose from the chair. He placed a hand on Bianca's shoulder in what he hoped was a consoling gesture. 'Someone wanted to kill her. They would have found a way, even if it didn't happen that night.'

'That's not the reassurance you think it is, because there's someone out there who had it in their mind to kill a teenage girl.'

'I don't have anything else to offer by way of kind words.' He headed back towards the front door. 'It's funny, but your Angela got me to leave in exactly the same fashion.'

Marmaduke left the bungalow and wandered back towards Ben's car. He'd done his job and found out who'd been sending the letters. He grinned at the thought that it had been Bianca Thistlethwaite the whole time. 'I should've known,' he said, as he settled into the passenger seat.

Chapter Twenty-One

When Alice awoke that morning, she hadn't planned on finding her ex-boyfriend and seeing him arrested for murder, but she was glad to finally have some answers. She supposed that she could thank Becky and Mrs Ambrose for that.

She rang Lorelai as she walked back to her car, but there was no response. Maybe she'd decided that she needed some time away from Alice and an active murder investigation. Whatever Lorelai's reasons for not answering her phone, Alice hoped that locating Thomas might set her mind at ease.

There wasn't much time to dwell on things as Duke had invited her to Thistlethwaite's for a debriefing about his recent errand. Ben had dropped him off because he'd been called back to the theatre due to an emergency with a polystyrene palm tree.

Mavis was sitting behind the counter when they arrived, reading a Catherine Cookson; despite declaring that she'd never been more upset than when she'd read *Tilly Trotter*, she'd yet to put her trust in a different author. She placed a piece of greaseproof paper between the pages and looked up at them. After a few blinks, she offered them a smile that could have been called welcoming, but which also had a reptilian quality that looked as though she was sizing them up for dinner.

'You're both having full Englishes and a pot of tea. It's been dead in here today and I'm not losing profits just because everyone is on a health kick.'

'I shouldn't, really,' Alice said. 'I had a takeaway last night.'

'And there's still not an inch of fat on you, so sit down and do as you're told.' Mavis had such a stony-faced expression on her face that she could have passed for a gargoyle.

Alice and Duke shrugged at one another and sat down at their usual table.

'How did your secret business go?'

'I don't think there will be any more poison pen letters in the future, and that's all I can say on the matter.'

'Is there a reason I couldn't meet the culprit?' Alice asked, busying herself by fiddling with the napkins in the middle of the table.

'I didn't see you rushing to invite me to go and catch a murderer.'

She couldn't ignore the disappointment in Duke's gruff tones. 'That's true, I suppose.'

They both went quiet, the silence only broken when Mavis delivered their pot of tea. Alice gazed at the skirting board in the corner of the room, debating how best she could clean off a spot of gravy that Mavis claimed had stained the wood years before. Meanwhile,

Duke stared out of the window, deep in thought.

After twiddling his thumbs for a few minutes, he harrumphed and said, 'I've been investigating Lucy Simpson's murder for nearly thirty years, and today I thought I might find some answers. Instead, I've found someone else with a vendetta against the local WI, who decided to spend their time writing blasted poison pen letters like a teenager with nothing better to do.'

Alice poured them each a cup of tea, adding the necessary three heaped spoonsful of sugar to Duke's. 'Why did they choose Lucy's murder?'

'Because she believes that certain folk who might've been involved think that they're safe from justice.' He slugged his tea, emptying the cup in an instant. The cup was still steaming when he set it down on the saucer. 'She wants to see everything solved before she carks it.'

'Is that likely to happen anytime soon?'

Duke clenched his jaw and nodded. 'That's one of the reasons she's come back. She's been told that she doesn't have much time left and wants to make things right before she goes.'

'And solving Lucy's murder will help?'

'I think she regrets not telling us what she saw back then.'

'It's a bit late now, isn't it? Her story could have helped find Joanna.'

Duke laid his hands flat on the table and met Alice's gaze. He had an unusually stern expression that gave him the look of a headmaster reprimanding a pupil who'd kept a gerbil in their desk. 'There are some things I'm going to keep to myself until I've heard her account of things. If I think about it too long, I might say things I shouldn't and ruin some friendships. When you're my age, you can't afford to do that.'

Mavis wandered over with a tray. She set down their food before placing a hand on top of Duke's and running her thumb along his knuckles. 'If I'd known what she'd been hiding, I would have told you straight away. I'm not usually one for apologies, but I'm sorry about this.'

Duke placed his hand on top of hers and held it tight. 'It's not your fault, Mavis. We all have our reasons for doing things, and I understand hers.'

'You're a good 'un, Marmaduke Featherstone. Now, get your breakfast eaten. I won't have it going around that I've started serving lukewarm food just because you decided to sit around and gab first.'

They offered each other meek smiles and she returned to the kitchen.

Alice picked up her cutlery. 'Well, I doubt anyone expected to see such a sombre moment in Thistlethwaite's.'

Duke chuckled. 'You should've seen the place when Little Pete Swadlincote lost his lottery ticket after his numbers came up. That wasn't just sombre, that was downright depressing.'

'He never found it, then?'

'He didn't, but his mother-in-law ran away to Mauritius about ten months later, never to return. She'd had a sudden windfall, apparently.' Duke raised his eyebrows in such a manner that it appeared as though a millipede was attempting a pasodoble across his forehead. 'It probably worked out in his favour. His mother-in-law made some good investments before she died. She choked on a boulette while watching the sunset over the Indian Ocean. Either way, her daughter inherited everything, so Little Pete didn't do too badly in the end, but I've never seen a man as sad as he was when he lost that winning ticket.'

They tucked into their food. While they ate, Alice related the day's events to him.

At the end of her tale, she looked across at him to find him grimacing.

Duke's face contorted in such a fashion that Alice couldn't be sure if he was about to ask a question or pass a gallstone; once he'd asked his question, she realised that she would have preferred the latter. He said, 'Are you sure that Ryan is the killer?'

She let the few baked beans she'd been balancing on her fork slip back to the plate. 'Who else could it be?'

'Any number of folk Gwen has conned before could have done her in,' he said with a shrug. 'There's also no saying that we only have one killer. Sandra Marsden might have been lying when she said she didn't recognise her mother. Besides, we shouldn't leave Indigo out of our thoughts. That's if Gloria Hebblethwaite didn't simply fall into the freezer. Just because Ryan admitted to -'

'Thomas.'

'Thomas?'

'Ryan's actually Thomas.'

'I suppose that's the new test for senility, remembering the aliases of every fool around. Moreover, you called him Ryan not two minutes ago.'

'Sorry.' Alice shrank into her jumper like a spooked snail.

'As I was saying, just because *Thomas* admitted to impersonating someone and attempting insurance fraud, it doesn't mean he killed anyone. He's also a forty-two carat plonker. Do you think he has the wherewithal for murder?'

'Maybe he never meant to kill anyone.'

They couldn't continue their conversation as Mavis came running in from the kitchen, her mobile phone in hand, the bright light of the screen giving her a ghostly pallor that wouldn't have looked out of place on an episode of *Most Haunted*.

'What's the matter?' Duke asked, wiping his hands on his handkerchief.

'They've found the gun,' she said, her eyes as wild as they'd been when the cost of margarine went up. 'It's all over social media. The police were called to Magwitch Road following an anonymous tip-off.'

Alice rubbed at a burgeoning ache in her forehead. 'That makes no sense.'

'What doesn't?' Mavis was scrolling through her phone so quickly that she would have won gold if it had been an Olympic sport.

'Ryan... Thomas was assaulted on Magwitch Road. Police would have searched the area, right?'

'You'd think that someone would notice a shotgun, at least.' Duke mumbled his agreement as he tried to dislodge a piece of bacon from between his incisors.

'But with his ties to the area, the police might assume he had something to do with it.'

'You've changed your tune. It's not five minutes since you had the lad pinned as a killer.'

'He's dozy, I admit. I just don't think he's that stupid.'

'Neither do I, but the police will follow procedure, check prints and the like. We just have to wait and see what they find.'

'I'm going to try Lorelai again.'

'Have you thought that she could be the killer?'

Alice stood up, removing her phone from her pocket. 'Lorelai couldn't be a killer. She wears too much suede.'

Alice went outside to make the call. This time, however, it went directly to voicemail. A sharp bud of anxiety bloomed in her sternum, but she pushed it down, reminding herself that she hadn't been friends with Lorelai for long enough to warrant such worry, even if her mind kept telling her that something wasn't quite right.

Chapter Twenty-Two

Over the years that Alice had owned the cottage, Jez had developed an annoying habit of appearing when she was otherwise indisposed. He'd seemed upset with her the last time they'd met, so she hadn't expected him to turn up while she was in the bath.

She was in the middle of performing a concert for her towels, using a shampoo bottle as a microphone and splashing water for dramatic effect, when someone tapped their hand on the bathroom door in time with the beat. Since Norman Bates never troubled himself with knocking, Alice supposed she wasn't dealing with a serial killer.

Clutching the shampoo bottle closer to her chest in case she needed to use it as a weapon, albeit a rather slippery one, she called, 'Who's there?'

'It's me.'

Jez's voice immediately put her at ease, though she

couldn't ignore the residual anger pulsing at her temples due to the fear he'd caused to rear its head. She set the shampoo bottle down, all thoughts of her adoring fans waiting for the grand finale washed away. She said, 'You could have warned me that you were coming around.'

'I'm going to go and make a brew. Do you want one?'

Alice slid further down into the water until it came up to her chin. 'I'll have a tea.'

She listened to Jez's footsteps as he descended the stairs, wandered into the kitchen, and opened the cupboard doors. Once she heard the kettle being switched on, she set about getting out of the bath. Alice had hoped for a long soak; there was something luxurious about taking a bath in the middle of the afternoon, listening to her favourite music as the sun began its descent towards dusk. The bath had cooled somewhat, and the tepid water had left her feeling as though she was lazing in a soup of her own filth, but she still felt untouchable being secreted away from the troubles of the town.

Ten minutes later, she was sitting on the settee in the living room, a mug of tea steaming in her hands. She'd changed into brushed cotton pyjamas and had a towel turban on her head.

Jez was sitting across from her in his favourite armchair.

They both remained silent for a few minutes. Alice couldn't gauge Jez's mood from his face; he had the same stoic expression that he regularly favoured so that she couldn't tell if he was brooding like Heathcliff or in need of a laxative.

After a slurp of his tea, he said, 'A Swiftie as well as a fan of Luther Vandross? At least your tastes are varied.'

Alice winced, before staring him dead in the eye and saying, 'I didn't know policemen were allowed to enter a property without permission.'

'We're not vampires, Alice,' he said. 'Besides, you haven't fixed your lock, and I had reason to believe someone on the premises was in distress.' He tried to hide a smirk behind his mug.

'If you mock my singing ability again then I'll tell everyone what you and Mark Burgess were doing behind the bike sheds.'

Jez blanched. 'We were playing conkers.'

'Is that a new slang term I haven't heard before? By all accounts, you gave a whole new meaning to woodwork.' Alice pressed her tongue against the back of her teeth.

'Nothing happened with Mark Burgess.'

'Ben told me.'

'He said he wouldn't tell anyone else.'

'There are no secrets in a marriage.'

'That's between the active matrimonial participants, not those who take an unhealthy interest in the sex lives of their friends.'

'It's perfectly normal to chat about it.'

Jez shook his head, staring at the carpet. 'I can't believe Ben told you.'

'To be fair to him, we'd drained an entire bottle of Kraken.'

This seemed to shock him more than the revelation about his antics with Mark Burgess. 'You were drinking rum?'

'And coke,' Alice said, with a nod.

'He hates rum.'

'Apparently not with coke.'

'When was this?'

Alice tilted her head to the side as though it would cause the memory to fall into place. 'You had your sister's hen party.'

'I was only gone for the weekend. He said he didn't get up to much.'

'Well, he didn't. He slept here on the Friday night. We were a little hungover on the Saturday, so we stayed in and watched *Real Housewives*, and on the Sunday, we walked from Lud's Church to The Roaches.'

Alice had never thought Jez was capable of slouching, but he did it then, falling back against the armchair so that his chin was against his chest. 'I can't believe it.'

'Just like I can't believe my boyfriend is a murderer.'

Jez's brow furrowed, giving him the look of a silverback gorilla. 'He isn't.'

'What do you mean?'

He sat up straight, pulling himself forward so that he was teetering on the edge of the armchair. His next declaration had Alice wondering why he'd never considered a career on the stage due to his confidence and the bass behind his words. 'Thomas isn't your boyfriend, nor is he a murderer. Your "relationship" didn't last as long as a tube of toothpaste. And he isn't our killer because his fingertips don't match, there's no gunpowder residue on his clothes and you were dousing him in alcohol at the time Gwen Mainwaring was killed.'

It was Alice's turn to slouch. 'I had a feeling he wasn't really the killing type.'

'I don't think there's a singular type of killer, Alice.'

She swallowed a mouthful of tea and said, 'I understand that, but Ryan – sorry, *Thomas* – never seemed capable. He struggled enough figuring out how to undo a bra, let alone firing a shotgun.'

'Either way, we had to let him go.'

Alice exhaled. 'Where is he now?'

'I can't tell you that.'

'Confidentiality again?'

Jez was mid-slurp when she asked her question. He swallowed hard before shaking his head and saying, 'I don't know where he went. By the time I got to work this morning, he'd been released. If it's any consolation, your new friend picked him up.'

'Lorelai?'

'Who else could it be? You're not so easy to get along with.'

'Sometimes I wonder how Ben copes being married to such a charmer.'

'You can ask him next time you arrange a weekend of binge drinking.'

'It wasn't the whole weekend,' she protested weakly. Her mind was elsewhere, specifically on how Lorelai had collected Thomas from the police station. 'I don't understand why Lorelai would come to collect him.'

'I can't say. After ringing a few times to see how he was doing, an officer on reception told her that we'd be releasing Thomas, and she said that she'd be there.'

Alice nodded. 'If he isn't the killer, do you have any idea who is?'

'We're following some leads. We lost a few days questioning Thomas. He might have intended to steal money from Gloria's life insurance policy by faking the death of a mannequin, but he made too many mistakes. Hopefully the embarrassment is punishment enough.'

Alice nodded mechanically. The police had some ideas about who the culprit was, and Jez didn't see fit to tell her. It made sense. Jez was a young officer; she couldn't have him ruining his career simply because she wanted to treat murder like a puzzle in a newspaper.

Still, she had more questions. 'Are you likely to question Sandra Marsden again?'

'Her husband has friends in the right places. Considering that no drugs were found on the premises, that she might have touched the body upon its discovery, and that she made a considerable donation to a charity of the PCC's choice, there's every chance we won't be speaking to her.'

'But she's Gloria's daughter.'

'There's no evidence to show that they'd talked to one another in the last forty years. We've just got a whole load of unfortunate coincidences.'

Alice groaned. She leaned forward, cradling her mug in her hands as though it was a rather rigid stress ball. 'I'm surprised you're not on constant medication for migraines, Jez, because this just keeps getting more confusing.'

He knocked back the remainder of his brew and set his empty mug on the table. 'We'll figure it out. Now that we know how everyone is connected, it's only a matter of time before we find out the truth.'

'It's great that you're so confident.'

'It's my job to reassure the public,' he said.

Alice swallowed hard and nodded. They offered meek smiles to one another; she was glad to have Jez back on her side, but there was still a killer walking the streets of Partridge Mews and the more that Alice thought about it, the more she found her mind veering towards a specific person.

She steeled herself before saying, 'I think it might be

a good idea for you to question Lorelai.'

'What's brought this on?'

'Since Thomas can't possibly have done it, and you've told me that Lorelai collected him from the police station even though she supposedly wanted nothing to do with him, I wonder if there's more to the story than she's letting on. For a start, we were both out on the night that Thomas was assaulted, but she left earlier than me.'

Jez nodded slowly as she spoke. 'I understand what you're saying, Alice, but it's all supposition. Sure, it can seem suspicious if you're that way inclined.'

'You don't think she did it?'

'I'm not saying that. I'm saying that we need proof before we go around throwing accusations at everybody willy-nilly.'

'I seem to do that often.'

'Give it time, Alice. We'll find out who killed Gloria and Gwen soon enough.'

She accepted his words and leaned back in her chair again, hoping that her face wasn't showing how fast her heart was battering her ribcage and threatening to escape, because her mind had started to spiral with the possibility that her most recent friend could be a murderer.

When Marmaduke arrived at Bianca's bungalow, he didn't expect to find her sitting on the same dining chair that she'd been sitting on the previous day. She leaned her head against the wall, her left hand pressed beneath her bust, breath rattling.

'You look even worse than you did yesterday,' he said, having let himself in. He made his way over the carpet of rubbish on the floor and sat down across from her, wincing at the hard wood; since he'd turned seventy, he'd

239

started to appreciate the comfort of cushions beneath his buttocks.

'That appointment just about took it out of me.' Every word was accompanied by a wheeze.

'Doctors will do that to you.'

All accusatory, she said, 'Who said anything about doctors? I were out following a lead.'

'Find anything?'

'All I'll say is that I confirmed some suspicions I've had for a long while, and that I'm sorry.'

It was Marmaduke's turn to raise an eyebrow. 'Why are you sorry?'

'I've got an ambulance on the way.'

'You're really keen on keeping these visits short, aren't you?' Marmaduke shook his head, chuckling to himself. 'Yesterday, you were saying you'd reveal everything, only to go and have a dramatic decline. At our age, we have to take each day as it comes.'

'I'm a damn sight older than you, Marmaduke Featherstone.'

'You don't have to tell me. I can tell by the yellowing of your eyes.'

They shared a laugh with each other, which descended into a fit of coughing for Bianca. She reached with shaky hands for a glass of water and gulped hastily, spilling it over her "I ♡ Blackpool" t-shirt. After setting her glass back down – aided by Marmaduke, who shifted a bag of mint humbugs – she grabbed a tea-towel and dabbed at her chest.

'Before you get carted off, is there anything you can tell me?'

'Your Joanna didn't disappear while looking into Lucy's murder,' Bianca said. 'She confronted who she thought was the killer.'

'Ash Grey?'

'The one and the same. Only I don't think that he did it.'

Marmaduke gave himself a moment to process the information, filing it for later, aware that he'd grown prone to allowing his thoughts to windmill when it came to news of his niece. 'Do you know who killed Lucy?'

Bianca hiccoughed, shaking her head. 'I sent those letters to the folk I thought were involved in covering it up.'

'Were they?'

'They were part of Violet Grey's inner circle, and they were the first to start throwing Walker McEwan's name around.'

'But you can't be sure?'

'I'm not one to cast nasturtiums.'

He smiled at the malapropism but carried on regardless. 'And because you're not the fondest of the Greys, anything you said wouldn't be taken seriously without hard evidence.'

'We've both been playing this game for a while.' She sighed. 'There's something else, Duke.'

'What?'

'Joanna didn't go missing. She went on the run.'

He went rigid in his chair. Although they'd been talking about a serious topic, the conversation had seemed friendly. But Bianca's words had struck a chord and Marmaduke immediately found himself sitting bolt upright. 'How could you know that? I've been looking into this for decades.'

'I helped Joanna to leave Partridge Mews.'

All of the air was vacuumed from Marmaduke's lungs.

'Why? What could have been so bad that she chose to run away?'

It was Bianca's turn to catch her breath, pressing harder on her chest, balling her fists in the fabric of her t-shirt. 'She thought that she killed a man.'

'Then why didn't she come to me? I could have helped her.'

'The police against the Greys? How do you think that would have gone? No, we sorted it out the old-fashioned way.'

He didn't want to know what that meant, recalling tales of men exposing themselves to young women in the local woodland. When that happened, the women and children were kept home and by morning the tale was over. The police turned a blind eye.

Bianca was telling him that there was a possibility that she'd helped his niece to get away with murder. He didn't want to consider what "we" meant or who else had helped Joanna, because that might mean that there were more folk in Partridge Mews that he couldn't trust.

Marmaduke despised the Greys; a husband and wife who believed that they ruled the town. The thought that they might have bred a killer didn't surprise him, but the idea that they'd made his niece into a murderer didn't bear thinking about. He clawed at his knees beneath the table.

'You've got some explaining to do here, Bianca Thistlethwaite, if you've kept my niece away from her family for nearly thirty years.' His eyes were magnified behind his spectacles with a fury he'd believed to be long gone; it turned out that it had just been slumbering in the pit of his stomach, waiting to fly again.

Bianca pursed her lips, inhaling a mere wisp of breath.

242

'I've written it all down,' she said. 'When I die, someone will send my notebook to you. Everything I know is in there.'

'Why can't you tell me now?' Every wrinkle on his face pleaded with her, like a basset hound after a sliver of chicken.

'I don't have the energy, Duke. I thought that I'd have time to find Lucy's killer, that I could bring Joanna back, but I failed. Now I'm just doing what I can to protect my family before I go.'

'Did your sister have something to do with this? She was friends with the Greys.'

'Our Doris knows nothing about this, and I want to keep it that way.' There was a determined set to her jaw as though she was preparing for a fight.

'What are you saying?'

'I'm protecting my niece. Something you would have done for yours if I'd let you have the chance.'

Marmaduke removed his glasses as they threatened to steam up. When Bianca reached for his hand, he let her take it, accepting the consoling rub of her thumb over his knuckles. He knew that she was right. If Joanna had fled to escape the wrath of the Greys, it was best that he wasn't involved, but there was more to it than that. Nobody could remember Ash Grey, and there had been no other bodies found or reported back then.

His mind alighted on Bianca's words. 'You said that Joanna *thought* she killed a man.'

'I know what I said, Duke. You've waited nearly thirty years for your answers and I'm asking you to wait a little longer.' Bianca held his hand tightly as the sirens of an ambulance announced its approach.

Chapter Twenty-Three

Hoping to take her mind off things, Alice went to visit her parents.

Her arrival coincided with Norman getting home from work. He had a midweek weariness about him, the kind where it feels as though the weekend is a distant mirage that's always over before it begins. The almost grey pallor to his skin brightened up slightly when he saw his daughter, a pink flush blooming on his cheeks.

They ordered food from their favourite Indian restaurant and shared a bottle of Pinot Grigio while they waited for it to arrive.

Primrose turned the conversation to how she'd managed to clear a few items out from the back bedroom so that it was nearly useable again. Any guests would have to hop over a treadmill if they wanted to sleep in the bed, but at least they wouldn't be dreaming beneath dumbbells; Alice was pretty sure that wasn't what the manufacturers meant by weighted blanket.

Norman enthused about a recent route he'd discovered through the woodland on the Greenfields Estate that backed onto Alice's garden; she was pleased for him, but she also hoped that he didn't make a habit of cycling by every time he took his bike for a spin.

It was nice to share food and innocuous conversation again, to reminisce with her parents and to hear how things were going for them. Earlier in the year, there had been a few months where she'd only seen them through video calls as they took a tandem on a charity bike ride. While it had strengthened their relationship, it had also made Primrose realise that she never wanted to cycle such a long way again and that in future, if her husband decided to traverse the country to raise funds for the local hospice, she'd simply donate to the cause – and buy him a properly padded seat.

Alice should have known that the sense of calm wouldn't last.

After agreeing that Norman could have the last onion bhaji, they opened a third bottle of wine and made their way into the living room. Their plan was to find a film – something they could watch without too much thinking – and while away the remainder of the evening. As her parents wondered aloud if it was appropriate to watch *Magic Mike* with their daughter, Alice checked her phone to find a text from Ben asking for her location.

Her parents were still debating the choice of film when he arrived at the house, accompanied by Lorelai.

Alice couldn't keep the confusion from her face; then again, she'd always seemed to lose control of her expressions when mildly inebriated. She hadn't expected to open the door and see the two of them standing beneath the porchlight in outfits that wouldn't have looked out of place on *Strictly Come Dancing*. 'What's going on?'

'Thomas has been in touch,' Lorelai said.

'Been in touch? You picked him up from the police station.'

'He called me.' She shrugged.

'You haven't been responding to any of my messages.'

'I've been busy with work, Alice.'

'Even Becky was worried.'

'She does that, but I only picked Thomas up and took him back to his boat. Now he's texted me.'

'So, you went to Ben?'

'She's just like you, Alice. She didn't even think about going directly to the police, and nor did she consider the fact that I'm married to a member of the local constabulary.' Ben scratched the back of his head. 'If Jez finds out, I'm going to have to perform some acts so depraved that I'll have to steer clear of crucifixes for a while.'

Alice quirked an eyebrow. 'I didn't know Jez had it in him.'

'Nor me. Had I known that my husband had such an adoration for karaoke, I'd have made him sign a pre-nup.'

'Karaoke?'

'He loves it.' Ben sighed. 'I wouldn't have minded a bit of light bondage, but he won't bring his handcuffs into the bedroom, says as he doesn't want to be reminded of work at home.'

'My parents can hear us, you know.'

'Good,' Lorelai said. 'That means we have witnesses if anything gets a bit messy.'

'Messy?' Alice pinched the bridge of her nose; the Pinot Grigio had started to take effect.

'With Thomas.'

'Thomas?'

'The message he sent. He says we should go to Gloria Hebblethwaite's house and that we'll find all the evidence we need in his bedroom.'

Once again, Alice found herself incensed by Thomas's behaviour. He knew that she wouldn't have been able to help herself and so had sent a message to another of his exes. 'If there's important evidence out there, then how come the police haven't found it already?'

'He says there's a loose floorboard beneath the bedside table.'

'That's convenient.'

Ben beamed as Norman stepped into the hall. 'Mr Valentine! You've never given up cycling? I almost didn't recognise you in such loose trousers.'

'Good evening to you too, Ben.' Norman placed a hand on Alice's shoulder and looked at her in a doleful fashion that was common among fathers. 'Are you sure that it's smart to visit Gloria's? We've had a fair amount of wine this evening.'

'How much has she had?'

'Because she seems okay to me. A little grizzly, but then that's just Alice. One minute she's a cuddly bear that you just want to squish against you, the next she's tearing your arm off and beating you with it.'

Alice couldn't believe her ears. 'I might be a little drunk, but I *am* here. Also, squish? Please never think about squishing me again.'

Lorelai exhaled in disbelief. 'Maybe you wouldn't be so fractious if you allowed a squish once in a while.'

'I didn't realise you knew her that well,' Ben said.

'I was just going to ask,' Norman said. 'Who are you?'

She grinned at Norman as she shook his hand. 'I'm Lorelai. I went to school with Alice. A decade later, she got with my ex – who now happens to be her ex – and while he *did* steal another man's identity, he's no longer a suspect in an ongoing murder investigation. His grandmother is dead, and so is the woman she was impersonating. Anyway, I think that it's the start of a great friendship. Me and Alice, I mean. Not me and Thomas, or me and the dead women.'

Norman stared dumbfounded at her. 'Are you always this chirpy?'

'I think I'm just excited.'

'Right,' he said. 'I want to reiterate that I don't think it's a good idea for any of you to be visiting a crime scene.'

'Look. We were just about to watch a film. Why don't we do that? I'll drink some water and flush out all the glorious Pinot Grigio that's currently swimming through my veins.'

'And then we'll go to Gloria's?' Lorelai grinned so hard that it looked as though her cheeks could crack at any moment.

'Sure,' Alice said with a shrug. 'But you're driving.'

Entering a crime scene with the husband of a detective and the ex-girlfriend of her ex-boyfriend probably wasn't one of Alice's best decisions, but if she was to rank all of the bad choices she'd ever made, she doubted it would make the top ten.

She held Ben's wrist tightly as they sneaked up the drive to Gloria's house. The place seemed more imposing in the dark, especially since the last time she'd visited there'd been a dead body in the living room. Alice kept expecting lightning to strike the gables as Bach's *Toccata and Fugue in D Minor* warned them against entering. It didn't. Apart from seeing their ghostly reflections in the windows, it was no more eerie than usual.

Alice was leading them towards the back when Lorelai whispered, 'Where are we going?'

'I'm hoping the back door is unlocked like last time.'

'But I have a key,' Lorelai said, taking it from her pocket.

'To the front door?'

Lorelai nodded.

Alice stared at the key twinkling in the light of the streetlamps; the faint glimmer had her biting her molars down on her tongue. This was yet another insult from Gloria Hebblethwaite.

'Gloria gave it to me when I was dating Ryan. Well, Thomas. I didn't plan on giving it back when we split. It's really convenient when I'm at work and need to pay a visit.'

'Why can't you use the toilet there?'

'I've got a socially awkward bowel, and no one dares go near the toilet when Yvette is in.'

'Who's Yvette?'

'The office administrator. She's very particular about paperclips.'

'Look, are we going in or not?' Ben asked. 'Only I'm freezing, and all this talk of lavatories isn't doing me any favours.'

Lorelai hurried to the front door and let them in.

Ben ran off to find the bathroom while Alice gawped at Lorelai. 'I can't believe Gloria gave you a key.'

'Don't think about it too much. You know what she was like.'

Alice ran her hands through her hair and unleashed a sigh the likes of which would insult an asthmatic. 'You're right,' she said. 'Let's forget about it and go and see what Ryan's talking about.'

'Should I switch on the lights?'

'Might as well. If the police turn up, we'll say that Ben had a bladder emergency, and you had a key. We came in without thinking.'

'Is it a good idea to lie to the police?'

Alice shrugged. 'It's all true, only the reasoning is off.'

Lorelai switched on the lights. 'I don't remember you being this sneaky at school.'

As they climbed the stairs, Alice said, 'We didn't hang out at school.'

'Do you think we'd be friends now if we'd known each other then?'

Alice stopped in her tracks and leaned back against the banister, holding onto the varnished oak. She couldn't meet Lorelai's eyes and instead stared straight ahead at a framed photograph on the wall; three young children and an older man in a grey checked blazer and trousers all grinning at the camera, with so many teeth on display that they could have been auditioning for an am-dram production of *Jaws*. 'Maybe not. I used to avoid everyone from high school. Sure, we were friends on social media, but I had no plans of ever getting close to them. I thought I'd find my people when I left university, but no one ever warns you that it's difficult to make friends as an adult. Jez only came back into my life because I found a dead detective.'

'Well, I plan to keep you as a friend.' Lorelai reached

out and took Alice's hand in hers, leading her upstairs. 'Come on, Al. Let's go find some clues.'

The back bedroom was reserved for Thomas. When Alice had been going out with him, they'd stayed there occasionally after their nights on the town resulted in a drunkenness that was too dangerous for a narrowboat. Alice would lie next to him, in the creaky double-bed, unable to sleep because of the lumpy mattress that made her spine ache; she also worried about making any sudden movements in case his grandmother thought they were making mischief.

Soon after entering the bedroom, the muffled sounds of *C'est La Vie* by B*Witched emanated from the pocket of Lorelai's jeans. She checked the caller ID and, having glanced at Alice to apologise, disappeared back downstairs.

Alice was wondering where Ben had got to when she heard him chatting as well. She hoped he'd also received a phone call; otherwise, she might have to speak to Jez. She sighed, thinking it was just her luck to go investigating with the two least attentive people in Partridge Mews. Duke wouldn't have been on his phone. Granted, he forgot where he'd left it half the time, but if he'd received a call while they were searching for clues, he would have let it go to voicemail – and then he would have never listened to the message, because he hadn't yet figured out how to use it.

Since the conversations didn't seem to be ending, Alice went to the bedside cabinet and knelt down. She ran her hands along the dusty floorboards until one rattled beneath her touch. After reminding herself to breathe, she lifted the loose floorboard and set it down beside her. Then she used the torch on her phone to see what was hidden beneath the floor: a navy-blue handbag, heavy and bulging. Alice took it, expecting to find it dusty, with the occasional cobweb and thin spider that was more leg than body. It wasn't. The handbag was clean – shining, almost – with an odour of shoe polish that reminded Alice of Sunday evenings.

She unzipped the handbag to find it filled with paperwork. Alice grinned and removed a wodge of crinkled and coffee-stained envelopes addressed to Mrs Gloria Hebblethwaite. She was about to see what was inside when she heard the front door slam. At first, she wondered if Lorelai had chosen to take her call outside, but then a masculine voice yelled, 'Hello?'

Alice jammed the papers back into the handbag and bolted out of the back bedroom. She ran down the landing towards an airing cupboard and flung herself inside, slamming the door shut behind her. It was a snug fit. Alice had to share the space with the boiler, an ironing board, and an old vacuum cleaner.

She'd chosen to hide in the airing cupboard because it was at the top of the stairs, and she could see through the slatted doors onto the landing without anyone being able to see inside. At least, that's what she was hoping. That had certainly been the case when she'd played hide and seek with her cousins as children.

Luckily, Lorelai and Ben had gone silent.

Alice listened to the man's footsteps as he wandered around downstairs. He no longer called out, but she heard him opening doors and moving things about. Soon enough, he began to climb the stairs. Through the slats in the door, Alice watched a tall, willowy figure approach.

She grew more aware of her breathing. It seemed much louder than normal, and she wasn't sure if it was because she was in such a small space or because she was being faced by a possible killer. She tried to hold her breath.

Once the man reached the top of the stairs, he took one look at the airing cupboard and reached for the handle. Of course he did; if Alice hadn't known about the loose floorboard and was casing the joint, she'd have done exactly the same. She grimaced at her short-sightedness and frantically glanced about the airing cupboard.

She took hold of the first thing that she came across and, as the man opened the door, thrust the ironing board towards him, pushing him until his back was against the wall.

She ran downstairs, vaguely aware of clattering behind her as the man chased after.

All the air was knocked from her lungs as he slammed into her back. She dropped the handbag and found herself thrown against the front door, the handle jammed into her side.

'What are you doing?' he exclaimed.

Alice would have answered if she'd had the chance. No sooner had she parted her lips to respond than the man crashed to the floor.

Alice turned around.

Thomas lay in a heap, sprawled out as broken pottery fell upon him from the remains of a lamp. Blood drained from his head, to be soaked up by an Afghan rug; at least it would add another element to the already intricate pattern.

'Thanks, Lorelai,' Alice said.

'My pleasure.' She looked smug. The lamp's wire dangled limply in front of her, like a sad cephalopod.

'You didn't let me finish. Thanks, Lorelai, you just made this a crime scene.'

Lorelai shrugged. 'Technically, it was already a crime scene. I just crimed it up a bit more.'

Alice caught sight of a shadow at the top of the stairs. Ben stood there, pointing at his phone. 'Would this be a bad time to say that I've spoken to Jez, and he says he's on his way?'

Alice gritted her teeth. 'Considering there's now an unconscious man lying feet away from where his grandmother was murdered, it's probably for the best.'

Moments later, the front door opened.

The three of them stood in a line and watched as Marmaduke entered, followed by Luke Sterling. 'Why am I not surprised?' said the latter.

'What are you doing here?'

'I received a call from Thomas saying that he was at this address and that he was worried for his safety. I can see that he was right to be worried.'

'But he texted us and told us to come here.'

Concern etched itself into Alice's brow. 'I'm worried, Duke. Something's not right.'

Chapter Twenty-Four

After a few minutes, Thomas came around, groaning. Ben helped him to his feet and led him into the kitchen – partly to treat his head wound, and partly because Lorelai seemed a bit too eager with the table lamp.

Before long, Jez arrived, seeming both afraid and confused.

Luke remained as scornful as ever. He glared at Alice with eyes so piercing that they could have belonged to a badger. 'I thought you said you were keeping out of this investigation, Miss Valentine.'

She nodded and reiterated the story she'd concocted earlier.

'And you just happened to come across Thomas, who you then assaulted?' he said, folding his arms.

Alice folded hers in retaliation. 'That was Lorelai. I just whacked him with an ironing board.'

'An ironing board?'

'To get him out of the way so I could run.'

'Why did you feel the need to run?'

'There was a creepy man in the house where someone was recently killed. Why wouldn't I feel the need to run?'

At that moment, Ben wandered back down the hall. He caught sight of the scowl on Jez's face and averted his gaze. 'So, it seems that "creepy man" has no idea about any text we received.'

'What are *you* doing here, Ben?' Jez asked.

'Hello to you, too, husband.'

'You're interfering with a police investigation.'

'No, I needed the loo. Lorelai had a key.'

'You could've held it.'

'And risk making a mess in our nice car? We only just had it valeted, Jez.' Ben reached for his husband's hand and brought it to his lips. 'Besides, we know from experience that a black man isn't likely to enter a house if he thinks there might be any threat to his life.'

'Someone was literally murdered here within the last fortnight, Ben.'

'Yes, but they're unlikely to come after me. One, I didn't know Gloria. And two, I'm the best drag queen that Partridge Mews has to offer. Kill me and you upset the entire queer community.'

Jez shook his head but couldn't hide the shy smile curling at the edge of his lips. 'Forget whoever killed Gloria, you'll be the death of me, Obinna Weatherill.'

Ben grinned. 'The full name? Someone is looking to score tonight.'

Jez blushed as Ben leaned in to steal a kiss.

'Do you mind?' Alice and Luke said in unison. They both looked at one another before glancing back at the pair.

'Spoilsports,' Lorelai said. She sat at the bottom of the

stairs, cradling the remains of the table lamp in her hands.

'So, Mr Mainwaring claims he didn't send any text message,' Luke prompted Ben, who seemed to have forgotten why they were at the house in the first place.

He gawped at Luke for a few seconds before his eyes lit up. 'Oh, that. Yes, he says that he's been staying here because someone trashed his boat.'

Alice rushed to the kitchen before anyone could stop her.

Thomas was sitting down and holding a bag of vegetable stir fry mix to the back of his head. He was leaning forward, water spilling between his fingers and trickling down his neck, his eyes dark and sunken into the hollows of their sockets. 'Come to finish the job?' he said, although he sounded more ogre than human.

'I'm not the one that whacked you around the head.'

'That's not as reassuring as you think.'

She sat down next to him as the others followed her into the kitchen. 'Put the kettle on, Jez.'

'This is still a crime scene.'

'Well, another crime has taken place, and I think we'd all benefit from a cuppa, so get a shift on.'

'What about milk? Gloria's been dead a while.'

'There's some UHT skimmed milk in the top cupboard. Perhaps your husband can get it down for you.'

Jez and Ben busied themselves as requested while Alice offered what she hoped was a smile to Thomas. However, she didn't get chance to speak as Luke said, 'Miss Valentine, do I really need to remind you that you're not a detective?'

'That's very presumptuous of you, Detective Sterling. You don't know what I was about to ask Tommy over here.'

'It's Thomas,' the man said.

Alice cocked her head to the side. 'Really?'

He nodded. 'My mother used to call me Tommy. I won't have anyone else calling me that.'

'But Ryan is fine?'

'Alice,' Luke warned. He took the seat on the opposite side of Thomas.

'*Luke.*' She fluttered her eyelashes in his direction.

'The police know that I didn't kill Gloria or Gwen, and I think that whoever did is after me.' Thomas sunk down in the chair. He dropped the stir fry mix to the table and ran his hands through his hair, tugging closest to his crown.

Something twirled in Alice's gut, and she stood up again. She looked down at Thomas and realised that she didn't know him at all. He'd already provided her with a testimony that she hadn't believed, and regardless of anything he said to her, she'd never be able to think of him in good terms. 'I'm sorry,' she said. 'I got carried away.'

He met her gaze. 'That's saying something.'

'You conned me, Thomas. You barrelled into my life without thinking about the consequences because you were so intent on getting your revenge. Now two women are dead and apparently you didn't do it, which is great, but why did you have to involve me?'

'Back at the bar, did you really wish I was dead?'

Alice looked around at the others in the kitchen. They all had expectant expressions on their faces, and she tried to pull some response from deep within, something tactful that wouldn't have her sounding so heartless, but the words weren't forthcoming, and it felt as though the pressure to talk was building. 'I need some air.'

'We'll come with you,' Ben said, beckoning Lorelai. 'Let's leave the real detectives to their work.'

'Why couldn't I lie to him? Just turn around and say, "No, Thomas, I just wanted to hurt you because you disappointed me. I thought I was going out with a man, not a ghost."'

Ben wrapped his arms around himself, his breath misting as he spoke. 'It's okay if you're not ready to forgive him.'

'I don't know why I dislike him so much. It's not as though I envisaged a future with him when we were going out together. I was only seeing him to pass the time. I wouldn't even have downloaded that dating app if I hadn't seen that Eloise Pigeon is engaged.'

Alice wandered over to the wall and leaned back against it, eyes closed, and head tilted towards the sky. She willed her mind to calm down, to think about all that she'd learned, but she kept going over the night's events. She focused on being left in Thomas's bedroom. Before she could stop herself, she said, 'Who called you?'

Lorelai looked like a rabbit in the path of a vixen, tears welling in her wide eyes. 'Before, do you mean?'

'When you left me in Thomas's bedroom, because I find it mighty convenient that he contacted you with details of the loose floorboard and then you disappeared just as he arrived. Perhaps you're all in this together.'

Lorelai blinked a couple of times, wiping her eyes on her sleeves. 'It was just Becky. You remember her? Cardigan. Soda water. Had a Judo tournament the morning after we went to see Elaine Closure. Probably needs her roots doing. She just wanted to check in and make sure I was okay.'

'And why would she do that?' Alice didn't mean for it to sound so spiteful.

'That's what friends do.'

'Alice, you've got to get a grip,' Ben said. 'Lorelai had no idea that Thomas lied about his identity. We don't know his reasons, but maybe when Luke and Jez finish talking to him, we'll have a few answers. Until then, I suggest you don't upset anyone else.'

Alice bit back any further insults and clenched her fists, pressing her nails into her palms. 'Sorry, Lorelai.'

'It's fine. I've heard much worse at the Quiz Night down the Hare and Horse. You should come along one night.'

'Maybe,' she said. 'Also, who could forget Becky?'

'She also asked me if you're joining us for clay pigeon shooting. You never replied to her message.'

Alice groaned. 'I meant to send her one back, but then I found Gloria's body.'

'There's no issue, just do it when you get the chance. Becky has this whole thing about respect.'

And in that moment, everything stilled in Alice's mind. She remembered how protective Becky was over Lorelai, how Thomas said that he'd been assaulted by a much bigger person, and how there was that photograph that Becky claimed had been for their work website. Maybe that had been a lie. 'Are you sure that she never saw you with Gwen?'

'Not that I remember. Why?'

'All along, we've believed that the murders were related to Gwen Mainwaring conning Gloria Hebblethwaite all those years ago. What if it was never about that?'

'What are you saying?' It might have been the cold of the night, but Lorelai's skin seemed to pale.

'What if it was about protecting you?' Alice allowed her words to sink in.

'Alice, I suggest you remember what I said a minute ago,' Ben said. 'Let's leave this one to the police.'

Lorelai's lips trembled. 'No. You're right.'

'About?'

'Becky killed Gloria and Gwen,' she said, her words shaky. 'She said that it was a mistake, and that it wouldn't have happened if she didn't have to protect me.'

'You knew?' Alice stared at her, disbelieving.

'I confronted her after we met for coffee, and she told me everything. She started going on about how she's seen me hurt too many times and if I keep ignoring her warnings, she'll have to be firmer. I didn't know what she meant, so I ran away.'

'That's why you wouldn't respond to my messages?'

Lorelai nodded. 'My uncle has a place in Penrith. I didn't tell anyone where I was going, but she found me.'

'Can she track your location from her phone?'

'I switched it off.'

'This is all getting too serious,' Ben said. 'We need to get inside and tell Luke and Jez what's going on.'

'Speaking of which, did Thomas tell you to come here?'

Lorelai shook her head, tears streaming down her face. 'She said that if I didn't get you all here then she'd hurt my family next.'

'What's she planning?' Ben asked, his voice quaking.

A gunshot responded.

The entire house rumbled as the sound of glass shattering resounded throughout the neighbourhood.

Alice ran for the back door, but Ben grabbed her and dragged her towards the hedge.

Another gunshot and more yelling from inside.

Lorelai sped across the garden, heading around to the front of the house.

Alice couldn't tell what Lorelai was screaming but held onto the idea that if she was making noise then she was still alive.

She stopped struggling against Ben's hold around her waist. As her legs buckled beneath her, they both sank to the ground. She tried to steady her breathing, thinking of everything she'd learned from her mother, but thoughts of Primrose only made things worse.

It felt as though the gunshots would never stop echoing in her head, but they were soon replaced by the sound of sirens.

Alice stared intently at the house, her mind on what might be happening within its walls. The longer she stared, the heavier the weight in her chest.

Blue and red lights glowed behind the house, and Alice hoped that meant that help was being provided to those who needed it.

An eternity seemed to pass before the back door opened and Duke appeared. His entire body trembled, illuminated by the light from the kitchen. He surveyed the garden, squinting into the darkness, before he caught sight of Alice and Ben huddled beside the hedge.

He moved as fast as Alice had ever known him to move. 'Did they get you?'

She couldn't find the words to answer. She stood up and wrapped her arms around him, burying her face in his neck. Molten tears burned down her cheeks. Her throat ached, unable to release the pearl of fear that had formed in her oesophagus.

Duke wrapped his arms more tightly around her. 'It's all right, I'm here.'

Those words triggered Alice's cries to break free. She shuddered in Duke's arms, unsure of what lay in wait in the house, unable to think straight, but knowing that she'd never experienced such terror and that she knew exactly who to blame.

Chapter Twenty-Five

Not longer after Alice and her new friends went into the back garden, Marmaduke heard a car door slamming. He'd been admiring a mahogany sideboard, remembering his mother's favourite crockery, when there was a crunching of stones as someone approached the house. He shivered, the hairs on the nape of his neck standing on end.

'What is it?' Luke asked.

'Nothing, lad. Someone just walked over my grave.' He rubbed his neck as the living room window exploded.

Marmaduke didn't know what was happening; he just felt the weight of Luke's body as he barrelled into him and pulled him to the ground. His knees slammed into the tiles, and he knew he'd pay for that later.

They crawled under the table alongside Jez and Thomas, the former already on his phone to dispatch.

The table wasn't built for four grown men to hide beneath it. Marmaduke grew aware of how cumbersome a body could be, knowing that while his broad shoulders made him a great human shield, they also made him the easiest target.

He heard Lorelai screeching and another woman saying something about "protection" before sirens silenced all other sound. Hope strangled the terror in his chest, and as much as he thought he should remain in place, his mind focused on Alice. He braced against the table and pulled himself to his feet before staggering over to open the back door.

Seeing Alice huddled on the ground with Ben caused an ache to swell in his throat.

Earlier in the evening, when Marmaduke had been enjoying a fish supper with his godson, he hadn't anticipated that within a few hours, he'd be hiding beneath a table after a shotgun had been fired at him.

'Considering the number of times, she fired, that Becky is a terrible shot. Maybe that's why she was trying to get you all clay pigeon shooting: to try and get some practice in.' He set a tray full of steaming mugs on the table. 'Now, I've put enough sugar in these teas to put a horse into a diabetic coma. I don't want any comments about calories or gym workouts, because you've all had a shock, and this will help.'

'Actually, Duke -'

Marmaduke silenced Jez with a look. They were all sitting around the kitchen table, looking drained. Admittedly, he wasn't feeling his best – by this time, he would usually have been in bed, dozing off to Dizzy Gillespie – but since everyone around him was understandably dazed, he'd taken control of the situation.

'How are you so calm?' That question came from

Thomas. Out of everyone there, he seemed to be the greyest of the bunch, as though he'd daubed his body in cement.

'That's not the first time I've been shot at.' Marmaduke knocked back a long glug of scalding tea, revelling in the sweetness and disregarding any worries about his weight. 'If you'd ever had to arrest a farmer then you'd know what I'm talking about. I had to bring in Dickie Gleason because of the mess he'd made of Petra Dichonne's Cortina when she parked it outside his gates. He responded by getting his two-two out.'

'Clive had you at gunpoint as well,' Alice said. She'd sipped her tea with distaste, but at least she was able to drink it.

'I don't know if he would have shot me, but I'm glad we didn't find out.'

Luke's phone rang and he headed out into the hall to answer it. They all remained silent, listening to his hushed voice. Ben rested his head on Jez's shoulder, and they held hands. Alice sat beside Thomas but kept herself as far away from him as possible, practically wedged against a table leg.

He knew that the lad had done wrong by Alice – that he'd been an idiot when it came to trying to commit a crime which could have led to the death of two women – but Marmaduke sympathised with Thomas. He was the only person at the table with no one to lean on. Marmaduke asked him, 'Do you have any family?'

A bewildered Thomas stammered, 'My parents live in Castleton. Dad's a joiner and Mum teaches children with special educational needs.'

Marmaduke stiffened. He'd thought that Thomas was alone in life, that he'd committed his misdeeds because he'd had no one around to properly guide him. 'Are they still together?'

Thomas nodded. 'Nearly forty years.'

'Any brothers and sisters?'

'Only brothers. There are three of us altogether. Harry works for my dad and Eddie is a gardener.' His skin brightened up as he talked about his family.

'And you all get along with each other?'

'Course! Me and Eddie were Harry's groomsmen.'

'Now, I'm going to ask a question that might upset you. This evening has been difficult for everyone. Some might say that you've had a difficult few weeks, having been assaulted -'

'Was that Becky?' Alice interjected.

Thomas shrank back in his seat and nodded. Marmaduke didn't know whether to be concerned or impressed by the effect she had on him. 'I'll get straight to the point, lad. Why the heck did you come to Partridge Mews?'

'Not this again,' he groaned. 'I saw that my nan had been up to her old tricks and decided to get revenge. When I was little, she was the best grandparent anyone could ask for. She looked after us when our parents were at work, helped teach us the alphabet, came to every school event. She was like a proper grandparent. Then she stole all that money from my grandad and disappeared.

'People say that children don't feel grief as keenly as adults, but when grandad died not long after nan did what she did, I felt like I'd lost everything. I couldn't see the point in life. I don't remember much about the next few years other than skipping school and being sad.

'I don't know if I wanted to avenge my grandad or to

267

have my nan back in my life, but I just needed to hear if she ever actually loved us, and I never got to find that out because she thought I'd only tracked her down to hurt her.'

'Wow,' Alice said.

'Alice,' Ben warned.

'No, I was just going to say that's the most heartfelt I've ever heard you.' She pushed her hair away from her face and went on, 'If the police are going to let you off because, let's face it, you're simply a twerp, then I think you should get back on board your narrowboat and return to Castleton.'

'Is that a polite way of telling me to get lost?'

She smiled. 'It is, but family clearly means a lot to you and now two families have lost grandparents that they didn't get to know. That didn't have anything to do with your stupid revenge plot and is the fault of a jumped-up admin assistant with a penchant for soda water, but the point remains that there's nothing here for you. So why stick around?'

'I never thought I'd see the day where Alice Valentine gave good advice.' Luke wandered back into the kitchen, pocketing his phone.

'I always give good advice. Those who don't follow it are simply gluttons for punishment.'

Marmaduke shook his head in disbelief at the pair of them. 'Have you had any news about this Becky?'

'We've asked online for anyone who sees her or her vehicle to let us know.'

'We have to wonder what made her scarper.'

'Lorelai,' Alice said. 'Everything Becky has done was to protect Lorelai. If she thought there was any threat to her, she'd have taken her away.'

'Do you think Lorelai ran to her to draw Becky away from us?' Ben asked.

'We know nothing about her, really. Before that night in the bar, I hadn't seen her for nearly a decade. People change a lot in that time. Jez is proof enough of that.'

'What's that supposed to mean?'

'My mistake. You're still as uptight as you were at high school.'

'I suppose you must be feeling better since you're already insulting folk,' Marmaduke said.

'It's a gift.' They smiled to one another. Alice turned to face Luke and said, 'Did you find anything in that handbag?'

'I find it highly suspicious that our officers inspected every nook and cranny of this place and never found the handbag, while you came across it in seconds. But I'll ignore that for now. It belonged to Gloria Hebblethwaite, and it includes a few life insurance policies.'

'Who are they made out to?' Thomas asked.

'I should've known that would interest you,' Alice said, with a shake of her head.

'I didn't kill -'

'It's not about whether you killed her or not. It's the fact that this entire scheme was about getting revenge on your grandmother, and you got it wrong at every turn. You might be remorseful now, but is it because of the murders or because you've lost out on some cash?'

'Who's to say I've lost out on anything?'

'Me,' Luke said. 'These policies are made out to Gloria's children. There's no mention of a Ryan Dewhurst or a Thomas Mainwaring. However, I *do* have a few pages of text messages between you and Gloria

269

talking about how you're going to take Gwen on the cruise and make sure she remains lost at sea.'

Thomas went so white that Marmaduke found himself reminded of a ghost. 'It's a good job Gwen never got on that cruise ship,' he said.

Thomas nodded. 'I never meant it.'

'Be that as it may, it looks like you got your wish in the end, even if you never got the reward you'd hoped for.'

They remained quiet for a while after that, considering Luke's words. It had been a difficult evening for them all, and further revelations about Thomas's behaviour would do nothing to diminish the shock they felt.

Once they no longer resembled phantoms, they left Gloria's home. Jez and Ben agreed to take Thomas with them for the night. Marmaduke reflected on how both of his visits to the place had ended terribly, and part of him wondered if it was cursed. He didn't have too long to think about it though, because Luke and Alice spent the entire journey home arguing about *The Walking Dead*, a television show that Marmaduke had never heard of before. By the time that they'd finished bickering with one another, he had no intention of ever watching it.

They arrived at Marmaduke's cottage to find a few police officers milling around outside.

'Just a precaution, Uncle Duke.'

'You'll have done the same for Alice, too, I suspect.' He was unable to stop himself from a saucy wink.

Luke's reddened face was illuminated by the light of a nearby streetlamp. 'There's an armed murderer out there.'

'It's fine, Duke. As long as they keep their truncheons to themselves, I don't mind.'

Marmaduke got out of the car, grateful that Luke hadn't brought the Land Rover, and headed down the garden path. He greeted the officers and stepped inside his cottage. He'd never been this happy to lock the world out behind him.

Chapter Twenty-Six

Alice was torn from a deeply pleasant dream about being on Cresswell Beach with Kenny Doughty by her phone's insistent buzzing. Before she had chance to do anything, it fell from the bedside cabinet. She opened one eye, looking out on indeterminate objects in the grey haze of pre-dawn. Slowly, everything coalesced and came into focus. Like a slug, she dragged her lethargic body to the edge of the bed and reached for her phone, trailing her fingers across the carpet until she landed upon it. The screen lit up to reveal several missed calls.

Her hands trembled as she dialled voicemail. All thoughts of her subconscious activities fled her mind as a robotic voice declared that she had a new message. It began to play. At first, all she heard was a racket of people yelling before a familiar voice said, 'Alice, I'm sorry.' After that, the line went dead, and she was left to wonder what Lorelai had meant.

She was about to listen to the message again when the

phone rang in her hand. She answered immediately.

'Mum, are you okay?'

'Morning, love. Now, I don't want to cause you any concern, but I've got a young woman here who says that she'd like you to come around for coffee.'

'Is it Becky? Are you okay?'

'That's right, love. We'll see you soon. And don't go bothering Jez or Luke with this. They've enough to be getting on with.'

'She could be a killer, Mum.'

'I don't doubt that for a second. She certainly has the ability and the equipment. Anyway, the sooner we finish this call, the sooner you'll be able to get here.' Primrose rang off.

Alice hadn't had chance to rub the sleep from her eyes, and so she hastily made herself presentable and rushed downstairs. After telephoning Jez, she called Duke, asking them both to make their way round.

An ache swelled in her throat, quickly becoming a rock that tried to block her oesophagus. She busied herself in the kitchen, grabbing mugs from the cupboard and throwing in teabags, attempting to focus on making a drink rather than rushing straight over to her parents' house and confronting a murderer.

Once the drinks were made, she gazed at the reflection in her tea. 'No one ever wakes you up early with good news.'

Alice located the biscuit tin and ate three chocolate digestives in quick succession before Jez and Luke wandered through the door. She offered them the biscuits. Both declined – a wise move on their part, considering that she was liable to bite off their heads if they had accepted; not that she was greedy, she was simply certain that the only way to assuage her rising anxiety was with copious amounts of chocolate, and possibly Pinot Grigio.

She glugged her tea, its reassuring warmth loosened the tightness in her throat enough for her to breathe and ask, 'Luke, are you likely to arrest me if I punch another murderer?'

'I'd be happy to,' he said.

She accepted his answer with a nod and pressed the heel of her hand against her forehead, trying to erase the anger that seemed to be rising like a marble beneath her skin.

'What is it?' Jez asked.

Alice was about to reply when the front door swung open and Duke walked in, looking mildly dishevelled. He was wearing grey jogging bottoms that were pocked with assorted stains, and he needed to fix his anorak, either by patching up the tears or setting the garment on fire. The nylon was so worn that goose feathers poked through in a variety of places. He'd had a go at combing his hair, but it still looked as though he'd been caught under a gorse bush.

'Since Duke's here, I think it's the perfect time to tell you that Becky is currently sitting in my mother's kitchen. She wants me to go around, without the police.'

'If you're serious, then we can't let you go.' Luke walked over to her. 'You've just reported a hostage situation to the police. I'll arrest you for your own safety if needs be.'

Alice clenched her fists. 'I'm not going to wait here in the hopes that your people get there before me.'

'I appreciate your feelings, but this –'

'Luke, I'm going to ask you to shut your mouth. I am

going to do this respectfully because you have already threatened to arrest me and, quite frankly, I can do without that right now. There are drinks in the kitchen for everyone, but we do not have long to drink them.

'I invited you around because I thought that you might be able to help. I'll be going to get my mother out of this situation, but if you want to concoct some sort of plan then I'll give you ten minutes. Becky said no police, and since she's already proven her ability and willingness to kill, I'm not going to give her any reason to do it again.'

His jaw twitched as he clenched and unclenched his knuckles a few times. 'All right then, Miss Valentine. What are you thinking?'

Alice headed towards the front door with trepidation. Unfortunately, this time it wasn't because she'd been so shamelessly inebriated that she'd slept in a farmer's field, lost a boot, thumbed a ride home with a concerned pensioner, and subsequently had to face her parents. She could have dealt with that. The rigid ache that tugged at her spine came from knowing that Becky was inside.

Before she had chance to put her key in the lock, the door opened. Primrose stood there, plastering a rictus grin to her face. 'She's just in the kitchen, love.'

'Where's Dad?'

'He's still in bed. You know how he gets after one of his sleeping pills.'

Alice's shoulders relaxed slightly as she released a sigh of relief. She followed her mother down the hall.

Becky was sitting at the kitchen table, looking as content as a cat on a radiator as she munched on a biscuit.

'If I knew you ate garibaldis, I'd have had you pegged

as the killer from the off.'

'Glad you could make it,' she said, grinning. 'It'll be nice to put an end to this sorry business.'

Alice knew it probably wasn't the best idea to stand within touching distance of a person who planned to kill her, but she'd never been one to know what was good for her. She'd once attended a pole fitness class after a severe bout of norovirus, the results of which were the employment of a biohazard team and Alice completely ruining the laminate flooring of the rehearsal room.

'Where's Lorelai?' she asked.

'That's none of your concern. Haven't you learned anything? If you'd all stayed away from Lorelai in the first place, I wouldn't have had to start killing people.'

'I thought you might say that.'

'Sit down, Alice.'

Although she didn't much care for being ordered around in her parents' home, she went and sat down at the opposite end of the table.

'I'll pop the kettle on,' said Primrose.

'Great idea. I'll have another coffee if you don't mind, Mrs Valentine. That last one was smashing.'

Primrose took Becky's mug with a smile and crossed the room to the counter.

'If you hurt my mum, you won't be the only killer in this house.'

Becky toyed with another garibaldi. 'I've no plans to hurt her. She's done nothing wrong.'

'And the others did?'

She mulled that over as she swallowed a bite of her biscuit, using her tongue as a toothpick to dislodge a tough currant from between her teeth. 'Maybe not Gloria.'

'The one in the freezer?'

'Considering that the one you called Gloria was actually Gwen and she deserved everything that happened to her? Yes.'

'Why did you kill them?'

Becky's eyes glazed over as she said, 'For her. For Lorelai.'

'Since we've established that you are, in actual fact, a murderer, would you mind telling us what you mean?'

'Lorelai is too trusting. She needs someone to look out for her.'

'There's looking out for someone and then there's killing for them.'

'It might not be as simple as that, love.' Primrose handed Becky her mug, taking care so that the recipient wouldn't burn her hands. 'Was there a threat to Lorelai's life?'

Becky beamed at Primrose. 'I knew you'd understand, Mrs Valentine. See, Lorelai has had issues with men in the past. Cheaters, slimeballs, ghosts. And when they inevitably break up, whose door does she run to? Mine. I've helped patch that girl's heart so many times that I'm surprised she can find the wherewithal for a relationship. Then Ryan Dewhurst came along.'

'He might have been bad at relationships, but that was no reason to try and kill him.'

Having hastily gulped back her coffee, steam issued from Becky's lips as she said, 'You're jumping the gun there. I battered him to protect Lorelai. Like most men, he was affectionate for the first few months, before giving it all up in favour of flatulence, forgetfulness, and a tendency to avoid holding hands in public.'

'Look, I know he was a fool.'

'He was worse than a fool. He was a liar.'

'But he wasn't a killer.' Alice glared at Becky; her fingers white from how tightly she'd wrapped them around her mug.

'Killing Gloria and Gwen was always the last resort. My main aim was always to make sure that Lorelai was safe.'

'Then what set you on the path towards killing two old women?'

Becky pulled the sleeves of her cardigan over her hands. She took a keen interest in a pulled stitch over her thumb as she mumbled, 'I killed Gloria by mistake.'

A dumbfounded Alice couldn't find the words to respond; she simply looked at Becky, questioning if she was really as overprotective as she made herself out to be or whether she had an as yet unknown idiotic streak.

Primrose took in her daughter's expression before turning to Becky and saying, 'That was a rather big mistake. Are you sure you didn't mean to end Gloria's life?'

'Not at first. When Lorelai gave me Gloria's address, I drove over to recce the place and saw Gwen and Gloria on the doorstep. Well, since I knew Gwen was a scam artist, I thought they couldn't be up to any good. That's when I decided to warn Ryan off. Not that it mattered. Lorelai dumped him because she was tired of his grandmother and his narrowboat.'

Alice nodded in solidarity. 'I get that. He really could have done with learning how to sweep up his mess.'

'I kept my ears open just in case he tried to get back with Lorelai, but next thing I knew, he was in a new relationship, and I was prepared to forget about him. Then I found out that she'd kept in contact with Gloria.'

'Gloria who's actually Gwen?' Primrose's forehead was screwed up with the effort of keeping track of who was who.

Becky shrugged. 'I didn't know that at the time.'

'You wanted to protect Lorelai so much that you stalked her, but you drew the line at finding out if you were about to murder the right person to protect her?' Alice was unable to hide the disbelief from her face.

'I never planned on killing Gloria.'

'How did it happen, then?'

'I found her on social media, saw that she volunteered for a charity in Wren's Lea, so I rang them up and asked for her. Luckily, they didn't care a jot about data protection and told me when she'd be there.'

'So, you went down and confronted her?'

'That makes it sound aggressive.'

'Have you heard yourself, Becky? You *are* aggressive. You're like a WWE wrestler in a wrap-around cardigan.'

Once again, Becky couldn't meet Alice's gaze; she simply stared at her reflection in the glass of the oven door. 'I just forget my own strength sometimes.'

Primrose reached out and rested her hand on Becky's. 'It happens to the best of us.'

'Mum, don't play devil's advocate for a murderer.'

'That's no reason to doubt what she says. When people look at me, they can't tell that I've been going to a boxing class every Tuesday for eight months.'

'I wouldn't have known that if Jez didn't tell me. Since when did you keep secrets?'

'It isn't a secret, love. If I'd told you then you would have mocked me for taking another class.'

She nodded. 'That's to be expected. I'm Alice.'

'I just wanted to see how I got on before telling you.'

'I really don't think it's fair for you to make your mum feel like this, Alice.' Becky placed her other hand on top of Primrose's, offering consoling caresses.

'I'm not about to take advice from a killer, if you don't mind.' Alice knocked back her tea so that she wouldn't have to look at the pair of them. The last time she'd confronted a murderer, they'd at least had the decency to threaten her with a shotgun, rather than making her feel bad about the way she treated her mother.

Primrose patted Becky's hand. 'Even so, she's entitled to an opinion.'

Alice gritted her teeth. 'Fine. You located the real Gloria Hebblethwaite, and then what?'

'I let her know that if she didn't leave Lorelai alone, there'd be trouble. When she said that she'd never met Lorelai in her life, I thought she was playing along.'

'But they stayed in contact?'

'I found out when Ryan got back from his cruise. Lorelai had been jittery for a few days and eventually came round and said she was concerned that Ryan had murdered his grandmother. She'd been checking the news and saw word of a body going overboard.'

'Because she didn't know that everything had already been disproven?'

'Exactly. She showed me some texts that she'd received from Gwen, posing as Gloria, saying how worried she was that Ryan wouldn't fake the death with a dummy as originally planned and that he'd kill her instead.'

Alice gulped back some of the slowly rising sadness at the idea that Thomas had been telling the truth. She'd also thought him capable of murder, and Becky had been able to find him because of that. To avoid thinking about it any further, she asked, 'Why did Gwen go to Lorelai?'

'I think it's because she was one of the only people to think she was actually Gloria, and she had a connection to Ryan. She also didn't much care for you.'

'The feeling was mutual, I assure you.'

'I can imagine. You're not an easy person to like.'

'Need I remind you that you're a killer?'

'And need I remind you that it mostly happened by mistake.' Becky leaned forward, her grip on Primrose's hand as strong as an anaconda wrapped around an antelope.

Primrose wriggled out of Becky's grip. She accidentally knocked the plate bearing the biscuits to the ground; bone china and garibaldis shattered on the linoleum. 'Blast, that was part of a set. Don't move, Becky. I don't want you getting hurt.'

Alice was sure that she saw Primrose draw something from her sleeve as she dropped beneath the table. Wishing to draw Becky's attention away, she said, 'Fast forward then, Becky. How did you become a murderer by mistake?'

'I suggested having a girl's night to take Lorelai's mind off everything. On the way there, I saw Gloria going into Marsden's, looking surprisingly well for a dead woman. I parked my car and went inside. See, I didn't know what I planned to do until it happened. I followed Gloria down the aisle but wasn't prepared for the floor to be so wet. I slipped forward and knocked into her. She fell straight into the freezer and the lid slammed down. By the time I'd got back onto my feet, she was on her back, banging on the lid, but it wouldn't budge. I can't remember why I did what I did next, but I was thinking how everyone already thought that she was dead, and that it would be an easy way to get her and Ryan out of Lorelai's life to avoid any further stress.'

'That's when you covered the lid of the freezer with boxes.'

Becky nodded in response.

Alice exhaled. She focused on her hands lying flat on the tabletop, examining the wrinkles of her knuckles, as the memory of Gloria Hebblethwaite's body lying in the freezer rose up in her mind.

'It was only an hour or two later that I found out she was the wrong Gloria,' Becky said. She drained the remainder of her mug and set it down on the table.

'What happened?'

'You came to the bar with Ryan, then you visited our table. I caught Lorelai mooning over a photo of the three of them together and saying that you'd never expect him to kill Gloria from the picture.'

'Only it wasn't Gloria, it was Gwen.'

Becky nodded, pressing down on the table with her index finger as though she could suppress all her rage with a single digit. 'That's when things started to click for me. In the beginning, I thought that something must be wrong if Gloria was the type to associate with people like Gwen Mainwaring. Then I realised that if there was some sort of insurance scam going on, it was more likely to be her.'

'When we left for the night, I went to visit Gwen. She had a shotgun.'

'It was Gwen's shotgun?' Alice sat up straight, perplexed.

Becky shrugged. 'I don't know if it was hers, but she had it. The funny thing is that she didn't remember me at all.'

'Did you talk to her?'

'I asked what was going on because Lorelai had it in her head that she'd spent the last few months speaking to Gloria Hebblethwaite. She revealed everything: how she'd been targeted after leaving prison, how she hadn't planned on stealing an identity again but couldn't help herself, how Ryan had come up with his scheme and how she realised he planned to kill her. That's when she told me he was also lying about his identity, so she could give me his motivation.

'As luck would have it, that was when he walked through the door.

'He saw the two of us together and immediately jumped to conclusions. See, he knew I was protective of Lorelai, but he also thought that Gwen and I were working together to kill him. Meanwhile, she was standing up and trying to steady herself to shoot him.

'After that, things got messy.

'Ryan – that's to say, Thomas – went for the gun. I knocked him to the ground and wrenched it out of Gwen's hands. That was when I shot her.'

Primrose came back out from beneath the table, broken biscuits and pieces of pottery in her hands. She wandered over to the bin and deposited the rubbish before heading back over to them and asking, 'Why, love?'

Strangely, Becky seemed unable to meet Primrose's gaze. 'It happened on the spur of the moment. I killed Gloria because I thought she'd been upsetting Lorelai, then I found out that I'd made a mistake, and that Gwen and Thomas were to blame. I was angry. I planned on shooting Thomas as well, but he'd already run off.'

'You tracked him down and battered him though,'

Alice said. 'Why didn't you just kill him then?'

'I thought that I had. I thought there was no way he could have survived the beating I gave him. I hoped that he'd do the decent thing and die, but some Samaritan came along and carted him off to hospital.'

'Last night, you had Lorelai bring us all to Gloria's house and shot at us. You could have killed us all.'

'I could have.'

'Why?'

Becky shot Alice a ferocious glare. 'Because I needed her to see that it's dangerous to spend time with people like you.'

'People like me? You're the one going around killing people.'

'To protect her! Why is that something you can't wrap your thick head around that?'

'It doesn't make any sense, that's why. Lorelai is a grown woman who's entirely capable of looking after herself.'

Becky shook her head, seemingly despondent. 'She might think that she is, but she isn't.'

'What have you done with her, Becky?'

'Kept her safe.' Alice couldn't be certain, but it seemed as though Becky was struggling to raise her head. Perhaps the lack of sleep was finally getting to her, regardless of the coffee she'd had.

'Where is Lorelai?'

'I'm not going to tell you, because you'll just try and corrupt her again.' Her words were argumentative but slurred slightly, like a drunk person protesting that they could walk a straight line.

'You made her collect Thomas from the police station, didn't you?'

Becky shrugged.

'Then you got us all together and tried to kill us. Do you honestly think that's going to make her feel safe and protected? No. It will make her feel like people could have died because of her. She probably already blames herself for Gloria and Gwen. We all know that it isn't her fault, but that won't matter.'

That caused Becky to pause, before doubling down and saying, 'All that Lorelai needs is a fresh start somewhere where we don't know anyone. I'll give her the time she needs to realise that I know what's best for her.'

'Becky, love is a strong emotion, but I don't think that Lorelai is looking for a girlfriend. Especially one who kills anyone who so much as looks at her the wrong way.'

Becky's eyes widened so much that they threatened to roll back in her head. 'A girlfriend? A *girlfriend*? I don't think of her that way. I'm just being a good friend. This is what friends do for each other, Alice. We protect each other.'

'I'm not sure that Lorelai will see it that way.'

'Once I'm finished here, I'm going to get in my car and take her away from all of this.'

'No, you're not.'

Becky scoffed. 'I'd like to see you try and stop me.'

'I don't need to. I have my mum,' Alice said, with a grin.

'Just because she boxes every Tuesday, you think she can fight me.' There was no hiding her amusement at the idea.

If anything, that caused Alice to beam wider. 'No, because she used to be a magician's assistant. See, your legs are currently tied to the table legs, and I can guarantee that those knots are going to take some untangling.'

Becky made to grab for Primrose who, in a flash of steel, handcuffed her to a nearby cupboard.

Primrose settled back against the kitchen counter. 'I also squashed a few strong sleeping pills into your coffee.'

'Don't be stupid, Mrs Valentine. They won't work with the amount of caffeine you've given me.'

From the way her shoulders settled, Alice could tell that her mother was disappointed. 'I don't like being called stupid, love. I've been kind to you while you've been here, even though you plan on killing my daughter. I doubt that you've had any sleep in a while, since you spent last night on a shooting spree in a cul-de-sac and presumably came straight here. You're basically surviving on adrenaline and exhaust fumes at this point. Frankly, I'm surprised you haven't collapsed already, but then you are of a sturdier build.'

'Did you just call me fat?'

'If there's anything I'd never do, love, it's body shame. I would, however, do anything within my power to keep my daughter safe. I suppose what I'm saying is that I understand what it means to be protective over someone, and maybe even to go so far as to kill for them.'

Becky hung her head. 'I'm sorry, Mrs Valentine.'

'I should think you are, love. I hope you understand that should you ever come near Alice again then things aren't likely to end well.'

'Mum, did you just threaten her?'

Becky's head lolled on her neck as though she was a ragdoll. Primrose launched forwards and grabbed her before she slammed down, gently settling her head

286

against the table.

She smiled at Alice. 'I'll always do what I can to stop you getting hurt.'

'Even if that's drugging a murderer?'

'I don't plan on making a hobby of it.'

'Good, because I don't think they teach that down the Adult Learning Centre.'

Alice crossed the kitchen and pulled her mother into a hug.

At that moment, Norman wandered in, yawning like an oversized dachshund in his navy-blue dressing gown. He surveyed the situation in the kitchen, before saying, 'I've missed a lot, haven't I?'

Chapter Twenty-Seven

Marmaduke ambled down the road, the mulchy leaves underfoot soaking the loose hems of his jogging bottoms. Children passed by on their way to school, chattering excitedly about the forthcoming day, while others wailed as they were all but dragged by their parents towards the gates. None of them were aware that there was a murderer holed up in a house just one street away. Indeed, that was the main reason why Marmaduke was walking – to take his mind off things. He knew that he shouldn't be concerned; after all, Alice had held her own against a murderer before, although that one had been a geriatric beanpole who looked like he'd disintegrate if hit with a good gust of wind.

Then there was the matter of Bianca Thistlethwaite. He didn't doubt that she'd reveal all she knew, but he couldn't dislodge the ball of worry that had lodged itself in his mind.

So, he walked.

He greeted a few folk, but soon gave it up as a bad job when he realised no one was paying him any attention. Half of them had headphones on, their heads down as they headed towards the purgatorial splendour of gainful employment, and the other half was filming themselves, making peace signs and sticking out their tongues, stumbling every few minutes because they refused to look where they were going.

Soon enough, bells were ringing, and Marmaduke found the nearby street empty, which was when he first heard the screaming. This wasn't the screaming of children in the playground, the raucous din that had plagued many a hungover parent on Monday morning. These were screams of terror.

A woman was calling for help while banging on something, adding to the racket.

Marmaduke stopped in his tracks. He glanced up and down the street at the cavalcade of 4x4s standing sentry beside the kerb, most of them black and fresh out of the factory. The screaming wasn't coming from any of the vehicles.

He wandered down the pavement until he reached a ratty green estate that was rocking from side to side. The screaming emanated from the boot of the car.

Marmaduke knocked on the roof. 'That wouldn't be Lorelai in there, would it?'

'Who's that?'

'Marmaduke Featherstone.'

'She's locked me in.'

'It's all right, I'll get you out.' People had told Marmaduke that he was loud enough to be heard in three counties, a fact that he hoped was still true.

After searching the pavement for a few minutes –

during which time, he'd reassured Lorelai that he hadn't gone anywhere – parents began to filter back out of the school gates. He received some odd looks, but that was something he'd grown accustomed to as he aged.

Eventually, a man who seemed unable to relinquish his adolescence stopped and asked, 'Is everything all right?'

Marmaduke held back laughter as he faced this wiry-haired individual in his bright blue raincoat, rucksack bouncing on his backside, headphones around his neck buzzing with music that sounded closer to white noise. Rather than guffaw or tell the man to grow up, Marmaduke said, 'There's a girl trapped in the boot of that car, and I was looking for something to smash its windows.'

The man nodded, the concern in his eyes transforming immediately to a simpering look. 'Gosh, that's brave of you. And why is the girl in the boot of that car?'

'She was kidnapped, you nitwit. Now, are you going to be useful, or are you going to stand around looking like the poster boy for millennial parenting?'

He gawped at Marmaduke, giving a great impression of a goldfish.

Another man approached, clapping the first on the back. 'All right, Andy? What're you on today?'

Marmaduke groaned, muttering, 'Not another one.'

'How're you doing, Gareth? I was just checking to see if this gentleman needed any help. He's looking for something so that he can break into that car because he says there's a girl trapped in the boot.'

The pair of young men exchanged knowing glances. Gareth seemed about to say something when Lorelai exclaimed, 'Will somebody get me out of here?'

Marmaduke glowered at Andy. 'Now, I might look senile, lad, but I don't go about smashing up cars in the hopes of finding a young lass inside. It's not a Kinder Egg.'

Having heard Lorelai's cries, the men busied themselves with helping out. Andy soon returned with a hefty branch which he handed to Marmaduke, his expression both apologetic and wary. 'You're sure you don't want one of us to have a go?'

'Because you're younger, stronger and fitter?'

They nodded.

'I wouldn't trust you to crack open a tin of beans.'

Marmaduke weighed the branch in his hand, swinging it a few times before he felt comfortable. He pressed his feet firmly into the ground and inhaled deeply through his nose and exhaled through his mouth. His mind went back to days spent playing cricket in the gardens at Greenfields.

He poised himself, raising the branch to shoulder level, and started to swing.

'Wait!'

Marmaduke lost his grip and the branch went flying.

The rear window shattered on impact. Not that there was any need to break the thing because as the glass sprayed over the upholstery, the car unlocked.

Marmaduke looked up to see Alice rushing down the pavement, holding the car keys. She was followed by Jez and Luke, both of whom looked harried; that was a side-effect of knowing Alice Valentine.

'Don't touch anything and step away from the vehicle, Uncle Duke,' Luke said as they reached him.

Andy and Gareth looked like schoolboys on the edge

of wetting their pants. 'We had nothing to do with this,' the latter said.

Marmaduke shot a glare in his direction. 'Coward.' He turned back to face Alice. 'You always have to spoil my fun.'

'Is this what happens when I'm not around?' she asked. 'You just gad about like some teenage hooligan smashing up cars.'

'Your friend is in the boot.'

Alice paid no mind to the broken glass. She flung the boot open without thinking about contaminating the crime scene.

Lorelai squinted at the sudden onslaught of light. Her clothes were wrinkled, and the scent of stale body odour emanated from the boot. Her hair was matted, her eyes red raw from crying. Her wrists and ankles were bound with rope.

'Alice?' she eked out. 'She said she was going to kill you.'

'I've never been very good at giving people what they want.' She leaned down and tried to untie the knots.

'It's no use. She was in the Girl Guides.' Lorelai struggled to stop a sob from escaping.

'Here, I have something.' Andy rushed forward, tearing off his rucksack and unzipping it. After rifling around for a few moments, he handed Alice a penknife.

'So, you can be useful when you put your mind to it,' Marmaduke said.

Alice cut through the rope and helped to ease Lorelai out of the car. She faced Luke and said, 'Can I take her back to my parents'?'

He considered her words. 'We'll need to collect a statement, but that can wait. Get her back, cleaned up and rested, and we'll speak to her in due course.'

They nodded to one another.

'How did you know where to find us?' Marmaduke asked.

'Becky had a tracker on everything. All we needed was her phone, and that was that.'

'I'm not paying for that windscreen.'

Alice stifled a chuckle. 'My mum is cooking breakfast. Let's go.'

Chapter Twenty-Eight

Alice always found it surreal how life continued as normal after such dark events had happened. On the day of Becky's arrest, everything seemed suddenly tumultuous as she made a statement to the police and dealt with reporters who seemed determined to ask insensitive questions. That quickly quietened down. Lorelai recognised that she needed some time away after the police discovered monitoring devices throughout her home, so she went to stay with her parents.

Alice took some shifts at Thistlethwaite's, but when she returned to the cottage of an evening, she found herself at a loss, and thus she did what she always did in times of boredom – she baked. Her kitchen counter was covered with dozens of cupcakes, a three-tiered sponge packed with jam and cream alongside other assorted desserts that she'd be ferrying around to friends for days.

That was one of the reasons why she invited Marmaduke over for tea and cake.

She made up a tray with a Royal Albert teapot at its centre – bedecked in a crocheted tea cosy she'd inherited with the house – along with matching teacups and small plates for the cake. She and Aunty Magdalena used to hold regular tea parties, and Alice had decided it was high time to reinstate the custom.

Once Duke was settled in the chair by the window, he asked, 'Has Thomas left town?'

Alice handed over a saucer laden with carrot cake. 'I watched him take his narrowboat down the canal myself.'

She hadn't planned on visiting the towpath to make amends, but she had a pineapple-upside-down cake going spare and couldn't think of anyone else who'd eat it. He looked suitably surprised when she handed it over. She said, 'It's really an offering to ask that you never come back.' He sagged slightly at that, although he nodded, saying that he understood. Alice supposed that she could've offered him some words of consolation, but they weren't forthcoming.

'Have all your boyfriends been such nuisances?' Duke asked, pulling her from her daydream.

'Jez said I didn't go out with him for long enough for him to qualify as a boyfriend.'

'He caused you a whole load of trouble for someone who wasn't your boyfriend.'

Alice shrugged and forked some cake into her mouth, savouring the flavour of the spices, the warm touch of ginger that tasted like the essence of autumn.

Despite everything that Thomas had done, she wondered if he was the worst of all the men she'd dated. There had been Grant, named after his mother's obsession with *Eastenders*; he was an online content creator who, up until recently, had worked in construction but had lost his job after making videos onsite that showed him laying more than bricks. Then there was the guy who'd believed every living creature on the planet was an automaton being operated by a jellyfish. Alice couldn't remember her name; she just remembered him going haywire when she asked if he included himself in his theory.

She supposed that neither of those men had embroiled her in familial disputes dating back half a century and nearly got her shot, and nor had they lied about their identity – except, perhaps, for jellyfish man – but there was something within her that said she no longer cared about Thomas; she'd never known him properly and had no wish to get to know him.

'I'm just glad it's over. The murderer has been caught, and you found the writer of the poison pen letters. How's she doing?'

Marmaduke swilled tea around his mouth like mouthwash to disperse the remnants of the cake he'd gobbled. 'She's doing as well as can be expected. One of the perils when you get to my age is that you regularly have to watch your friends die.'

'And there's really nothing they can do for her?'

'She's lasted longer than anyone thought she would.'

'Does she have any family?'

'Her sister is due back in the next day or two.'

'What will you do then?'

'I'll wait for her to die, and then someone will bring her notebook to my door.'

'Which hopefully contains all of the answers you're looking for.' Alice finished her slice of cake and set the saucer on the table.

'I think that if Bianca had discovered the murderer, or

found Joanna, then she would have told me. What she's written down is more than likely going to be her version of events and some leads she's never been able to follow up.'

'So, we're no further along in finding answers?'

'At least I know that Joanna didn't die, and I have to hope that she's out there somewhere.'

'Hope is a good thing to hold onto, and I'm glad that you have it.'

Duke finished off his tea and helped himself to another. 'It's been a long time since I had tea from a pot.'

'It just seemed right to serve it that way.'

'Nice to keep up with tradition, though. Back in the day, wherever I visited there would always be a pot of tea stewing in the kitchen in case of visitors.' After slurping, he sighed. 'Anyway, now that Thomas is out of the picture, how do you see things going with you and Luke?'

Alice all but choked on her tea. 'What do you mean "you and Luke"? There is no me and Luke. There will never be a me and Luke because he's an unutterable swine.'

'See, he said something similar about you.'

'You talked to him about this?' Alice felt like she was screeching; she was certainly being more high-pitched than she wanted to be.

'You both seem to delight in upsetting each other.'

'I wouldn't say that I delight in it. There's just something pleasurable about goading him.'

Duke chuckled, unable to look at Alice.

'What is it?'

'Nothing,' he said. 'I suppose that's all right, as long as it's a pleasurable goading.' With that, he fell about laughing again, having to keep a firm hold on his cup so that he didn't spill tea everywhere.

Alice looked at him, bewildered. She'd once been attracted to Luke Sterling, but that had been when she was a teenager, and he was the grandson of her Aunty Magdalena's neighbour. He'd seemed unobtainable and mysterious. Years later, she wished that he'd remained such an enigma.

Duke stuck around for another slice of cake before heading out. Visiting hours at the hospital were due to start, and he wished to see his friend one more time before her sister returned to town. Alice offered to drive him, aware that it was likely to be a sad occasion, but he declined.

With nothing planned for the afternoon, she was about to settle down in front of the television to watch some reruns of *Friends* when she received a phone call from her father. Norman was frantic as he asked, 'Have you seen your mother today?'

'No. Is she meant to be coming around? I told her that I might have a few cupcakes for her.'

'She's done it again. I can't believe she's actually done it again.'

Alice sat upright on the sofa. 'Dad, calm down. What do you mean?'

'She's left me, Alice. Her suitcase has gone and so has the car, and her side of the bed was cold when I got up this morning.'

She massaged her forehead with the heel of her hand. 'Just wait there, I'll be right around.'

She rang Jez on the way. 'I need you to meet me at my parents' house.'

'I'm already there.'

'Did my dad call you?'

'I think it best that you just get here, Alice.'

His tone left her even more worried as she sped towards Wren's Lea.

When she arrived, the front door was open. Alice stepped over the threshold to discover Jez and Norman standing in the hall. 'Have you found Mum?'

'There's been no sign of her.'

'This is serious.'

'Pointing out the obvious there, Jez. My mum has gone missing.'

'Technically, we have to wait until she hasn't been seen for twenty-four hours. It's serious because I was coming here to question Primrose.'

Alice's heart was beating so hard that it was threatening to shatter her ribcage. 'What's Becky claiming now?'

'It's got nothing to do with Becky.'

'Then what's this about?'

'The coat that Gloria Hebblethwaite was wearing.'

'Why are the police interested in her coat?'

'Because it wasn't her coat.'

'So, Gloria was a thief as well as a murder victim? These things aren't mutually exclusive.'

'On the night that she was murdered, Gloria had been at the church hall, sorting through donations for their next jumble sale.'

All the moisture in Alice's mouth evaporated; her tongue felt as rough as sandpaper, her throat practically constricting in its need for water. She remembered finding Gloria's body in the freezer and that she was wearing a mauve anorak. Only the day before, Alice had seen her mother shove a similar coat into a bin bag for the jumble sale. 'She thought it was an unwanted gift from my grandmother. She had no idea where it came from.'

'There was a name tag sewn into the collar and an ID in the pocket. It once belonged to Joanna Hollinshead, and your mother's fingerprints are all over it.'

'She didn't even know where it came from! There's got to be some chance that it was planted in the back bedroom.' Alice sent a pleading gaze towards Norman. 'That's got to be what happened, right?'

Norman set a hand on her shoulder. 'She's been emptying the house for weeks, and now she's gone missing.'

Alice clung to her father's arm as theories spiralled through her mind. 'She behaved weirdly when she found out about the poison pen letters. Could she have received one?

Norman shrugged and headed towards the kitchen. 'If she did then she kept it secret from me.'

Alice barged past him and rushed over to the tea cupboard. She pulled canisters down, ignoring the dust that caught the sunlight and brushed against her cheeks, until she found an old shortbread tin, complete with an image of a typical Victorian winter scene. Primrose had kept it at the back of the cupboard for decades.

She slammed it down on the counter and tore off the lid, hands frenzied.

The tin was filled with papers, photographs, the odd toy out of a cereal box and her Blue Peter badge. Alice searched until she found the least tattered piece of paper, which was pale purple and folded in two.

Her attempts to steady her breathing proved futile. She unfolded the paper and a newspaper clipping fell to the floor.

Norman rushed over and picked it up.

Meanwhile, Alice read the note. "YOUR SECRET IS NO LONGER SAFE".

'What does this mean?' Norman asked. He and Alice exchanged their respective papers, but neither could make head nor tail of what they were reading. The strip of yellowing newspaper showed a photograph of a tall, spindly woman sitting on a bench with a poised smile upon her face. She was holding a small trophy. Beneath the image, a caption read "Mrs Violet Grey won best private garden in a recent competition held by the Partridge Mews Women's Institute."

They handed the papers to Jez.

Alice breathed deep and said, 'Duke knows who sent the poison pen letters. If you find her, she might be able to tell you Mum's location.'

'Last time, she disappeared to Nepal,' Norman said. 'Maybe you should check the airports.'

'Dad!'

'Or do you think she's been practising those magic tricks again and has accidentally made herself disappear? Suppose she's got herself stuck beneath the kitchen sink and this has all been some massive magical mistake.' Alice thought her heart might shatter when she recognised the grief in her father's eyes. She longed for the shelter of his arms, but the way he was talking about her mother had her wanting to keep him at a distance.

Jez finished reading the note and the article, brow furrowed. 'Has Mrs Valentine behaved out of character recently?'

'Apart from tidying the back bedroom? She said she was decluttering. Now, I'm not too sure.'

'Jez, please tell me you're not taking this seriously. My mum couldn't have anything to do with Joanna leaving town. She knows the effect everything had on Duke.'

'We have to consider every possibility, Alice. I'm not accusing her of any wrongdoing, I just have questions. But if she *has* fled then things don't look too good, do they?'

Alice chewed her lips. 'Do you think Duke knew about the poison pen letter that Mum got? Could that be why he didn't want me joining the rest of his investigation?'

'I think that's a question you'll have to ask him. I'm sure he'll have his own questions about your mum's involvement in his niece's disappearance and whether it relates to the murder of Lucy Simpson.'

All the breath fled Alice's lungs as though someone had taken a sledgehammer to her chest.

She leaned against the kitchen counter, looking down at the contents of the tea caddy. There was a photo from her parents on their wedding day; an image that had always exuded love and safety. Considering Jez's news, she wondered if everything she believed to be true was false, and as they discussed the consequences of Primrose's actions, Alice wondered if she'd ever truly known her mother.

She's groggy as she comes around. The cloying odour of diesel envelops her, invading her nostrils.

Cold wind blasts against her cheeks, accompanied by the sting of raindrops.

Her chest throbs and her head pulses. It feels like her brain is trying to break through her skull. A myriad of women's voices filter in from outside, but she can't tell what they're saying because of the thundering in her ears.

She wonders if she's trapped inside a tornado.

Her head lolls on her neck, feeling as heavy as it had when she tried absinthe for the first time, but she raises it and opens her eyes.

She sees nothing but shadows.

Still, the women's voices call to one another.

She remembers what happened. Ash. The beating. The brakes.

And she wishes her Uncle Marmaduke were here to fix everything. He told her to leave well alone, to go to him with any worries, but she didn't. She thought she could solve everything by herself, and now she's alone in a car in the middle of the night and she's killed a man.

She needs to see him. She removes her seatbelt, but it proves too much, and nausea racks her body. She keels over and rests her head on the dashboard, ignoring the press of glass against her skin.

She grinds her head from side to side against the hard plastic before falling back against the seat once more.

Anger and fear blend and, without thinking, she screams. Screeches and bellows tear through her throat like daggers through silk, but she can't stop herself. She's certain she'll scream for all eternity, that she's destined to be little more than a banshee, haunted by all that has happened in the last few months.

The passenger door opens, and a torch is shone into the car.

She stops screaming abruptly, pulled into a hug. She stares out at several people, shining torches at their faces, each offering their version of a sympathetic look.

The woman hugging her, murmurs in her ear, 'It's okay, love, it's all going to be okay.'

Joanna has a ton of questions, but nothing escapes her lips except, 'Primrose?'

Acknowledgements

Thanks are due to my beta-readers, Brian Bruce, Cathryn Heathcote, Emily Novelle, and Joy Winkler. You provided much-needed insight to help me improve this second outing for Alice and Duke.

Also, thanks to Dane Cobain for agreeing to return and edit what sometimes felt like the most challenging book I ever tried to write.

www.ingramcontent.com/pod-product-compliance
Lightning Source LLC
Chambersburg PA
CBHW030423180626
46812CB00005B/2146